NOTES OF A DIRTY OLD MAN

NOTES OF A DIRTY OLD MAN

Charles Bukowski

First published in Great Britain in 2008 by
Virgin Books Ltd
Thames Wharf Studios
Rainville Road
London
W6 9HA

Published in the United States in 1969 by City Lights Books,
San Francisco

A catalogue record for this book is available from
the British Library.

ISBN 978 0 7535 1382 8

Typeset by TW Typesetting, Plymouth, Devon
Printed and bound in Great Britain by
CPI Bookmarque Ltd, Croydon, CR0 4TD

1 3 5 7 9 10 8 6 4 2

Mixed Sources
Product group from well-managed
forests and other controlled sources
www.fsc.org   Cert no. TT-COC-002227
© 1996 Forest Stewardship Council

FSC

The Random House Group Limited supports The Forest Stewardship Council (FSC),
the leading international forest certification organisation. All our titles that are
printed on Greenpeace approved FSC certified paper carry the FSC logo.
Our paper procurement policy can be found at *www.rbooks.co.uk/environment.*

FOREWORD

More than a year ago John Bryan began his underground paper OPEN CITY in the front room of a small two story house that he rented. Then the paper moved to an apartment in front, then to a place in the business district of Melrose Ave. Yet a shadow hangs. A helluva big gloomy one. The circulation rises but the advertising is not coming in like it should. Across in the better part of town stands the *L.A. Free Press* which has become established. And runs the ads. Bryan created his own enemy by first working for the *L.A. Free Press* and bringing their circulation from 16,000 to more than three times that. It's like building up the National Army and then joining the Revolutionaries. Of course, the battle isn't simply OPEN CITY vs. FREE PRESS. If you've read OPEN CITY, you know that the battle is larger than that. OPEN CITY takes on the big boys, the biggest boys, and there are some *big* ones coming down the center of the street, NOW, and real ugly big shits they are, too. It's more fun and more dangerous working for OPEN CITY, perhaps the liveliest rag in the U.S. But fun and danger hardly put margarine on the toast or fed the cat. You give up toast and end up eating the cat.

Bryan is a type of crazy idealist and romantic. He quit, or was fired, he quit *and* was fired – there was a lot of shit flying

CHARLES BUKOWSKI

– from his job at the *Herald-Examiner* because he objected
to them airbrushing the cock and balls off of the Christ child.
This on the cover of their magazine for the Christmas issue.
"And it's not even my God, it's theirs," he told me.

So this strange idealist and romantic created OPEN CITY.
"How about doing us a weekly column?" he asked off-
handedly, scratching his red beard. Well, you know, thinking
of other columns and other columnists, it seemed to me to be
a terribly drab thing to do. But I started out, not with a
column but a review of *Papa Hemingway* by A. E. Hotchner.
Then one day after the races, I sat down and wrote the
heading, NOTES OF A DIRTY OLD MAN, opened a beer,
and the writing got done by itself. There was not the
tenseness or the careful carving with a bit of a dull blade, that
was needed to write something for *The Atlantic Monthly*.
Nor was there any need to simply tap out a flat and care-
less journalism (er, journalesé??). There seemed to be no
pressures. Just sit by the window, lift the beer and let it come.
Anything that wanted to arrive, arrived. And Bryan was
never a problem. I'd hand him some copy – in the early days
– and he'd flit through it and say, "OK, it's in." After a while
I'd just hand him copy and he wouldn't read it; he'd just jam
it into a cubbyhole and say, "It's in. What's going on?" Now
he doesn't even say, "It's in." I just hand him the copy and
that's that. It has helped the writing. Think of it yourself:
absolute freedom to write anything you please. I've had a
good time with it, and a serious time too, sometimes; but I
felt mainly, as the weeks went on, that the writing got better
and better. These are selections from about fourteen months
worth of columns.

For action, it has poetry beat all to hell. Get a poem
accepted and chances are it will come out 2 to 5 years later,
and a 50-50 shot it will never appear, or exact lines of it will
later appear, word for word, in some famous poet's work,
and then you know the world ain't much. Of course, this isn't
the fault of poetry; it is only that so many shits attempt to
print and write it. But with NOTES, sit down with a beer and

hit the typer on a Friday or a Saturday or a Sunday and by Wednesday the thing is all over the city. I get letters from people who have never read poetry, mine or anybody else's. People come to my door – too many of them really – and knock to tell me that NOTES OF A DIRTY OLD MAN turns them on. A bum off the road brings in a gypsy and his wife and we talk, bullshit, drink half the night. A long distance telephone operator from Newburgh, N.Y., sends me money. She wants me to give up drinking beer and to eat well. I hear from a madman who calls himself "King Arthur" and lives on Vine Street in Hollywood and wants to help me write my column. A doctor comes to my door: "I read your column and I think that I can help you. I used to be a psychiatrist." I send him away.

I hope that these selections help you. If you want to send me money, o.k. Or if you want to hate me, o.k. too. If I were the village blacksmith you wouldn't fuck with me. But I am just an old guy with some dirty stories. Writing for a newspaper, which, like me, might die tomorrow morning.

It's all very strange. Just think, if they hadn't airbrushed the cock and balls off the Christ child, you wouldn't be reading this. So, be happy.

Charles Bukowski
1969

NOTES OF A DIRTY OLD MAN

some son of a bitch had held out on the money, everybody claiming they were broke, card game finished, I was sitting there with my buddy Elf, Elf was screwed-up as a kid, all shriveled, he used to lay in bed for years squeezing these rubber balls, doing crazy exercises, and when he got out of bed one day he was as wide as he was tall, a muscled laughing brute who wanted to be a writer but he wrote too much like Thomas Wolfe and, outside of Dreiser, T. Wolfe was the worst American writer ever born, and I hit Elf behind the ear and the bottle fell off the table (he'd said something that I disagreed with) and as the Elf came up I had the bottle, good scotch, and I got him half on the jaw and part of the neck under there and he went down again, and I felt on top of my game, I was a student of Dostoevski and listened to Mahler in the dark, and I had time to drink from the bottle, set it down, fake with a right and lend him the left just below the belt and he fell against the dresser, clumsily, the mirror broke, it made sounds like a movie, flashed and crinkled and then Elf landed one high on my forehead and I fell back across a chair and the thing flattened like straw, cheap furniture, and then I was in deep – I had small hands and no real taste for fighting and I hadn't put him away – and he came on in like some zany two-bit vengeful individual, and I got in about one for three, not very good ones, but he wouldn't quit and the furniture was breaking everywhere, very much noise and I kept hoping somebody would stop the damned thing – the landlady, the police, God, anybody, but it went on and on and on, and then I didn't remember.

when I awakened the sun was up and I was *under* the bed. I got out from under and found that I could stand up. large cut under chin. scraped knuckles. I'd had worse hangovers. and there were worse places to awaken. like jail? maybe. I looked around. it *had* been real. everything broken and smeared and shattered, spilled – lamps, chairs, dresser, bed, ashtrays – gored beyond all measure, nothing sensible, everything ugly and finished. I drank some water and then walked to the closet. it was still there: tens, twenties, fives, the money I had thrown into the closet each time I had gone to piss during the card game, and I remembered starting the fight about the MONEY. I gathered up the green, placed it in my wallet, put my paper suitcase on the slanting bed and began to pack my few rags: laborer's shirts, stiff shoes with holes in the bottom, hard and dirty stockings, lumpy pants with legs that wanted to laugh, a short story about catching crabs at the San Francisco Opera House, and a torn Thrifty Drugstore dictionary – "palingenesis – recapitulation of ancestral stages in life-history."

the clock was working, the old alarm clock, god bless it, how many times had I looked at it on 7:30 a.m. hangover mornings and said, fuck the job? FUCK THE JOB! well, it said 4 p.m. I was just about to put it into the top of my suitcase when – sure, why not? – there was a knock on my door.

YEAH?
MR. BUKOWSKI?
YEAH? YEAH?
I WANT TO COME IN AND CHANGE THE SHEETS.
NO, NOT TODAY. I'M SICK TODAY.

OH, THAT'S TOO BAD. BUT JUST LET ME COME IN AND CHANGE THE SHEETS. THEN I'LL GO AWAY.

NO, NO, I'M TOO SICK, I'M JUST TOO SICK. I DON'T WANT YOU TO SEE ME THE WAY I AM.

it went on and on. she wanted to change the sheets. I said, no. she said, I want to change the sheets. on and on. that landlady. what a body. all body. everything about her screamed BODY BODY BODY. I'd only been there 2 weeks. there was a bar downstairs. people would come to see me, I wouldn't be in, she'd just say, "he's in the bar downstairs, he's always in the bar downstairs." and the people would say, "God and Jesus, man, who's your LANDLADY?"

but she was a big white woman and she went for these Filipinos, these Filipinos did tricks man, things no white men would ever dream of, even me; and these Flips are gone now with their George Raft pulldown widebrims and padded-shoulders; they used to be the fashion leaders, the stiletto boys; leather heels, greasy evil faces – where have you gone?

well, anyhow, there was nothing to drink and I sat there for hours, going crazy; jumpy, I was, gnatz, lumpy balls, there I sat with $450 easy money and I couldn't buy a draft beer. I was waiting for darkness. darkness, not death. I wanted out. another shot at it. I finally got the nerve up. I opened the door a bit, chain still on, and there was one, a little Flip monkey with a hammer. when I opened the door, he lifted the hammer and grinned. when I closed the door he took the tacks out of his mouth and pretended to pound them into the rug of the stairway leading to the first floor and the only door out. I don't know how long it went on. it was the same act. everytime I'd open the door he'd lift the hammer and grin. *shit monkey!* he just stayed on the top step. I began to go crazy. I was sweating, stinking; little circles whirling whirling whirling, light flanks and flashes of light in my dome. I really felt like I was going to go screwy. I walked over and got the suitcase. it was easy to carry. rags. then I took the typewriter. a steel portable borrowed from the wife

3

of a once-friend and never returned. it had a good solid feel: gray, flat, heavy, leery, banal. the eyes whirled to the rear of my head and the chain was off the door, and one hand with suitcase and one hand with stolen typewriter I charged into machinegun fire, the mourning morning sunrise, cracked-wheat crinkles, the end of all.

HEY! WHERE YOU GO?

the little monkey began to raise to one knee, he raised the hammer, and that's all I needed – the flash of electric light on hammer – I had the suitcase in the left hand, the portable steel typer in the right, he was in perfect position, down by my knees and I swung with great accuracy and some anger, I gave him the flat and heavy and hard side, greatly, along the side of his head, his skull, his temple, his being.

there was almost a shock of light like everything was crying, then it was still. I was outside, suddenly, sidewalk, down all those steps without realization. like luck, there was a yellow cab.

CABBY!

I was inside. UNION STATION.

it was good, the quiet sound of tires in the morning air. NO, WAIT, I said. MAKE IT THE BUS DEPOT.

WHATZ MATTA, MAN? the cabby asked.

I JUST KILLED MY FATHER.

YO KILLED YO FATHA?

YOU EVER HEARD OF JESUS CHRIST?

SHORE.

THEN MAKE IT: BUS DEPOT.

I sat in the bus depot for an hour waiting for the bus to New Orleans. wondering if I had killed the guy. I finally got on with typewriter and suitcase, jamming the typewriter far into the overhead rack, not wanting the thing to fall on my head. it was a long ride with much drinking and some involvement with a redhead from Fort Worth. I got off at Fort Worth too, but she lived with her mother and I had to get a room, and I got a room in a whorehouse by mistake. all night the women hollering things like, "HEY! you're not

going to stick THAT thing in ME for ANY kind of money!"
toilets flushing all night. doors opening and closing.

the redhead, she was a nice innocent thing, or bargained
for a better man. anyhow, I left town without getting into her
pants. I finally made New Orleans.

but the Elf. remember? the guy I fought in my room. well,
during the war he was killed by machinegun fire. I've heard
he lay in bed a long time, 3 or 4 weeks before he went. and
the *strangest* thing, he had told me, no, he had *asked* me
"suppose some STUPID son of a bitch puts his finger to a
machinegun and cuts me in half?"

"then, it's your fault."

"well, I know you ain't going to die in front of any god
damned machinegun."

"you're sure as shit right, I ain't, babe. unless it's one of
Uncle Sam's."

"don't give me that crap! I know you love your country. I
can see it in your eyes! love, real love!"

that's when I hit him the first time.

after that, you've got the rest of the story.

when I got to New Orleans I made sure I wasn't in any
whorehouse, even though the whole town looked like one.

---

we were sitting in the office after dropping another one of
those 7 to 1 ballgames, and the season was halfway over and
we were in the cellar, 25 games out of first place and I knew
that it was my last season as manager of the Blues. our
leading hitter was batting .243 and our leading home run
man had 6. our leading pitcher stood at 7 and 10 with an
e.r.a. of 3.95. old man Henderson pulled the pint out of the
desk drawer, took his cut, shoved the bottle at me.

"on top of all this," said Henderson, "I even caught the
crabs about 2 weeks ago."

"jesus, sorry, boss."

"you won't be calling me boss much longer."

"I know. but no manager in baseball can pull *these* rummies out of last place," I said, knocking off a third of a pint.

"and worse," said Henderson, "I think it was my wife who gave me the crabs."

I didn't know whether to laugh or what, so I kept quiet.

there was a most delicate knock on the office door and then it opened. and here stood some nut with paper wings glued to his back.

it was a kid about 18. "I'm here to help your club," said the kid.

he had on these big paper wings. a real nut. holes cut in his suit. the wings are glued to his back. or strapped. or something.

"listen," said Henderson, "will you please get the hell out of here! we've got enough comedy on the field now, just playing it straight. they laughed us right out of the park today. now, get *out* and *fast!*"

the kid reached over, took a slug from the pint, set it down and said, "Mr. Henderson, I am the answer to your prayers."

"kid," said Henderson, "you're too young to drink that stuff."

"I'm older than I look," said the kid.

"and I got somethin' that will make you a little older!" Henderson pressed the little button under his desk. that meant Bull Kronkite. I ain't sayin' the Bull has ever killed a man but you'll be lucky to be smoking Bull Durham out of a rubber asshole when he gets through with you. the Bull came in almost taking one of the hinges off the door as he entered.

"which ONE, boss?" he asked, his long stupid fingers twitching as he looked about the room.

"the punk with the paper wings," said Henderson.

the Bull moved in.

"don't touch me," said the punk with the paper wings.

the Bull rushed in, AND SO HELP ME GOD, that punk began to FLY! he flapped around the room, up near the ceiling. Henderson and I both reached for the pint but the old man beat me to it. the Bull dropped to his knees:

"LORD IN HEAVEN, HAVE MERCY ON ME! AN ANGEL! AN ANGEL!"

"don't be a jerk!" said the angel, flapping around, "I'm no angel. I just want to help the Blues. I been a Blues fan ever since I can remember."

"all right. come on down. let's talk business," said Henderson.

the angel, or whatever it was, flew on down and landed in a chair. the Bull ripped off the shoes and stockings of whatever it was and started kissing its feet.

Henderson leaned over and in a very disgusted manner spit into the Bull's face: "fuck off, you subnormal freak! anything I hate is such sloppy sentimentality!"

the Bull wiped off his face and left very quietly.

Henderson flipped through the desk drawers.

"shit, I thought I had me some contract papers in here somewhere!"

meanwhile, while looking for the contract papers he found another pint and opened that. he looked at the kid while ripping off the cellophane:

"tell me, can you hit an inside curve? outside? how about the slider?"

"god damned if I know," said the guy with the wings, "I been hiding out. all I know is what I read in the papers and see on TV but I've always been a Blues fan and I've felt very sorry for you this season."

"you been hidin' out? *where?* a guy with wings can't hide out in an elevator in the Bronx! what's your *hype?* how've you made it?"

"Mr. Henderson, I don't want to bore you with all the details."

"by the way, what's your name, kid?"

"Jimmy. Jimmy Crispin. J.C. for short."

"hey, kid, what the *fuck* you tryin' to do, get funny with *me?*"

"oh *no*, Mr. Henderson."

"then shake hands!"

they shook.

7

"god damn, your hands is sure COLD! you had anything to eat lately?"

"I had some french fries and beer with chicken about 4 p.m."

"have a drink, kid."

Henderson turned to me. "Bailey?"

"yeh?"

"I want the full friggin' ballteam down on that field at 10 a.m. tomorrow morning. no exceptions. I think we've got the biggest thing since the a-bomb. now let's all get outa here and get some sleep. you got a place to sleep, kid?"

"sure," said J.C. then he flew down the stairway and left us there.

we had the park locked tight. nobody in there but the ball-team. and with their hangovers and looking at the guy with the wings they thought it was some publicity gag. or a practice for one. they put the team on the field and the kid at the plate. but you should have been there to see those bloodshot eyes OPEN when the kid tapped a roller down the 3rd base line and FLEW to first base! then he touched down and before the 3rd base man could let go of the ball the kid flew on down to 2nd base.

everybody just kind of swayed in the early 10 p.m. sunlight. playing for a team like the Blues you figured you were crazy anyway but this was something else.

then as the pitcher got ready to throw to the batboy who we had put at the plate, J.C. flew on down to third base! he jetted on down! you couldn't even *see* the wings, even if you had had time for two alka seltzers that morning. and by the time the ball got to the plate, this thing had flown in and touched home plate.

we found the kid could play the *whole* outfield. his flying speed was tremendous! we just brought in the two other outfielders and put them in the infield. that gave us two shortstops and two second basemen. and as *bad* as we were, we were hell.

that night would be our first league game with Jimmy Crispin in the outfield.

first thing I did when I got in was to phone Bugsy Malone.

"Bugsy, what are the odds against the Blues finishing first?"

"ain't no odds. the bet is off the board. no damn fool would bet the Blues even at 10,000 to one."

"what'll you give me?"

"are you serious?"

"yeah."

"250 to one. you wanna bet a dollar, is that it?"

"one grand."

"one *grand*! now wait a minute! let me call you back in two hours."

the phone rang in an hour and forty-five minutes. "all right, I'll take you. I can always use a grand. somehow."

"thanks, Bugsy."

"you're welcome."

that first night game, I'll never forget it. they thought we were pulling some laugh stunt to get the crowds in but when they saw Jimmy Crispin rise into the sky and pull down an obvious home run that would have cleared the left centerfield fence by ten feet, then the game was on. Bugsy had flown down to check things out and I watched him in his box seat. when J.C. flew up to grab that one Bugsy's five dollar cigar dropped out of his mouth. but there was nothing in the rulebook that said a man with wings couldn't play baseball so we had them by the balls. and how. we took that game easy. Crispin scored 4 times. they couldn't hit anything out of our infield and anything in the outfield was a sure out.

and the games that followed. how the crowds came in. it was enough to drive them mad to see a man flying in the sky but the fact that we were 25 games out and with such little time left was also what kept them coming. the crowd loves to see a man get off the deck. the Blues were driving. it was the miracle of the times.

LIFE came to interview Jimmy. TIME. LIFE. LOOK. he told them nothing. "I just want to see the Blues win the pennant," he said.

but it was still tough, mathematically, and like a storybook ending it came down to the last game of the season, tied with the Bengals for first place and playing the Bengals, and winner take all. we hadn't lost a game since Jimmy joined the team. and I was pretty close to $250,000.00. what a manager I was!

we were in the office just before that last night game, old man Henderson and I. and we heard the noise on the stairway, and then a guy fell through the door, drunk. J.C. his wings were gone. just stumps.

"they sawed off my motherfucking wings, the rats! they put this woman on me in the hotel room. what a woman! what a broad! man, they loaded my drinks! I got on top of this cunt and they began SAWING MY WINGS OFF. I couldn't move! I couldn't even get my nuts! what a FARCE! and all the time, this guy smoking a cigar, laughing and cackling in the background . . . – oh god, what a beautiful woman, and I couldn't get it . . . – oh, shit . . ."

"well, baby, you aren't the first guy a woman has fucked-up. is there any bleeding?" asked Henderson.

"no, it's just bone, a bone-thing, but I'm so sad, I've let you fellows down, I've let the Blues down, I feel terrible, terrible, terrible."

they felt terrible? I was out 250 grand.

I finished the pint on the desk. J.C. was too drunk to play, wings or no wings. Henderson just put his head down on the desk and began crying. I found his luger in the bottom drawer. I put it into my coat and went out of the tower and down into the reserve section. I took the box right behind Bugsy Malone and some beautiful woman he was sitting with. it was Henderson's box and Henderson was drinking himself to death with a dead angel. he wouldn't need that box. and the team wouldn't need me. I'd phoned down to the dugout and told them to turn the thing over to the batboy or somebody.

"hello, Bugsy," I said.

it was our field so they had first at bats.

"where's your center fielder? I don't see him," said Bugsy, lighting up a five buck cigar.

"our center fielder has gone back to heaven due to one of your $3.50 Sears-Roebuck hacksaws."

Bugsy laughed. "a guy like me can piss in a mule's eye and come up with a mint julep. that's why I am where I am."

"who's the beautiful lady?" I asked.

"oh, this is Helena. Helena, this is Tim Bailey, the worst manager in baseball."

Helena crossed those nylon things called legs and I forgave Crispin for everything.

"nice to meetcha, Mr. Bailey."

"yeah."

the game began. it was old times. by the 7th inning we were behind 10 to 0. Bugsy was feeling damn good by then, feeling this broad's legs, rubbing up against her, having the whole world in his pocket. he turned to me and handed me a five buck cigar. I lit up.

"was this guy really an angel?" he asked me, kind of smiling.

"he said to call him J.C. for short, but damned if I know."

"looks like Man has beat God nearly everytime they have tangled," he said.

"I don't know," I said, "but the way I figure it, cutting a man's wings off is kind of like cutting his cock off."

"maybe so. but the way I see it, the strong make things go."

"or death makes things stop. which one *is* it?"

I pulled the luger out and put it at the back of his head.

"for Christ's sake, Bailey! get hold of yourself! I'll give you half of everything I've got! no, I'll give you everything I've got – this broad, everything, the works – just take that gun away from my head!"

"if you think killing is strong, then TASTE some strong!"

I pulled the trigger. it was awful. a luger. parts of eggshell head, and brain and blood everywhere: over me, over her nylon legs, her dress . . .

the game was held up an hour while they got us out of there – the dead Bugsy, his crazy hysterical woman, and me. then they finished out the innings.

God over Man; Man over God. mother preserved strawberries while everything was so very sick.

it was the next day in my cell when the screw handed me the paper:

"BLUES PULL IT OUT IN 14th INNING, WIN 12-11 GAME AND PENNANT."

I walked to the cell window, 8 floors up. I balled the paper up and jammed it through the bars, I jammed and jolted the paper up and shoved it through the bars and as it fell through the air I watched it, it spread, it seemed to have wings, well, horseshit on that, it floated down like any piece of unfolding paper does, toward the sea, those white and blue waves down there and I couldn't touch them, God beat Man always and continually, God being Whatever It Was – a cocksucker machinegun or the painting of Klee, well, and now, those nylon legs folding around another damn fool. Malone owed me 250 grand and couldn't pay off. J.C. with wings, J.C. without wings, J.C. on a cross, I was still a little alive and I walked back across the floor, sat upon that prison pot without a lid and began to shit, x-major league manager, x-man, and a slight wind came through the bars and a slight way to go.

———

it was hot in there. I went to the piano and played the piano. I didn't know how to play the piano. I just hit the keys. some people danced on the couch. then I looked under the piano and saw a girl stretched out under there, her dress up around her hips. I played with one hand, reached under and copped a feel with the other. either the bad music or copping that feel woke up the girl. she climbed out from under the piano. the people stopped dancing on the couch. I made it to the couch and slept for fifteen minutes. I hadn't slept for two nights and two days. it was hot in there, hot. when I awakened I vomited in a coffee cup. then that was full and I had to let go on the couch. somebody brought a large pot. just in time. I let it go. sour. everything was sour.

I got up and walked into the bathroom. two guys were in there naked. one of them had some shaving cream and a brush and was lathering up the other guy's cock and balls.

"listen, I got to take a shit," I told them.

"go ahead," said the guy being lathered, "we ain't bothering you."

I went ahead and sat down.

the guy with the brush said to the guy being lathered, "I hear Simpson got fired from Club 86."

"KPFK," said the other guy, "they can more people than Douglas Aircraft, Sears Roebuck and Thrifty Drugs combined. one wrong word, one sentence out of line with their pre-baked conceptions of humanity, politics, art, so forth, and you've had it. the only safe guy on KPFK is Eliot Mintz – he's like a kid's toy accordion: no matter how you squeeze him you get the same sound."

"now go ahead," said the guy with the brush.

"go ahead what?"

"rub your dick until it gets hard."

I dropped a big one.

"jesus!" said the guy with the brush, but he no longer had the brush. he'd thrown it in the sink.

"jesus what?" said the other guy.

"you got a head on that thing like a mallet!"

"I had an accident once. it caused it."

"I wish I could have an accident that way."

I dropped another one.

"now go ahead."

"go ahead what?"

"bend way back and slip it between your upper legs."

"like this?"

"yeah."

"now what?"

"bring your belly down. slide it. back and forth. make your legs tight. that's it! see! you'll never need another woman!"

"oh Harry, it just *ain't* like pussy! what you giving me? you're giving me a lot of shit!"

"it just takes PRACTICE! you'll see! you'll see!"

I wiped, flushed and got out of there.

I went to the refrigerator and got another can of beer, I got 2 cans of beer, opened them both and began on the first one. I figured that I was someplace in North Hollywood. I sat across from some guy with a red tin helmet on and a two foot beard. he'd been brilliant for a couple of nights but was coming down off the speed and was out of speed. but he hadn't hit the sleep stage yet, just the sad and vacant stage. just maybe hoping for a joint but nobody was showing anything.

"Big Jack," I said.

"Bukowski, you owe me 40 dollars," said Big Jack.

"listen, Jack, I have this idea that I gave you 20 dollars the other night. I really have this idea. I remember this 20."

"but you don't *remember, do* you Bukowski? because you were *drunk*, Bukowski, that's why you don't remember!"

Big Jack had this thing against drunks.

his girl friend Maggy was sitting next to him. "you gave him a 20, all right, but it was because you wanted some more to drink. we went out and got you some stuff and brought you the change."

"all right. but where are we? North Hollywood?"

"no, Pasadena."

"Pasadena? I don't believe it."

I had been watching these people go behind this big curtain. some of them came out in ten or twenty minutes. some of them never came out. it had been going on for 48 hours. I finished the 2nd beer, got up, pulled the curtain back and went in there. it was very dark in there but I smelled grass. and ass. I stood there and let my eyes adjust. it was mostly guys. licking assholes. reaming. sucking. it was not for me. I was square. it was like the men's gym after everybody had worked out on the parallel bars. and the sour smell of semen. I gagged. a light colored negro came up to me.

"hey, you're Charles Bukowski, aren't you?"

"yeh," I said.

"wow! this is the thrill of my life! I read *CRUCIFIX IN A DEATHHAND*. I consider you the greatest since Verlaine!"

"Verlaine?"

"yeah, Verlaine!"

he reached out and cupped a hand around my balls. I took his hand away.

"what's the matter?" he asked.

"not just yet, baby, I'm looking for a friend."

"oh, sorry . . ."

he walked on off. I kept looking around and was just about ready to leave when I noticed a woman kind of leaning against a far corner. she had her legs open but seemed rather dazed. I walked on over and looked at her. I dropped my pants and shorts. she looked all right. I put the thing in. I put in what I had.

"oooh," she said, "it's good! you're so curved! like a gaff!"

"accident I had when I was a child. something with the tricycle."

"oooooh . . ."

I was just going good when something RAMMED into the cheeks of my ass. I saw flashes before my eyes.

"hey, what the HELL!" I reached and pulled the thing out. I was standing there with this guy's thing in my hand. "what do you think you're doing, buddy?" I asked him.

"listen, friend," he said, "this whole game is just one big deck of cards. if you want to get into the game you have to take whatever comes up in the shuffle."

I pulled up my shorts and pants and got out of there.

Big Jack and Maggy were gone. a couple of people were passed out on the floor. I went and got another beer, drank that and walked outside. the sunlight hit me like a squad car with the red lights on. I found my short pushed into somebody else's driveway with a parking ticket on it. but there was still room to get out of the driveway. everybody knew just how far to go. it was nice.

I stopped at the Standard Station and the man told me how to get on the Pasadena freeway. I made it home. sweating. biting my lips to stay awake. there was a letter in the mailbox from my x-wife in Arizona.

". . . I know you get lonely and depressed. when you do, you ought to go to The Bridge. I think that you would like those people. or some of them, anyhow. or you ought to go to the poetry readings at the Unitarian Church . . ."

I let the water run into the bathtub, good and hot. I undressed, found a beer, drank half, set the can on the ledge and got into the tub, took the lather and the brush and began dabbing at the string and knobs.

————————

I met Kerouac's boy Neal C. shortly before he went down to lay along those Mexican railroad tracks to die. his eyes were sticking out on ye old toothpicks and he had his head in the speaker, jogging, bouncing, ogling, he was in a white t-shirt and seemed to be singing like a cuckoo bird along with the music, *preceding* the beat just a shade as if he were leading the parade. I sat down with my beer and watched him. I'd brought in a six pack or two. Bryan was handing out an assignment and some film to two young guys who were going to cover that show that kept getting busted. whatever happened to that show by the Frisco poet, I forget his name. anyhow, nobody was noticing Neal C. and Neal C. didn't care, or he pretended not to. when the song stopped, the 2 young guys left and Bryan introduced me to the fab Neal C.

"have a beer?" I asked him.

Neal plucked a bottle out, tossed it in the air, caught it, ripped the cap off and emptied the half-quart in two long swallows.

"have another."

"sure."

"I thought I was good on the beer."

"I'm the tough young jail kid. I've read your stuff."

"read your stuff too. that bit about climbing out the bathroom window and hiding in the bushes naked. good stuff."

"oh yeah." he worked at the beer. he never sat down. he kept moving around the floor. he was a little punchy with the action, the eternal light, but there wasn't any hatred in him. you liked him even though you didn't want to because Kerouac had set him up for the sucker punch and Neal had bit, kept biting. but you know Neal was o.k. and another way of looking at it, Jack had only written the book, he wasn't Neal's mother. just his destructor, deliberate or otherwise.

Neal was dancing around the room on the Eternal High. his face looked old, pained, all that, but his body was the body of a boy of eighteen.

"you want to try him, Bukowski?" asked Bryan.

"yeah, ya wanta go, baby?" he asked me.

again, no hatred. just going with the game.

"no, thanks. I'll be forty-eight in August. I've taken my last beating."

I couldn't have handled him.

"when was the last time you saw Kerouac?" I asked.

I think he said 1962, 1963. anyhow, a long time back.

I just about stayed with Neal on the beer and had to go out and get some more. the work at the office was about done and Neal was staying at Bryan's and B. invited me over for dinner. I said, "all right," and being a bit high I didn't realize what was going to happen.

when we got outside a very light rain was just beginning to fall. the kind that really fucks up the streets. I still didn't know. I thought Bryan was going to drive. but Neal got in and took the wheel. I had the back seat anyhow. B. got up in front with Neal. and the ride began. straight along those slippery streets and it would seem we were past the corner and then Neal would decide to take a right or a left. past parked cars, the dividing line just a hair away. it can only be described as hairline. a tick the other way and we were all finished.

after we cleared I would always say something ridiculous like, "well, suck my dick!" and Bryan would laugh and Neal would just go on driving, neither grim or happy or sardonic, just there – doing the movements. I understood. it was necessary. it was his bull ring, his racetrack. it was *holy* and necessary.

the best one was just off Sunset, going north toward Carlton. the drizzle was good now, ruining both the vision and the streets. turning off of Sunset, Neal picked up his next move, full-speed chess, it had to be calculated in an instant's glance. a left on Carlton would bring us to Bryan's. we were a block off. there was one car ahead of us and two approaching. now, he could have slowed down and followed the traffic in but he would have lost his *movement*. not Neal. he swung out around the car ahead of us and I thought, this is it, well, it doesn't matter, really it doesn't matter at all. that's the way it goes through your brain, that's the way it went through my brain. the two cars plunged at each other, head-on, the other so close that the headlights flooded my back seat. I do think that at the last second the other driver touched his brake. that gave us the hairline. it must have been figured in by Neal. that movement. but it wasn't over. we were going very high speed now and the other car, approaching slowly from Hollywood Blvd. was just about blocking a left on Carlton. I'll always remember the color of that car. we got that close. a kind of gray-blue, an old car, coupe, humped and hard like a rolling steel brick thing. Neal cut left. to me it looked as if we were going to ram right through the center of the car. it was obvious. but somehow, the motion of the other car's forward and our movement left coincided perfectly. the hairline was there. once again. Neal parked the thing and we went on in. Joan brought the dinner in.

Neal ate all of his plate and most of mine too. we had a bit of wine. John had a highly intelligent young homosexual baby-sitter, who I now think has gone on with some rock band or killed himself or something. anyhow, I pinched his buttocks as he walked by. he loved it.

I think I stayed long past my time, drinking and talking with Neal. the baby-sitter kept talking about Hemingway, somehow equating me with Hemingway until I told him to shove it and he went upstairs to check Jason. it was a few days later that Bryan phoned me:

"Neal's dead, Neal died."

"oh shit, no."

then Bryan told me something about it. hung up.

that was it.

all those rides, all those pages of Kerouac, all that jail, to die alone under a frozen Mexican moon, alone, you understand? can't you see the miserable puny cactii? Mexico is not a bad place because it is simply oppressed; Mexico is simply a bad place. can't you see the desert animals watching? the frogs, horned and simple, the snakes like slits of men's minds crawling, stopping, waiting, dumb under a dumb Mexican moon. reptiles, flicks of things, looking across this guy in the sand in a white t-shirt.

Neal, he'd found his movement, hurt nobody. the tough young jail kid laying it down alongside a Mexican railroad track.

the only night I met him I said, "Kerouac has written all your other chapters. I've already written your last one."

"go ahead," he said, "write it."

end copy.

————

the summers are longer where the suicides hang and the flies eat mudpie. he's a famous street poet of the '50's and still alive. I throw my bottle into the canal, it's Venice, and Jack is holing up at the place for a week or so, giving a reading somewhere in a few days. the canal looks strange, very strange.

"hardly deep enough for self-destruction."

"yeah," he says in the Bronx movie voice, "you're right."

he's gray at 37. hook-nose. slumped. energetic. pissed. male. very male. a little Jewish smile. maybe he's not Jewish. I don't ask him.

he's known them all. pissed on Barney Rosset's shoe at a party because he didn't like something Barney said. Jack knows Ginsberg, Greeley, Lamantia, on and on, and now he knew Bukowski.

"yeah, Bukowski came to Venice to see me. scars all over his face. shoulders slumped. very tired-looking man. doesn't say much and when he does it's kind of dull, kind of commonplace. you'd never think he'd written all those books of poems. but he's been in the post office too long. he's slipped. they've eaten his spirit out. damn shame, but you know how it works. but he's still boss, real boss, you know."

Jack knows the inside, and it's funny but real to know that people aren't much, it's all a motherfucking jive, and you've known it but it's funny to hear it said while sitting by a Venice canal trying to cure an extra-size hangover.

he goes through a book. photographs of poets mostly. I am not in there. I began late and lived too long alone in small rooms drinking wine. they always figure that a hermit is insane, and they may be right.

he goes through the book. jesus christ, it's a catsass sitting there with that hangover and the water down there, and here is Jack going through the book, I see spots of sunlight, noses, ears, the sheen of the photographic pages. I don't care, but I guess we need something to talk about and I don't talk well and he is doing the work, so here we go, Venice canal, the whole chicken-shit sadness of living it out –

"this guy went nuts about 2 years ago."

"this guy wanted me to suck his dick in order to get my book published."

"did you?"

"did I? I belted him out! wit' dis!"

he shows me the Bronx fist.

I laugh. he's comfortable and he's human. every man is afraid of being a queer. I get a little tired of it. maybe we should all become queers and relax. not belting Jack. he's good for a change. there are too many people afraid to speak against queers – intellectually. just as there are too many people afraid to speak against the left wing – intellectually. I don't care which way it goes – I only know: there are too many people afraid.

so Jack's good meat. I've seen too many intellectuals lately. I get very tired of the precious intellects who must speak diamonds every time they open their mouths. I get tired of battling for each space of air for the mind. that's why I stayed away from people for so long, and now that I am meeting people, I find that I must return to my cave. there are other things beside the mind: there are insects and palm trees and pepper shakers, and I'll have a pepper-shaker in my cave, so laugh.

the people will always betray you.

never trust the people.

"the whole poetry game is run by the fags and the left-wing," he tells me, staring into the canal.

there is a kind of truth here that it is bitter and false to dispute and I don't know what to do with it. I am certainly aware that there is something wrong with the poetry game – the books of the famous are so very dull, including Shakespeare. was it the same *then*?

I decide to throw Jack some shit.

"remember the old *poetry* mag? I don't know if it was Monroe or Shapiro or what, now it's gotten so bad I don't read it anymore, but I remember a statement by Whitman:

"'to have great poets we need great audiences.' well, I always figure a Whitman a greater poet than I, if that matters, only this time I think he got the thing backwards. it should read:

"'to have great audiences we need great poets.'"

"yeah, so, all right," Jack said, "I met Creeley at a party this time and I asked him if he ever read Bukowski and he got frozen real solid, wouldn't answer me, man, like you know what I mean."

"let's get the fuck outa here," I say.

we go out toward my car. I've got a car, somehow. a lemon, of course. Jack's got the book with him. he's still turning pages.

"this guy sucks dick."

"oh yeah?"

"this guy married a schoolteacher who belts his ass with a whip. horrible woman. he ain't writ a word since his marriage. she's got his soul in her cunt-strap."

"you talking about Gregory or Kero?"

"no, this is *another* one!"

"holy Jesus!"

we keep walking toward my car. I feel rather dull but I can FEEL this man's energy, ENERGY, and I realize that it might be possible that I am walking next to one of the few immortal and unschooled poets of our time. and then, that doesn't matter either, after I think about it a moment.

I get on in. the lemon starts but the gearshift is fucked-up again. I've got to drive in low all the way and the bitch stalls at every signal, battery down, I pray, one more start, no cops, no more drunk-driving raps, no more christs of any kinds on anybody's kind of Cross, we can choose between Nixon and Humphrey and Christ and be fucked anyway we turn, and I turn left, brake up at the address and we get out.

Jack's still at the pages.

"this guy's o.k. he killed himself, his father, his mother, wife, but didn't shoot his three children or the dog. one of the best poets since Baudelaire."

"yeah?"

"yeah, shit."

we get out of the lemon as I make the sign of the Cross for one more start on the mother battery.

we walk up and Jack bangs a door.

"BIRD! BIRD! this is Jack!"

the door opens and there is the Bird. I look twice. I can't see whether it is a woman or a man. the face is the distilled essence opium of untouched beauty. it's a man. the motions are man. I know it but I also know that he can catch hell and ultimate brutality every time he hits the streets. they will kill him because he has not died at all. I have died nine-tenths but keep the other one-tenth like a gun. I can walk down the street and they can't tell me from the news vendor, even tho the news vendors have more beautiful faces than any president of the united states, but then, that's no task either.

"Bird, I need 20," says Jack.

Bird peels off a g.d. twenty. his movement is smooth, without worry.

"thanks, baby."

"sure, can you come on in?"

"all right."

we move in. sit down. there's the bookcase. I lay my eyes across it. there doesn't seem to be a dull book in there. I catch all the books I've admired in there. what the hell? is it a dream? the kid's face is so beautiful that everytime I look I feel good, like you know, chili and beans, hot, after coming off a bad one, the first food in weeks, well, fuck, I am always on guard.

the Bird. and the ocean down there. and bad battery. a lemon. the cops patrolling their stupid dry streets. what a bad war it is. and what an idiot nightmare, only this momentary cool space between us, we are all going to be smashed, very quickly into broken children's toys, into those highheels that ran so gaily down the stairway to be flicked out of it forever, forever, dunces and fools, dunces and tools, god damn our weak bravery.

we sit down. a quart of scotch appears. I pour a quarter of a pint down without pause, ah, I gag, blink, idiot, working toward 50, still trying to play Hero. asshole hero in a fusillade of puke.

the Bird's wife comes in. we are introduced. she is a liquid woman in a brown dress, she just flows flows her eyes laughing, she flows, I tell you, she flows,

"WOW WOW WOW!" I say.

she looks so good I've got to pick her up, hug her, I carry her on my left hip, spin her, laugh. nobody thinks that I am crazy. we all laugh. we all understand. I put her down. we sit down.

Jack likes me coming on. he's been carrying my soul and he's tired. he grins the grin. he's o.k. once in a rare lifetime have you ever been in a roomful of people who only helped you when you looked at them, listened to them. this was one of those magic times. I knew it. I glowed like a fucking hot tamale. it didn't matter. o.k.

I smacked down another quarter pint out of embarrassment. I realized that I was the weaker of 4 people and I did not want to harm, I only wanted to realize their easy holiness. I loved like a crazy jackoff dog turned into a pen of heated female bitches, only they had miracles to show me beyond sperm.

the Bird looked at me.

"see my collage?"

he held up a very shitty-looking thing with a woman's earring and some other dab of shit hanging upon it.

(by the way . . . I realize I switch from present to past tense, and if you don't like it . . . ram a nipple up your scrotum. – printer: leave this in.)

I go into a long boring hartang harrangue about how I don't like this or that, and about my sufferance in Art Classes . . .

the Bird pulls the stop out of me.

by yanking the thing apart it's only a popneedle and then he grins at me, but then I too know the inside: that perhaps, as I am told, from inside, the only junky who can make it is Wm. Burroughs, who owns the Burroughs Co., almost, and who can play it tough while all along being a sissy fat wart-sucking hog inside. this is what I hear, and it's kept very quiet. is it true? for it all, true or not, Burroughs is a very dull writer and without the insistence of knowledgeable pop in his literary background, he would be almost nothing, as Faulkner is nothing except to very dry Southern extremists like Mr. Corrington, and Mr. Nod, and Mr. Suck-Dry-Shit.

"Baby," they start saying to me, "you are drunk."

and I am. and I am. and I am.

there's nothing now but be turned into the heat or sleep. they make a place for me.

I drink too fast. they talk on. I hear them, gently.

I sleep. I sleep in comradeship. the sea will not drown me and neither will they. they love my sleeping body. I am an asshole. they love my sleeping body. may all God's children come to this.

jesus jesus jesus
who cares about a dead
battery?

---

jesus, mother, it was terrible – here they came pounding out of the vast cuntholes in the earth spinning me about with my paper suitcase up near Times Square.

I finally managed to ask one of them where the Village was and when I got to the Village I found a room and when I opened my wine bottle and took off my shoes I found that the room had an easel, but I wasn't a painter, just a kid looking for luck, and I sat behind the easel and drank my wine and looked out the dirty window.

when I went out to get another bottle of wine I saw this young guy standing in a silk bathrobe. he wore a beret and sandals, had a half-diseased beard and spoke into the hall phone:

"oh, yes yes, darling, I *must see* you, oh yes, I *must*! I shall slash my wrists otherwise . . . ! yes!"

I've got to get out of here, I thought. he wouldn't slash his shoelaces. what a sickening little snip. and outside, they sat in the cafes, very comfortable, in berets, in the get-up, pretending to be Artists.

I stayed there a week drinking, finishing out the rent, and then I found a room outside the Village. for the looks and size of the room it was very cheap and I couldn't understand why. I found a bar around the corner and sipped at beers all day. my money was going but, as usual, I hated to look for a job. each drunken and starvation moment contained some type of easy meaning for me. that night I bought two bottles of port wine and went up to my room. I took off my clothes, got into bed in the dark, found a glass and poured the first wine. then I found why the room was so cheap. the "L" ran right past my window. and that's where the stop was. right outside my window. the whole room would be lit by the train. and I'd look at a whole trainload of faces. horrible faces: whores, orangutans, bastards, madmen, killers – all my masters. then, swiftly the train would start up and the room would be dark again – until the next trainload of faces, which was always too soon. I needed the wine.

a Jewish couple owned the building and also ran a tailor and cleaning shop across the street. I decided that my few rags needed cleaning. job-hunting time was belching and farting across my mad horizon. I went in drunk with my rags.

". . . need these cleaned or washed or something . . ."

"poor boy! why you are living in THREADS! I couldn't wash the windows with this stuff. tell you what . . . oh, Sam!"

"yeh?"

"show this nice boy that suit the man left!"

"oh yes, it's such a *nice* suit, mama! I don't *understand* how that man left it!"

I won't go through all the dialogue. mainly I insisted that the suit was too small. they said it wasn't. I said if it wasn't too small it was too high. they said seven. I said, broke. they said six. I said, I'm broke. when they got down to four I insisted that they get me inside the suit. they did. I gave them the four. went back to my room, took the suit off and slept. when I awakened it was dark (except when the "L" came by) and I decided to put on my new suit and go out and find a woman, a beautiful one, of course, to support a man of my still-hidden talents.

as I got into the pants the entire crotch split up the back. well, I was game. it was a little cool but I figured the coat would cover. when I got into the coat the left arm ripped out at the shoulder spilling out a sickening gummy padding.

taken again.

I got out of what remained of the suit and decided that I'd have to move again.

I found another place. a rather cellar-like structure, down the steps and in between the tenants' garbage cans. I was finding my level.

the first night out after the bars closed I found I had lost my key. I only had on a thin white Calif. shirt. I rode a bus back and forth to keep from freezing. finally the driver said it was the end of the line or the ride was over. I was too drunk to remember.

when I got out it was still freezing and I was standing outside of Yankee Stadium.

oh Lord, I thought, here is where my childhood hero Lou Gehrig used to play and now I am going to die out here. well, it's fitting.

I walked about a bit, then found a cafe. I walked in. the waitresses were all middle-aged negresses but the coffee cups were large and the doughnut and coffee hardly cost anything.

I took my stuff over to a table, sat down, ate the doughnut very quickly, sipped at the coffee, then took out a king-sized cigarette and lit it.

I started hearing voices:

"PRAISE THE LORD, BROTHER!"

"OH, PRAISE THE LORD, BROTHER!"

I looked around. all the waitresses were praising me and some of the customers too. it was very nice. recognition at last. the *Atlantic* and *Harper's* be damned. genius would always out. I smiled at them all and took a big drag.

then one of the waitresses screamed at me:

"NO SMOKING IN THE HOUSE OF THE LORD, BROTHER!"

I put the cigarette out. I finished the coffee. then I went outside and looked at the lettering on the window:

FATHER DIVINE'S MISSION.

I lit another cigarette and began the long walk back to my place. when I got there nobody would answer the bell. I finally stretched out on top of the garbage cans and went to sleep. I knew that down on the pavement the rats would get me. I was a clever young man.

I was so clever that I even got a job the next day. and the next night, hungover, shaky, very sad, I was at work.

two old guys were to break me in. they'd each been on the job since the subways were invented. we walked along with these heavy sheets of cardboard under the left arm and a little tool in the right hand that looked like a beercan opener.

"all the people in New York have these little green-colored bugs all over them," one of the old guys said.

"izzat so?" I said, not giving the least damn what color the bugs were.

"you'll see 'em on the seats. we find 'em on the seats each night."

"yeh," said the other old man.

we walked along.

good god, I thought, did this ever happen to Cervantes?

"now watch," said one of the old guys. "each card has a little number. we replace each card with the little number with another card with the same number."

flip, flip. he beercan-opened the strips, flipped in the new advertisement, replaced the strips, took the old advertisement and put it on the bottom of the pile of cards under his left arm.

"now you try it."

I tried it. the little strips didn't want to give. I had a bum can opener. and was sick and shaky.

"you'll get it," said an old guy.

I AM getting it, you fuck, I thought.

we moved along.

then we stepped out of the rear of the car and they went ahead stepping along the railroad ties between the tracks. the space between each board was about three feet. a body could easily fall through without even trying. and we were elevated about 90 feet from the street. and it must have been 90 feet to the new car. the two old guys skipped over the boards with their heavy cardboard load and waited for me at the new car. there was a train stopped across the way picking up passengers. it was well-lit around there, but that was all. the lights from the train clearly showed me the three foot gap between the boards.

"COME ON! COME ON! WE'RE IN A HURRY!"

"god damn you and your hurry!" I screamed at the two old guys. then I stepped out on the boards with my load of cardboard under my left arm and the beercan opener in my right hand. one step, two steps, three steps . . . hungover, sick.

then the train that was loading pulled out. it was dark as a closet. darker than a closet. I couldn't see. I couldn't take the next step. and I couldn't turn around. I just stood there.

"come on! come on! we got a lot more cars to do!"

finally my eyes refocused a bit. I began the wobbly steps again. some of the boards were soft, were worn round and splintered. I ceased to hear their shouting. I took the transfixed strides one after the other, expecting each next step to be the one that sent me on down through.

I made the other car and threw the cardboard ads and the can opener on the floor.

"watza matta?"

"watza matta? watza matta? I say, 'FUCK IT!' "

"what's wrong?"

"one misstep and a man can get killed. don't you idiots realize that?"

"nobody's gotten killed yet."

"nobody drinks like I do, either. now, come on, tell me, how do I get the hell out of here?"

"well, there's a stairway down to the right but you've got to walk across the tracks instead of along them and that means stepping over two or three third rails."

"fuck it. what's a third rail?"

"that's the power. you touch one and you're gone."

"show me the way."

the old boys pointed to the stairway down. it didn't seem too far away.

"thank you, gentlemen."

"watch the third rail. it's gold. don't touch it or you'll burn."

I stepped on out. I could sense them watching me. each time I reached a third rail I stepped high and fancy. they had a soft and calm look to them in the moonlight.

I reached the stairway and was alive again. at the bottom of the stairway there was a bar. I heard people laughing.

I went into the bar and sat down. some guy was telling stories about how his mother took care of him, made him take piano and painting lessons and how he managed to get money out of her, one way or the other, to get drunk on. the whole bar was laughing. I began laughing too. the guy was a genius, giving it away for nothing. I laughed until the bar closed and we broke up, each going our different ways.

I left New York soon after, never went back, never will. cities are built to kill people, and there are lucky towns and the other kind. mostly the other kind. in New York you've got to have all the luck. I knew I didn't have that kind. next thing I knew I was sitting in a nice room in east Kansas City listening to the manager beat up the maid because she'd failed to sell me a piece of her ass. it was real and peaceful and sane again. I listened to the screams while sitting up in bed, reached for my glass, had a good one, then stretched out among the clean sheets. the guy could really lay it on. I could hear her head bouncing against the wall.

maybe the next day when I wasn't so tired from the bus trip I'd let her have a little. she had a nice ass. at least he wasn't beating on that. and I was out of New York, almost alive.

———

those were the nights, the old days at the Olympic. they had a bald little Irishman making the announcements (was his name Dan Tobey?), and he had *style*, he'd seen things happen, maybe even on the riverboats when he was a kid, and if he wasn't *that* old, maybe Dempsey-Firpo anyhow. I can still see him reaching up for that cord and pulling the mike down slowly, and most of us were drunk before the first fight, but we were easy drunk, smoking cigars, feeling the light of life, waiting for them to put two boys in there, cruel but that was the way it worked, that is what they did to us and we were still alive, and, yes, most of us with a dyed redhead or blonde, even me. her name was Jane and we had many a good ten-rounder between us, one of them ending in a k.o. of me. and I was proud when she'd come back from the lady's room and the whole gallery would begin to pound and whistle and howl as she wiggled that big magic marvelous ass in that tight skirt – and it *was* a magic ass: she could lay a man stone cold and gasping, screaming lovewords to a cement sky. then she'd come down and sit beside me and I'd lift that pint like a coronet, pass it to her, she'd take her nip, hand it back, and I'd say about the boys in the gallery: "those screaming jackoff bastards, I'll kill them."

and she'd look at her program and say, "who do you want in the first?"

I picked them good – about 90 percent – but I had to see them first. I always chose the guy who moved around the least, who looked like he didn't want to fight, and if one *guy* gave the Sign of the Cross before the bell and the other guy didn't you had a winner – you took the guy who didn't. but it usually worked together: the guy who did all the shadow boxing and dancing around usually was the one who gave the Sign of the Cross and got his ass whipped.

there weren't many bad fights in those days and if there were it was the same as now – mostly between the heavyweights. but we let them know about it in those days – we tore the ring down or set the place on fire, busted up the seats. they just couldn't afford to give us too many bad ones. the Hollywood Legion ran the bad ones and we stayed away from the Legion. even the Hollywood boys knew the action was at the Olympic. Raft came, and the others, and all the starlets, hugging those front row seats. the gallery boys went ape and the fighters fought like fighters and the place was blue with cigar smoke, and how we screamed, baby baby, and threw money and drank our whiskey, and when it was over, there was the drive in, the old lovebed with our dyed and vicious women. you slammed it home, then slept like a drunk angel. who needed the public library? who needed Ezra? T.S. E.E.? D.H. H.D.? any of the Eliots? any of the Sitwells?

I'll never forget the first night I saw young Enrique Balanos. at the time, I had me a good colored boy. he used to bring a little white lamb into the ring with him before the fight and hug it, and that's corny but he was tough and good and a tough and good man is allowed certain leeways, right?

anyway, he was my hero, and his name might have been something like Watson Jones. Watson had good class and the flair – swift, quick quick quick, and the PUNCH, and he *enjoyed* his work. but then, one night, unannounced, some-body slipped this young Balanos in against him, and Balanos had it, took his time, slowly worked Watson down and took him over, busted him up good near the end. my hero. I couldn't believe it. if I remember, Watson was kayoed which made it a very bitter night, indeed. me with my pint screaming for mercy, screaming for a victory that simply would *not* happen. Balanos certainly had it – the fucker had a couple of snakes for arms, and he didn't *move* – he slid, slipped, jerked like some type of evil spider, always getting there, doing the thing. I knew that night that it would take a very excellent man to beat him and that Watson might as well take his little lamb and go home.

it wasn't until much later that night, the whiskey pouring into me like the sea, fighting with my woman, cursing her sitting there showing me all that fine leg, that I admitted that the better man had won.

"Balanos. good legs. he doesn't think. just reacts. better not to think. tonight the body beat the soul. it usually does. goodbye Watson, goodbye Central Avenue, it's all over."

I smashed my glass against the wall and went over and grabbed me some woman. I was wounded. she was beautiful. we went to bed. I remember a light rain came through the window. we let it rain on us. it was good. it was so good we made love twice and when we went to sleep we slept with our faces toward the window and it rained all over us and in the morning the sheets were all wet and we both got up sneezing and laughing, "jesus christ! jesus christ!" it was funny and poor Watson laying somewhere, his face slugged and pulpy, facing the Eternal Truth, facing the six rounders, the four rounders, then back to the factory with me, murdering eight or ten hours a day for pennies, getting nowhere, waiting on Papa Death, getting your mind kicked to hell and your spirit kicked to hell, we sneezed, "jesus christ!" it was funny and she said, "you're blue all over, you've turned all BLUE! jesus, look at yourself in the mirror!" and I was freezing and dying and I stood in front of the mirror and I was all BLUE! ridiculous! a skull and shit of bones! I began to laugh, I laughed so hard I fell down on the rug and she fell down on top of me and we both laughed laughed laughed, jesus christ we laughed until I thought we were crazy, and then I had to get up, get dressed, comb my hair, brush my teeth, too sick to eat, heaved when I brushed my teeth, I went outside and walked toward the overhead lighting factory, just the sun feeling good but you had to take what you could get.

———

Santa Anita, March 22, 1968, 3:10 p.m. I can't catch Quillo's Babe the even-money shot with Alpen Dance. the 4th race is over and I haven't touched a thing, I am $40.00 down, I should have had Boxer Bob in the 2nd with Bianco, one of the best unknown riders at the track at 9/5; any other jock, say Lambert or Pineda or Gonzales, the horse would have gone at 6/5 or even-money. but I've got an old saying (I make up old sayings as I walk around in rags) that knowledge without follow-through is worse than no knowledge at all. because if you're guessing and it doesn't work you can just say, shit, the gods are against me. but if *you know* and don't do, you've got attics and dark halls in your mind to walk up and down in and wonder about. this ain't healthy, leads to unpleasant evenings, too much to drink and the shredding machine.

all right. old horseplayers don't just fade away. they die. hard and finally, on east 5th or selling papers out front with a sailor's cap on, pretending it's all a lark, your mind split in half, your guts dangling, your cock without sweet pussy. I think that it was one of Freud's favorite pupils, who has now become a philosopher of some renown – my x-wife used to read him – who said that gambling was a form of masturbation. very nice to be a bright boy and say these things. and there is always a minor truth contained in almost every saying. if I were an easy bright boy I think I would say something like, "cleaning the fingernails with a dirty fingernail file is a form of masturbation." and I would probably win a scholarship, a grant, the king's sword on shoulder and 14 hot pieces of ass. I will only say this, out of a background of factories, park benches, two-bit jobs, bad women, bad weather of Life – the reason the average person is at the track is that they are driven screwy by the turn of the bolt, the foreman's insane face, the landlord's hand, the lover's dead sex; taxation, cancer, the blues; clothes that fall apart on a 3rd wearing, water that tastes like piss, doctors that run assembly-line and indecent offices, hospitals without heart, politicians with skulls filled with pus ... we can go on and on but would only be accused of being bitter and demented, but the world makes madmen (and women) of us all, and even the saints are demented, nothing is saved. so shit. well. according to my figures I've only had 2500 pieces of ass but I've watched 12,500 horse races, and if I have any advice to anybody it's this: take up watercolor painting.

but what I am trying to tell you is, that the reason most people are at the racetrack is that they are in agony, ey yeh, and they are so desperate that they will take a chance on further agony rather than face their present position (?) in life. now the big boys are not as half-ass as we think they are. they sit on mountain tops studying the ant-swirl. don't you think Johnson is proud of his bellybutton? and don't you realize, at the same time, that Johnson is one of the biggest assholes ever fomented upon us? we are hooked, slapped and chopped silly; so silly that some of us finally love our tormentors because they are there to torment us along logical lines of torture. this seems so reasonable, since there isn't anything else showing. it's got to be right because that's all there is. what? Santa Anita is there. Johnson is there. and, one way or another we keep them there. we build our own racks and scream when our genitals are torn off by the subnormal keeper waving the big silver cross (gold is out). let this explain, then, why some of us, if not most of us, if not all of us are there, say on a day like March 22, 1968, an afternoon in Arcadia, Calif.

end of 5th race won by the 12 horse Quadrant. the board reads 5/2 and I have to win on the nose. horse won big, running past horses in the stretch and drawing out. I have ten win and am $40.00 down and wait on the official sign. a 5/2 shot pays between $7.00 and $7.80 and so ten win means a return of between $35.00 and $39.00. so I figure I am about even. the horse was three on the line and never moved from 5/2 all during the betting. the official payoff was flashed on the board:

5:40.

right on the toteboard. $five-four-oooh. which lies halfway between 8/5 and 9/5 and is not 5/2 at all. earlier in the week, in an overnight gesture, the track doubled the parking fee from 25 cents to 50 cents. I doubt that the parking lot attendants' salaries were doubled. also they snatched the whole $2.00 instead of the $1.95 on entering. now, $5.40. god damn. a slow unbelievable moan went across the grandstand and through the infield. in watching nearly 13,000 races I had never seen an occurrence like this. the board is not infallible. I have seen a 9/5 pay $6.00, and other slight variances, but never have I seen a 5/2 pay close to 8/5 nor have I ever seen a 5/2 drop in one flash (the last one) from 5/2 to close to 8/5. it would have taken an almost unbelievable amount of money bet at the last moment to do this.

the crowd began to BOOOOO BOOOOOO BOOOOO! it died, then began again. BOOO, BOOOOOO, BOOOOO! and each time it began it lasted longer. the mob smelled rotten fish plus greed. the mob had been knifed, again. $5.40 meant a return to me of $27.00 instead of a possible $39.00. and I wasn't the only one affected. you could feel the mob writhing, stung; to many out there each race meant rent or no rent, food or no food, car payment or no car payment.

I looked down at the track and there was a man out there waving his program, pointing at the board. he was evidently talking to a track steward. then the man waved his program at the crowd, waving them in, asking them to come out onto the track. one man came through, leaping the rail. the crowd cheered. another man found the gateway opening in the rail. now there were three. the crowd cheered. people were feeling better. now they came, more and more and the crowd cheered. everybody was feeling better. a chance. a chance? something of some sort. more came. there must have been between 40 and 65 people spread across the track.

the announcer came on over the speaker: "LADIES AND GENTLEMEN, WE ARE ASKING YOU TO PLEASE CLEAR THE TRACK SO THAT WE MAY BEGIN THE 6th RACE!"

his voice was not kindly. there were ten track policemen down there in their Santa Anita grays. each man carried a gun. the crowd booed, BOOOOOOOED!

then one of the players down there noticed that the next race was on the turf. hell, they were blocking the dirt track. the crowd moved on over to the grass infield which circles inside the dirt track as the horses came out for the post parade. there were eight horses led by the outrider in his red hunting jacket and black cap. the crowd spread across the track.

"PLEASE," the announcer said, "CLEAR THE TRACK! PLEASE CLEAR THE TRACK! THE TOTEBOARD WAS UNABLE TO REGISTER THE LAST FLASH DOWN IN THE BETTING. THE PRICE IS CORRECT!"

the horses moved slowly toward the waiting crowd. those horses looked very big and nervous.

I asked Denver Danny, a guy who has hung around the tracks much longer than I, "what the hell gives, Denver?"

"the board reads properly," he said, "that's not the bitch. each dollar bet is recorded. when the machines closed the board read 5/2; the board flashed again and there were the final variances but the 5/2 remained. now the French have an old saying, 'who is to guard the guards themselves?' as you recall, Quadrant was the obvious winner a 3rd of the way down the stretch, drawing out. a number of things could have happened. perhaps the machines were never locked during the running. when Quadrant was the obvious winner management could have stood there and kept punching out winning tickets. others say that one or two machines can be fixed to remain open and in use when the others are locked. I really don't know. all I know is that some SHIT went on and everybody else here knows it too."

the horses moved on toward the crowd. the outrider and the front horse, a monster, RICH DESIRE, br. g.4, Pierce up, moved toward the line of waiting people. one of the boys called the track police something very filthy and three of the cops took him over to the rail and roughed him up a bit. the crowd got on them and they let him go and ran back to their positions in front of the line of people spread across the track. the horses kept moving forward, and you could see that they intended to go through. the orders were in. this was the moment: men on horses against men with nothing. two or three guys lay down in front of the horses, right in front of the line of march. this was it. the outrider's face distorted suddenly, it got as red as his hunting jacket, and he grabbed the number one horse, RICH DESIRE, by the rein, spurred his horse and rammed through human flesh, eyes shut. the horse got through. I'm not sure whether he broke anybody's back or not.

but the outrider had earned his salary. a good management boy. and some of the few scabs in the stands cheered. but it wasn't over. a few of the guys grabbed at the number one horse and tried to pull the jock out of the saddle and to the ground. then the police moved in. the other horses got on through but the boys momentarily had the number one horse and Pierce was almost pulled out of the saddle. this was the final sway of the tide.

I'm sure that if they could have gotten Pierce out of the saddle they would have ended up burning the grandstands and smashing up the whole damn dumb scene. meanwhile the cops were working over the boys pretty good. no guns were pulled but it looked like the cops were enjoying the action, especially one cop who kept hitting an old man along the top of the head, back of the neck and along the spine. Pierce got on through with RICH DESIRE, an aptly named gelding, and the horse warmed up for their mile and one half on the turf. the cops seemed particularly vicious and energetic and the protesters didn't seem too interested in fighting back. the game was lost. so the track was cleared.

the next voice that went up was: "DON'T BET! DON'T BET! DON'T BET!"

what a thing that would have been, eh? not a dollar for the vultures – fat subnormal slobs thrown out of Beverly Hills homes. all too good. there was already six grand in the mutuels when they started to holler, "DON'T BET!" we were hooked, bleeding, gotten forever … there was nothing we could do but bet again and again and again and take it.

ten cops stood along the infield rail. proud and true and sweating, they'd earned a hard day's pay. the winner of the 6th was OFF, who read nine to one and paid that. if the board has paid eight or seven there would be no Santa Anita today.

I read that the next day, Saturday, there were around 45,000 people at the track, which was about normal.

I was not there and I was not missed and the horses ran and I wrote this.

March 23, 8 p.m., Los Angeles the same damn sadness and no place to go.

maybe next time we'll get that number one horse.

it takes practice, a little laughter and some luck.

––––––––

this guy in the army fatigues came up to me and said, "now that it happened to Kennedy you'll have something to write about." he claims to be a writer, why doesn't *he* write about it? I've always got to pick up their messy balls and put them into a little literary sack for them. I think we've got enough experts on the case now – that's what this decade is: the

Decade of the Experts and the Decade of the Assassins. and neither one of them worth crystallized dog turds. the main problem with a thing like that last assassination is that we not only lose a man of some worth but we also lose political, spiritual and social gains, and there *are* such things, even if they do seem high-sounding. what I mean is, that in an assassination crisis the anti-human and reactionary forces tend to solidify their prejudices and to use all ruptures as a means of knocking natural Freedom off the goddamned end seat at the bar.

I don't want to get as holy about being *active* and involved with mankind as Camus did (see his essays) because basically most of mankind sickens me and the only saving that *can* be done is a whole new concept of Universal Education-Vibration understanding of happiness, reality and flow, and that's for the little children who ain't murdered yet, but they will be, I'll lay you twenty-five to one, for no new concept will be allowed – it would be too destructive to the power gang. no, I'm no Camus, but, sweetheart, it bothers me to see the Klankheads making hay out of Tragedy.

Gov. Reagan's statement, in part: "The average man, decent, law-abiding, God-fearing, is as disturbed and worried as you and I about what happened.

"He, and all of us, are the victims of an attitude that has been growing in our land for nearly a decade – an attitude that says a man can choose the laws he must obey, that he can take the law into his own hands for a cause, that crime does not necessarily mean punishment.

"This attitude has been spurred by demagogic and irresponsible words of so-called leaders in and out of office."

but, God, I can't go on. it's so dreary. the Father-Image with ye old razor strop to whip our ass. now the good governor is going to take away our toys and put us to bed without dinner.

lord lord, I didn't murder Kennedy, either one of them. or King. or Malcom X. or the rest. but it's fairly obvious to me that the Left Wing Liberal forces are being picked off one by

one – *whatever* the reason (a suspect who once worked in a
health food store and hated Jews) – *whatever* the reason, the
left-wingers are being murdered and put into their graves
while the right-wingers don't even get grass-stains upon their
pantscuffs. and weren't Roosevelt and Truman also shot at?
Democrats. how very odd.

that the assassins are sick, I will admit, and that the
Father-Image is also sick, I will also admit. I'm also told by
the God-fearing that I have "sinned" because I was born a
human being and once upon a time human beings did
something to one Jesus Christ. I neither killed Christ or
Kennedy and neither did Gov. Reagan. that makes us even,
not him *one* up. I see no reason to lose any judicial or
spiritual freedoms, small as these may be now. who is
bullshitting who? if a man dies in bed while fucking, must the
rest of us stop copulating? if one non-citizen is a madman
must all citizens be treated as madmen? if somebody killed
God, did I want to kill God? if somebody wanted to kill
Kennedy did I want to kill Kennedy? what makes the
governor, *himself*, so right and the rest of us so wrong?
speech-writers, and not very good ones at that.

a very curious aside: I had no reason to drive throughout
town June 6th and 7th and in the Negro districts nine out of
ten cars had their headlights burning in daylight in tribute to
Kennedy; driving North the ratio lessened until along Hollywood Blvd. and along Sunset between La Brea and Normandie it became one in ten. Kennedy was a white man, babies.
I am white. as I drove my headlights did not burn. neverthe-
less, while driving between Exposition and Century, I got
some cool and wonderful chills that made me feel better.

but like I say, everybody including the governor has a
mouth and almost everybody let go, ingraining their prejudices, making personal hay outa tragedy. those who *got*
wanta keep and they are going to tell you how wrong
everything is that might strip them of their golden drawers. I
am apolitical but with these murky curve-balls these reaction-
aries throw, I might get pissed and into the game yet.

even the sportswriters got into the game, and as anybody knows the sportswriters are the worst of the worst when it comes to writing and especially when it comes to thinking. I don't know which is worse, their writing or their thinking, but whichever is on top it is a union which will only bear illegitimate and unendearing monsters. as you must realize, the worst form of humor takes its dreary tool in extreme exaggeration. so does the worst form of ego-patronizing and emotional-patronizing type of thinking.

one sportswriter on our largest non-striking newspaper came on like this, in part (while R. Kennedy was in surgery):

"The Violent State of America: A Nation in Surgery"

". . . once again America the Beautiful has taken a bullet to the groin. The country is in surgery. The Violent States of America. One bullet is mightier than one million votes . . .

"It's not a Democracy, it's a Lunacy. A country that shrinks from punishing its criminals, disciplining its children, locking up its mad . . .

"the President of the United States is chosen in a hardware store, a mail order catalogue . . .

"Freedom is being gunned down. The 'right' to murder is the ultimate right in this country. Sloth is a virtue. Patriotism is a sin. Conservation is an anachronism. God is over thirty years old. To be young is the only religion – as if it were a hardwon virtue. 'Decency' is dirty feet, a scorn for work. 'Love' is something you need penicillin for. 'Love' is handing a flower to a naked young man with vermin in his hair while your mother sits home with a broken heart. You 'love' strangers, not parents.

"I like people with curtains on the window, not people with 'pads.' The next guy that calls money 'bread' should be paid off in whole wheat. I am sick of being told I should try to 'understand' evil. Should a canary 'understand' a cat?

"The Constitution was never conceived as a shield for degeneracy. You start out burning the flag and you end up burning Detroit. You do away with the death penalty for everyone but Presidential candidates – and presidents . . .

"... Men of God become men of the Mob. The National Anthem is a scream in the night. Americans can't walk in their own parks, get on their own buses. They have to cage themselves.

"'Get off your knees, America!' people cry, but it is ignored. Bare your teeth, they say. Threaten to fight back. The lion bares his teeth and the jackals slink away. A cowering animal invites attack. But America is not listening.

"... neurotic students with their feet on desks they couldn't make, pulling down universities they wouldn't know how to rebuild.

"... it all begins with that, the deification of drifters, wastrels, poltroons – insolent guests at the gracious table of democracy overturning it on their dismayed hosts ...

"... Pray God our healers can repair Bobby Kennedy. Who is going to repair America?"

do you want this guy? I thought so. too easy. pre-graduate purple prose colored only from a survival viewpoint of present position. do you drive a garbage truck? don't feel bad. there are better jobs, done worse.

lock up the mad. but who *is* mad? we all play our little game, depending upon the positions of the pawns, the knights, the castles, the king, the queen, ah, what the hell, I'm beginning to sound like *him*.

and now we will have the headshrinkers, the thinkers, the panels, the appointed presidential boards trying to figure out what's wrong with us. who's mad, who's glad, who's sad, who's right, who's wrong. lock up the mad, when fifty-nine out of sixty men you meet on the street are cuckoo with industrial neuroses and wives and strives and no time to loosen up and find out where they are or why, and when money which has kept them boosted and blinded for so fucking long, when that's no good no longer, then what we gonna *do*? come, baby, the assassins have been with us for a long time. only it ain't been a blast, just a man with a face like sawdust and eyes like shitstains, so many men like that and women too. millions of them.

and soon we will have the reports from the headshrinker panels, which like the poverty panels which told us that some men are starving downstairs, they will tell us that some men are starving upstairs; and then everything will be forgotten until the next little emotional little murder or city burning, and then they will assemble again and utter their dull little expected words, rub their hands and disappear like turds down a flushing pot. it really seems that they don't care so long as the balance board is maintained. and those little headshrinkers, flashing their magic aces, conning us with words, saying this is so because your mother had a clubfoot and your father drank and a chicken shitted in your mouth when you were three years old and therefore you are a homosexual or a punchpress operator. everything but the truth: simply that some men feel bad because life is bad for them the way it is and that it could easily be made better. but, no, the headshrinkers with their mechanistic baubles that will some day be proven completely false, they will continue to tell us that we are all mad and they will be well-paid to do so. we're just not taking it right. remember some of the songs?:

"lucky lucky me
I can live in luxury
because I've got a pocketful of
dreams . . ."

"it's my universe
even with an empty purse
because I've got a pocketful of
dreams . . ."

or:
"no more money in the bank
no more people we can thank
what to do about it
oh, what to do about it:
let's turn out the lights and
go to sleep."

what they *won't* tell us is that our madmen, our assassins *do* spring from our present mode of life, our good old All-American way of living and dying. Christ, that we are all not *outwardly* raving, that's the miracle! and since we have been rather sombre here, let's end it on the light fantastic, speaking, as we are, about madness. I was down in Santa Fe one time speaking to, no, rather drinking with, a friend of mine who was a headshrinker of some renown, and in the middle of one of our drunks I leaned forward and asked him, –

"Jean, tell me, am I crazy? come on, babe, let me have it. I can take it."

he finished his drink, put it on the coffee table and told me, "you'll have to pay me my fee first."

then I knew that at least one of us was crazy. Gov. Reagan and the Los Angeles sports writers were not there. and the second Kennedy had not yet been assassinated. but I got the odd feeling, sitting in that room with him that things were not well, not well at all, and would not be, would not be for another couple of thousand years at least.

and, so now, my friend in the army fatigues, you write yours . . .

––––––––

"it's over," he said, "the dead have won."

"the dead have won, have won, have won," said Moss.

"who won the ballgame?" Anderson asked Moss.

"I dunno."

Moss walked to the window. he saw a male American walking by. he shouted out the window – "hey, who won the ballgame?"

"Pirates, 3 to 2," answered the male American.

"you heard it, didn't you?" asked Moss of Anderson.

"yeh. Pirates, 3-2."

"I wonder who won the ninth race?"

"I know that one," said Moss. "Spaceman II. 7 to 1."

"who rode?"

"Garza."

they sat down to their beer. they were not quite drunk.

"the dead have won," said Anderson.

"tell me something new," said Moss.

"well, I've got to get some pussy pretty soon or I'll go goofy."

"the price is always too high. forget it."

"I know. but I can't forget it. I'm starting to have crazy dreams. I screw chickens in the ass."

"chickens? does it work?"

"in the dream it works."

they sucked at their beer. they were two old friends in their mid-thirties with dull jobs. Anderson had been married once, divorced once. two children somewhere. Moss married twice, divorced twice. one child somewhere. it was Saturday evening at Moss' apartment.

Anderson tossed an empty beer bottle through the air in a great arc. it landed on top of the others in the large wastebasket. "you know," he said, "some men just aren't any good with women. I never was any good with women. the whole thing seems a terrible bore, and when it's over you feel like you really been screwed."

"you tryin' to be funny?"

"you know what I mean: gyped, short-changed. the panties on the floor there with just the slightest of a summer shit-stain on them and her plodding to the bathroom, victorious. you lay there looking at the ceiling with your limp meat and wonder what the hell it means, knowing you've got to listen to her empty-headed chatter the rest of the evening . . . and I've got a daughter too. umm, listen, do you think I'm Victorian or queer or something?"

"naw, man. I know what you mean. you know, reminds me, one time at this gal's place, I knew her only slightly, a friend had more or less sent me over. I showed up with a pint and slipped her a ten. it wasn't bad and I figured no spiritual intimacy, no soul-stuff. I rolled off feeling fairly free, stared at the ceiling, stretched, and waited for her to make her bathroom run. she reached under the springs and pulled out this rag and handed it to me to wipe off with. it took the heart out of me. the damn rag was almost stiff all over. but I played the pro. I found a soft spot and wiped off. it took some searching to find the soft spot. then *she* used the rag. I got out of there fast. and if you want to call that Victorian, go ahead, call it Victorian."

they were both quiet a while, drinking the beer.

"but let's not be pricks," said Moss.

"uhhh?" asked Anderson.

"there *are* some good women."

"uuhh?"

"yeah, I mean when everything works well. I had a girl friend once, jesus, it was pure heaven. and no demands on soul or anything like that."

"what happened?"

"she died young."

"tough."

"tough, yes. I damn near drank myself to death."

they worked at their beer.

"how come?" asked Anderson.

"how come what?"

"how come we agree on almost everything?"

"that's why we're friends, I guess. that's what friendship means: sharing the prejudice of experience."

"Moss and Anderson. a team. we should be on Broadway."

"the seats would be empty."

"yeah."

(silence, silence, silence) then:

"beer keeps getting flatter and flatter. they sure make it lousy anymore."

"yeah. Garza. I could never hit with Garza."

"his percentage ain't high."

"but now that Gonzales lost his bug maybe he'll get better mounts."

"Gonzales. he ain't big and strong enough. his horses always drift out on the turns."

"he makes more money than we do."

"that's no miracle."

"no."

Moss tossed his beer bottle toward the basket, missed.

"I was never an athlete," he said. "god, in school they always chose me next to last when they chose teams. right before the subnormal idiot. Winchell was his name."

"whatever happened to Winchell?"

"now president of a steel company."

"god."

"want to hear the rest?"

"why not?"

"the hero. Harry Jenkins. now at San Quentin."

"god. are the right men in jail or the wrong men in jail?"

"both: the right and the wrong."

"you've been in jail. what's it like?"

"it's the same."

"what do you mean?"

"I mean, it's a society of the world in another element. they grade themselves according to their trade. the swindlers don't hobnob with the car thieves. the car thieves don't hobnob with the rapists. the rapists don't hobnob with the indecent exposure cases. all men are graded according to what they got caught at doing. for instance, a maker of dirty films is graded fairly high while a man who molested a child is graded damn low."

"how do you grade them?"

"all the same: caught."

"all right, then. what's the difference between a guy in the big-house and the average guy you pass on the street?"

"the guy in the bighouse is a Loser who has *tried*."

"you win. I still need some pussy."

Moss went to the refrigerator and brought out some more beer. sat down and cracked two open.

"ah, pussy," he said. "we talk like kids of fifteen. I just can't get *at* it anymore, I just can't jump through all the boring loopholes, do the little niceties. some men just have the natural touch. I think of Jimmy Davenport. christ what a vain terrible little shit he was, but the ladies just loved him. a horrible monster of a person. after he finished screwing them he used to go to their refrigerators and piss onto the open bowls of salad and into the cartons of milk, anywhere he could. he thought it was very funny. then she'd come out and sit down, her eyes just mushrooming with love for the bastard. he took me around to his girl friend's places to show me how he did it, and even lined me up a bit now and then, so that's why I was there and saw it. but it seems that the most beautiful women always go for the most horrible shits, the most obvious fakes. or am I just jealous, is my vision distorted?"

"you're right, man. the woman loves the fake because he lies so well."

"well, then, presuming this is true – that the female procreates with the fake – then doesn't this destroy a law of Nature? – that the strong mate with the strong? what kind of a society does this give us?"

"society's laws and nature's laws are different. we have an *un*natural society. that's why we are near to being blown to Hell. intuitively the female knows that the fake survives in our society and that is why she prefers him. she is only interested in bearing the child and bringing him through safely."

"then you say the female has brought us to the edge of hell where we sit today?"

"the word for that is 'misogynist.'"

"and Jimmy Davenport is King."

"King of the Pissers. the pussy has betrayed us and their atomic eggs lay stacked all about us . . ."

"call it 'misogyny.'"

Moss lifted his beer bottle:

"to Jimmy Davenport!"

Anderson lifted his:

"to Jimmy Davenport!"

they drained their bottles.

Moss opened two more. "two lonely old men blaming it on the ladies . . ."

"we're really a couple of shits," said Anderson.

"yeah."

"listen, you sure you don't know a couple of pussy somewhere?"

"maybe."

"whyn't you try?"

"you're a jerk," said Moss. then he got up and went to the phone. dialed a number.

he waited.

"Shareen?" he said. "oh yeah, Shareen . . . Lou. Lou Moss . . . you remember? the party on Katella Ave. Lou Brinson's place . . . a hell of a night. sure, I *know* I was nasty but we made it, remember? I always liked you, it's the face, I think it's the face, so classical-like. no. just a couple of beers. how's Mary Lou? Mary Lou's a fine person. I've got this friend . . . what? he teaches philosophy at Harvard. no kidding. but a natural guy. I *know* Harvard's a Law School! but what the hell, they still have these Immanuel Kants running around! what? a '65 Chevvy. just made my last payment. when? do you still have that green dress with that screwy belt that hangs way down around your tail? I'm *not* being funny. very sexy. and beautiful. I keep dreaming of you and chickens. what? a joke. how about Mary Lou? o.k. fine. but tell her this guy is very deferential. brainy. bashful. all that . . . oh, a distant cousin. Maryland. what? oh hell, I've got a *powerful* family! oh, is that right? now *you're* being funny. anyhow, he's in town and loose. no, of *course* he isn't married! why would I lie? no, I keep thinking of you – that low-hanging belt – I know it sounds corny – class. you're top class. sure, radio and heater. the Strip? just a bunch of kids down there now. why don't I just bring a bottle? . . . all right, sorry. no, I'm not *saying* you're old. Christ, you know me, me and my mouth. no, I would have called but they sent me out of town. how old? he's 32 but looks younger. I think he's on some kind of grant, going to Europe soon. to teach at Heidelberg. no, no shit. what time? all right, Shareen. see you, sweets."

Moss hung up. sat down. picked up his beer.

"we've got an hour's freedom, professor."

"an hour?" asked Anderson.

"an hour. they've got to powder their pussies, all that. you know how it works."

"to Jimmy Davenport!" said the professor from Harvard.

"to Jimmy Davenport!" said the punch-press operator.

they drank them down.

---

the phone rang.

he was sitting on the rug. he pulled the whole phone to the floor by the wire. then he picked up the receiver. there was a sound.

"hello?" he said.

"McCuller!"

"yowp?"

"it's been 3 days."

"since what?"

"since you've been to work."

"I'm building a Leyden Jar."

"what's that?"

"an apparatus for storing static electricity, invented by Cuneus of Leyden in 1746."

he hung the phone up and then threw it across the room. the receiver fell off. he finished his beer and went in to shit. he zipped up and walked back into the other room.

"DA DA!" he sang,

"DA DA
    DA DA
        DA DA DA DA!"

he liked Herb A's T. Brass. jesus, what sour melancholy.

"RA DA
    RA DA

RA DA DA DA –"

when he sat down in the center of the rug, there was his three and one-half year old daughter. he farted.

"hey! you FARTED!" she said.

"I FARTED!" he said.

they both laughed.

"Fred," she said.

"yowp?"

"I gotta tellya somethin'."

"shoot."

"mama got all this shit pulled outa her ass."

"yes?"

"yes, these people reached up into her ass with their fingers and pulled all this shit outa there."

"what makes you talk that way? you know that didn't happen."

"yes, it did, it *did!* I *saw* it!"

"go get me a beer."

"o.k."

she ran off into the other room.

"RA DA,"

he sang,

"RA DA

RA DA

RA DA DA DA!"

his daughter came back with the beer.

"sweetheart," he said, "I want to tell you something."

"all right."

"the pain is now almost *entirely* total. when it gets entirely total I will not be able to last any longer."

"why don't you get blue like me?" she asked.

"I'm already blue."

"why don't you get blue like me and the flowers?"

"I'll try," he said.

"let's dance to 'The Man of La Mancha,'" she said.

he put on "The Man of La Mancha." they danced. he six feet tall and she about ⅓ or ¼ his size. they danced separately with different movements and were very serious, yet sometimes laughed at the same time.

the record stopped.

"Marty slapped me," she said.

"what?"

"yes, Marty and mama were hugging and kissing in the kitchen and I was thirsty and asked Marty for a glass of water and Marty wouldn't give me one and then I cried and then Marty slapped me."

"go get me a beer!"

"a beer! beer!"

he got up and walked over and hung the phone up. as soon as he did, it rang.

"Mr. McCuller?"

"yowp?"

"your auto insurance has expired. your new rate is $248 a year and must be paid in advance. you have picked up three traffic violations. each violation is viewed by us in the same light as an auto accident . . ."

"horseshit!"

"what?"

"an auto accident costs you money; a so-called violation costs me money. and the boys on their bikes, who protect us from ourselves, have a sixteen to thirty a day ticket quota to meet in order to buy their homes, their new cars, and clothing and trinkets for their lower-middle class wives. don't give me all your shit. I've stopped driving. I pushed my car off the pier last night. I only have one regret."

"what's that?"

"that I wasn't inside that fucking car when it went down."

McCuller hung up and took the beer his daughter had brought him.

"little maiden," he said, "may at least some of your hours be more gentle than mine."

"I love you, Freddie," she said.

she reached around and put her arms around his body but the arms would not go entirely around.

"I squeeze you! I love you! I squeeze you!"

"I love you too, little maiden!"

he reached around her and squeezed her. she glowed and glowed and if she had been a cat she would have purred.

"man, man, it's a funny world," he said. "we've got everything but we can't have it."

they got down on the floor and played a game called "BUILD A CITY." there was some argument over where the railroad tracks were and just what and who was allowed to use the rail-road tracks.

then the bell rang. he got up and opened the door. his daughter saw them:

"Mama! Marty!"

"get your stuff, sweety, it's time to go!"

"I wanna stay with Freddie!"

"I said, 'Get your stuff!'"

"but I wanna stay with Freddie!"

"I'm not going to tell you again! get your stuff or I'll paddle your behind!"

"Freddie, *you* tell them I want to stay!"

"she wants to stay."

"you're drunk again, Freddie. I *tole* you I don' want you to drink 'round the kid!"

"well, *you're* drunk!"

"don't call her drunk, Freddie," said Marty, lighting a cigarette. "I don't like you anyhow. I always thought you were about half-queer."

"thank you for telling me what you think I am."

"just don't call her drunk, Freddie or I'll whip your ass . . ."

"just a moment, I have something to show you."

Freddie walked back into the kitchen. when he came out he was singing:

"RA DA
  RA DA
    RA DA DA DA!"

Marty saw the butcher knife. "what do you think you're going to do with *that* thing? I'll jam it up your ass."

"no doubt, but I wanted to tell you. the lady from the business office of the phone company phoned me and said that my service would be disconnected because retributions for past bills had not been made. I told her that I'd like to fuck her and she hung up."

"so what?"

"I mean, I *too* can disconnect."

Freddie moved very fast. the quickness was a still magic. the butcher knife sliced four or five times across Marty's throat before he fell back, down, halfway down the steps . . .

"geezus . . . don' kill me, please don' kill me."

Freddie walked back into the front room, threw the knife into the fireplace and sat on the rug again. his daughter sat down with him:

"now we can finish our game."

"sure."

"no cars on the railroad tracks."

"hell no. the police would arrest us."

"and we don't want the police to arrest us, do we?"

"uh uh."

"Marty's fulla blood, isn't he?"

"sure is."

"is that what we're made of?"

"mostly."

"mostly what?"

"mostly blood and bones and pain."

they sat there and played Build a City. you could hear the sirens. one ambulance, too late. three squad cars. a white cat walked by, looked at Marty, lifted its nose, ran off. one ant crawled on the sole of his left shoe.

"Freddie."

"what?"

"I wanna tell ya somethin'."

"shoot."

"these people reached into mama's ass and pulled all that shit outa there with their fingers . . ."

"o.k., I believe you."

"where's mama, now?"

"I don't know."

mama was running up and down the streets telling all the newsboys and grocery clerks and bartenders and subnormals and sadists and motorcycle riders and salt-eaters and x-seamen and loafers and hustlers and readers of Matt Weinstock, and so forth and so forth, and the sky was blue and the bread was in wrappers, and for the first time in years her eyes were live and beautiful. but death was really boredom, death was really boredom, and even the tigers and ants would never know how and the peach would someday scream.

---

all the rivers are going to get higher, and yet it's tight, the schoolteachers whack you with rulers and the worms eat the corn; they are mounting the mgs on tripods and the bellies are white and the bellies are black and the bellies are bellies. men are beaten simply for the sake of *beating;* courts are places where the ending is written first and all that precedes is simply vaudeville. men are taken into rooms for questioning and come out half-men or no-men at all. some men hope for revolution but when you revolt and set up your new government you find your new government is still the same old Papa, he has only put on a cardboard mask. the Chicago boys sure made a mistake busting the big press boys on the head – that knock on the head *might* get them to thinking and the big presses – aside from an earlier *New York Times* and some editions of *The Christian Science Monitor* – stopped thinking with the declaration of World War One. you can bust OPEN CITY for printing a normal portion of the human body but when you kick the editorial writer of a million circulation newspaper in the ass you better watch out, he just might start writing the truth about Chicago and everyplace else, advertisers be damned. he might only be able to write one column but that one column might get a million readers thinking – for a change – and nobody could tell what might happen then. but the lock's on tight: when you are given a choice between Nixon and Humphrey it's like being given a choice between eating warm shit or cold shit.

there just isn't much change anywhere. the thing in Prague has dampened a lot of boys who have forgotten Hungary. they hang in the parks with the Che idol, with pictures of Castro in their amulets, going OOOOOOOOMMMMM OOOOOOOMMM while William Burroughs, Jean Genet and Allen Ginsberg lead them. these writers have gone, soft, cuckoo, eggshit, female – not homo but female – and if I were a cop I'd feel like clubbing their addled brains myself. hang me for that. the writer of the streets is getting his soul cock-sucked by the idiots. there is only one place to write and that is ALONE at a typewriter. a writer who has to go INTO the streets is a writer who does not know the streets. I have seen enough factories, whorehouses, jails, bars, park orators to last 100 men 100 lifetimes. to go into the streets when you have a NAME is to go the easy way – they killed Thomas and Behan with their LOVE, their whiskey, their idolatry, their cunt, and they half-murdered half a hundred others. WHEN YOU LEAVE YOUR TYPEWRITER YOU LEAVE YOUR MACHINE GUN AND THE RATS COME POURING THROUGH. when Camus began giving speeches before the academies his writing died. Camus did not begin as a speechmaker, he began as a writer; it was not an automobile accident that killed him.

when some of my few friends ask, "why don't you give poetry readings, Bukowski?" they simply do not understand why I say "no."

and so we have Chicago and so we have Prague and it's no different than it has ever been. the little boy is going to get his ass beat and when (and if) the little boy gets big he is going to beat on ass. I'd rather see Cleaver president than Nixon but that's no big thing. what these god-damned revolutionaries who lay around my place drinking my beer and eating my food and showing off their women must learn is that the thing must come from inside out. you just can't give a man a new government like a new hat and expect a different man inside that hat. he's still going to have chickenshit proclivities and a full belly and a complete set of Dizzy Gillespie ain't going to change that. a lot of people swear that there is going to be a revolution but I'd hate to see all those people get killed for nothing. I mean, you can kill most people and you aren't killing anything but a few good men are bound to go. and then what do you end up with: a government OVER the people. a new dictator in sheep's clothing; the ideology was only to keep the guns going.

the other night some kid told me (he was sitting in the center of the rug looking very spiritual and beautiful):

"I'm going to shut off all the sewers. the whole city will be floating in turds!"

why, the kid had already told me enough shit to bury the whole city of L.A. and halfway up into Pasadena.

then he said, "got another beer, Bukowski?"

his whore crossed her legs high and showed me a flash of pink panty so I got up and got the kid a beer.

revolution sounds very romantic, you know. but it ain't. it's blood and guts and madness; it's little kids killed who get in the way, it's little kids who don't understand what the fuck is going on. it's your whore, your wife ripped in the belly with a bayonet and then raped in the ass while you watch. it's men torturing men who used to laugh at Mickey Mouse cartoons. before you go into the thing, decide where the spirit is and where the spirit will be when it is over. I don't go with Dos – CRIME AND PUNISHMENT – that no man has a right to take another man's life. but it might take a bit of thinking first. of course, the gall is that they have been taking our lives without firing a bullet. I too have worked for dismal wages while some fat boy has raped fourteen-year-old virgins in Beverly Hills. I've seen men fired for taking five minutes too long in the crapper. I've seen things I don't even want to talk about. but before you kill something make sure you have something better to replace it with; something better than political opportunist slamming hate horseshit in the public park. if you are going to pay through the nose get something better than a 36 month warranty. as yet, I have seen nothing but this emotional and romantic yen for Revolution; I've seen no solid leader or no realistic platform to insure AGAINST the betrayal that has always, so far, followed. if I am going to kill a man I don't want to see him replaced by a carbon copy of the same man and the same way. we have wasted history like a bunch of drunks shooting dice back in the men's crapper of the local bar. I am ashamed to be a member of the human race but I don't want to add any more to that shame, I want to scrape a little of it off.

it's one thing to talk about Revolution while your belly is full of another man's beer and you're traveling with a sixteen-year-old runaway girl from Grand Rapids; it's one thing to talk about Revolution while three jackass writers of international fame have you dancing to the OOOOOOO-OOOMMM game; it's another thing to bring it about, it's another thing to have happen. Paris, 1870–71, 20,000 people murdered in the streets, the streets as red with blood as with rain, and the rats coming out and eating at the bodies, and the people hungered, ravaged, no longer knowing what it meant, coming out and yanking the rats off the corpses and eating the rats. and *where* is Paris tonight? and *what* is Paris tonight? and my buddy is going to add shit on top of this and he smiles. well, he's twenty and mostly reads poetry. and poetry is just a wet rag in the dishpan.

and pot. they always equate pot with Revolution. pot just isn't that *good*. for Christ's sake, if they legalized pot half the people would stop smoking it. prohibition created more drunks than grandmother's warts. it's only what you can't do that you want to do. who wants to fuck their own wife every night? or, for that matter, even once a week?

there are a lot of things I would like to do. first off, I would like to stop getting such *very* ugly looking people for presidential nominees. then, I'd change the museums. there is nothing as depressing or quite as *stinky* as a museum. why there hasn't been a greater percentage of three-year-old girls molested on museum steps I'll never know. first off, I'd install at least one bar on each floor; this alone would pay all the salaries and would allow for regeneration and salvation of some of the paintings and the dropping sabre-toothed tiger whose asshole is beginning to look more like the 8-ball sidepocket. then I'd install a rock-band, a swing-band and a symphony band for each floor, plus three or four good-looking women to walk around and look good. you don't learn anything *or see* anything unless you vibrate. most people look at that sabre-tooth behind all that hot glass and just slink by, a little bit ashamed and a little bit bored.

but can't you see a guy and his wife, each a beer in hand, looking at the sabre-tooth, and saying, "god damn, look at those *tusks!* a little bit like an elephant, huh?"

and she'd say, "honey, let's go home and make love!"

and he'd say, "your *ass!* not until I go down to the basement and see that 1917 Spad. they say Eddie Ricken-backer flew it himself. got seventeen hun. besides, I hear they got the Pink Floyd down there."

but the Revolutionaries are going to burn the museum. they figure burning answers everything. they'd burn their grandmother if she couldn't run fast enough. and then they are going to look around for water or for somebody who can do an appendectomy or somebody who can keep the truly insane from cutting their throats as they sleep. and they are going to find out how many rats live in a city, not human rats but rat-rats. and they are going to find that the rats are the last things that drown, burn, starve; that they are the first things that can find food and water because they have been doing so for centuries without help. the rats are the true revolutionaries; the rats are the true underground, but they don't want your ass except to nibble on and they are not interested in OOOOOOOOOMMM.

I'm not saying give up. I'm for the true human spirit wherever it is, wherever it has been hiding, whatever it is. but beware of the cowboys who make it sound so good and leave you out on a plateau with 4 hard-core cops and eight or nine national guard boys and only your bellybutton as a last prayer. the boys screaming for your sacrifice in the public parks are usually the furthest away when the shooting begins. they want to live to write their memoirs.

it used to be the religion con. not the big church con, that was a drag. everybody bored, including the preacher. but the little storefront places, painted white. Jesus, how they carried on. I used to go in drunk and sit there and watch. especially after I was 86'd at the bars. it beat going home and beating my meat. the best religious con places were L.A., followed by N.Y. and Philly. those preachers were artists, man. they almost had me rolling on the floor too. most of those preachers recovering from hangovers, bloodshot eyes, needing more $$$ for something to drink or maybe even a pop, hell, I don't know.

they almost had me rolling on the floor and I was pretty cool and pretty tired. it was better than a piece of ass even if it only caught you halfway. I wish to thank these babies, most of them negroes, pardon me, blacks, for some entertaining nights; I think that if I have ever written any poetry that I might have stolen *some* of it from them.

but now that game is fading. God just didn't pay the rent or come up with that bottle of wine no matter how much they hollered or got their last clean clothes dirty on that floor. God said WAIT and it's hard to WAIT when your belly is empty and your soul don't feel so good and maybe you can only live to be 55 and the last time God showed up was almost 2,000 years ago and then He just did a few cheap carnival tricks, let some Jew outfox him, then blew the scene. a man gets g.d. tired of suffering. the teeth in his mouth are enough to kill him or the same same woman in the same same small room.

the religious con boys are moving in with the revolutionary con boys and you can't tell asshole from pussy, brothers. realize this, and you have a beginning. listen carefully, and you have a beginning. swallow it all, and you're dead. God got out of the tree, took the snake and Eden's tight pussy away and now you've got Karl Marx throwing golden apples down from the same tree, mostly in blackface.

if there is a battle, and I believe that there is, always has been, and that's what has made Van Goghs and Mahlers as well as Dizzy Gillespies and Charley Parkers, then please be careful of your leaders, for there are many in your ranks who would rather be president of General Motors than burn down the Shell Oil station around the corner. but since they can't have one, they take the other. these are the human rats of the centuries who have kept us where we are. this is Dubcek coming back from Russia a half-man, afraid of psychic death. a man must finally learn that it is better to die with his balls slowly cut off than to live any other way. foolish? no more foolish than the greatest miracle. but if you are caught in the trap, always understand what it is that you are trading for, exactly, or the soul will give way. Casanova used to run his fingers, his hands up the ladies dresses as men were torn apart in the king's courtyard; but Casanova died too, just an old guy with a big cock and a long tongue and no guts at all. to say that he lived well is true; to say that I could spit on his grave without feeling is also true. the ladies usually go for the biggest damn fool they can find; that is why the human race stands where it does today: we have bred the clever and lasting Casanovas, all hollow inside, like the chocolate Easter bunnies we foster upon our poor children.

the nest of the Arts like the nests of the Revolutionaries crawl with the most unimaginable licecovered freaks, seeking coca-cola solace because they can neither find jobs as dishwashers or paint like Cezanne. if the mold don't doesn't want you, the only thing to do is to pray or work for a new mold. and when you find that *that* mold doesn't want you, then why not another? everybody pleased in his certain way.

yet, old as I am, I am particularly pleased to live in this certain age. THE LITTLE MAN HAS SIMPLY GOTTEN TIRED OF TAKING TOO MUCH SHIT. it's happening everywhere. Prague. Watts. Hungary. Vietnam. it ain't government. it's Man against govt. it's Man who can no longer quite be fooled by a white Christmas with a Bing Crosby voice and dyed Easter eggs that must be hidden from kids who must WORK TO FIND THEM. of future presidents of America whose faces on TV screens must make you run to the bathroom and puke.

I like this time. I like this feeling. the young have finally begun to think. and the young have become more and more. but everytime they get a spearhead for their feelings that spearhead is murdered. the old and the entrenched are frightened. they know that the revolution can come through the voting polls in the American manner. we can kill them without a bullet. we can kill them by simply becoming more real and more human and voting out the shits. but they are clever. what do they offer us? Humphrey or Nixon. like I said, cold shit, warm shit, it's all shit.

the only thing that has kept me from being assassinated is that I am small shit, I have no politics, I observe. I have no sides except the side of the human spirit, which after all does sound rather shallow, like a pitchman, but which means mostly *my* spirit, which means *yours* too, for if I am not truly alive, how can I see you?

man, I'd like to see a good pair of shoes on every man walking the streets and see that he gets a good piece of ass and a bellyfull of food too. Christ, the last piece of ass I've had was in 1966 and I've been jacking off ever since. and there just ain't no jackoff compared to that wonder-hole.

it's tough times, brothers, and I don't know quite what to tell you. I'm white but I've got to agree – don't too much quite trust that paint job – it's soft and I don't too much like softshits either, but I've seen a lot of you black boys who can make me puke all the way from Venice West to Miami Beach. the Soul has no skin; the soul only has insides that want to SING, finally, can't you hear it, brothers? softly, can't you hear it, brothers? a hot piece of ass and a new Cadillac ain't going to solve a god-damned thing. Popeye will have one eye and Nixon will be your next president. Christ slipped off the cross and we are now nailed to the motherfucker, black and white, white and black, completely.

our choice is almost no choice. if we move too quickly, we are dead. if we do not move fast enough, we are dead. it isn't our deck of cards. how you gonna shit with a 2,000-foot Christian cork jammed up your ass?

to learn, do not read Karl Marx. very dry shit. please learn the spirit. Marx is only tanks moving through Prague. don't get caught this way please. first of all, read Celine. the greatest writer of 2,000 years. of course, *THE STRANGER* by Camus must fit in. *CRIME AND PUNISHMENT. THE BROTHERS.* all of Kafka. all the works of the unknown writer John Fante. the short stories of Turgenev. avoid Faulkner, Shakespeare, and especially George Bernard Shaw, the most overblown fantasy of the Ages, a real true-blown shit with political and literary connections beyond belief. the only younger guy I can think of with the road paved ahead for him and kissing ass whenever necessary was Hemingway, but the difference between Hemingway and Shaw was that Hem wrote some good early work and Shaw wrote completely flip and dull crap all the way through.

so, here we are mixing Revolution with Literature and they both fit. somehow everything fits, but I grow tired and wait for tomorrow.

will the Man be at my door?

who gives a damn?

I hope this made you spill your tea.

———

is this the way it ends? Death through the nose of Everywhere? how inexpensive. how plagiaristic. how brutal. – raw hamburger forgotten and stinking on the stove.

he vomited across his chest, too sick to move his body.

never mix pills with whiskey. man, they weren't kidding.

he could feel his soul floating out from under his body. he could feel it hang upside down there like a cat, its feet gripping the springs.

motherfucker, come back! he said to his soul.

his soul laughed, you've treated me too bad too long, baby. you're gettin' what you need.

it was about three a.m. in the morning.

with him it wasn't dying that mattered. with him it was the unsolved and loose parts left behind – a four-year-old daughter in some hippy camp in Arizona; stockings and shorts on the floor, dishes in the sink; an unpaid for car, gas bills, light bills, phone bills; and parts of him left in almost every state in the Union, parts of him left in the unwashed pussies of half a hundred whores; parts of him left on flagpoles and firescapes, empty lots, Catholic Church Communion classes, jail cells, boats; parts of him left in band-aids and down in sewers; parts of him left in thrown-away alarm clocks, thrown away shoes, thrown-away women, thrown-away friends . . .

it was so sad, so very sad. who could blow the blues the way they really were? nobody could. that's it. nobody could or ever did. they could only try and get bluer than blue because there was no way home.

he heaved again, then lay still. he could hear the crickets. crickets in Hollywood crickets along Sunset Blvd. healthy crickets: that's all he had.

I blew it, Jesus, I blew it, he thought.

yeah, brother, you blew it, said his soul.

but I want to see my little girl again, he said to his soul.

your little girl again? you're no artist! you're no *man*! you're *soft*!

I'm soft, he answered his soul, you're right, I'm soft.

he'd reached the end of cures. beer wouldn't go down. not even water. no pills, no pop, no hash, no grass, no love, no breeze, no sound – just crickets – no hope – just crickets – not even a match to burn the fucking place down.

then it got worse.

the same tune started playing over and over again in his head: "you'd better tend to business Mr. Business man,

while you can . . ."

and that was it. the same melody over and over again:

"you'd better tend to business Mr. Business man,

while you can . . ."

"you'd better tend to . . ."

"you'd better . . ."

"you'd . . ."

with an effort borrowed only from the madness of space (who can blow the blues? nobody can.) he reached up and turned on the little overhead lamp, which was then just an exposed electric bulb, the shade long ago smashed off (who can blow the blues?) and he picked up a postcard found in the mailbox a few days back and the postcard said:

"dear – : we slap greetings at you while drenched in German beer and Schnapps,

in stained-glass waiting . . ."

the lines fell off into that sloppy and impolite scrawl of fat boys who live luckily upon the land without the need of excessive wit or courage.

something about leaving for England tomorrow. poems slowly coming. too much grease and few visitations. too much the world hanging by the tip of its cock.

"we consider you the greatest poet since Eliot."

then the professor's signature and his pet student's signature.

only since Eliot? what a short inch that was. he'd taught these bastards how to write a living poetry of clarity and now they were joyriding and finger-fucking Europe while he died alone in a skid-row room in Hollywood.

"you'd better tend to business Mr. Business man,

while you can . . ."

he threw the postcard down on the floor. it didn't matter. if he could only feel some real good ace-high self-pity or some two-bit anger or some chickenshit vengeance, it could save him. but it was all dry inside of him, dry and silly and the way it had been for a long time.

the professors had begun knocking at the door about two years ago, trying to find out where it came from. and there was nothing to tell them. the professors were all the same – a bit pretty and rather rested in a female sort of way, gangling long legs, large picture window eyes, and finally rather stupid, and so their visits didn't please him at all. they were, in reality, only the fat-head nobles of a changing structure, which like an idiot in a candy store, refused to see the walls burning down. their candy was the mind.

– the clinging to the intellect, the clinging to the intellect, the clinging . . .

"you'd better tend to business, Mr. Business man, while you can . . ."

and Jesus, *he* was soft. all the hard poems; he'd played hard-man all his life but he was soft. everybody was soft, really. – the hard was only there to protect the soft. what a ridiculous asshole trap.

he felt the need to get out of bed. it cost him. he heaved along the whole hallway. the retches brought up a pulpy green-yellow and some blood. first heat, then chills; then chills, then heat. and legs like rubbery elephant legs. flump. flump. flump. – and look (he winked at somebody somewhere): the moaning and terrified Eye of Confucius upon his last drink.

blow the blues.

he got into the front room thinking –

I am lucky to have a rented front room, even *now* –

"hey, Mr. Business man . . ."

and tried to sit on a chair, missed, hit the monkey tailbone hard on the floor, laughed, then looked at the telephone.

this is the way a Loner ends up: dead alone. dying alone.

a Loner should get ready early.

all my poems ain't gonna help. all the women I ever screwed ain't gonna help. and all the women I didn't screw surely ain't gonna help. I need somebody to blow me the blues. I need somebody to say, I understand, kid, now take it on in and die.

he looked at the phone. he thought and he thought and he thought, he thought about who he might phone who could blow him the blues, just say the easy word, and he went through the few that he knew out of the billions – he went through them one by one, the few that he knew, and he also knew that it was too early in the morning, hardly a convenient time to die, it wasn't right, and that they'd only think that he was clowning or drunk or faking or maudlin or insane, and he couldn't hate them or blame them for it – everybody was locked-off, jacked-off, chopped-off, everybody was in their own little cell. hey, Mr. Business man . . .

Motherfuck!

who'd ever invented the game had worked up a neat little masterwork. call him God, He had a shot over the eye coming. but He never showed so you could get Him in the sights. the Age of the Assassins had missed the Biggest One of all. earlier they'd almost got the Son, but He'd slipped on out and we still had to go on staggering over slippery bathroom floors. the Holy Ghost never showed; He just layed back and whipped his dick. the cleverest One of all.

if I could only phone my little daughter I could die happy, he thought.

his soul walked out of the bedroom holding to an empty can of beer. "ah, you soft, you soft soft *fuck*! your little daughter is in a hippy camp while her mother rubs the balls of idiots. *take* it, Loner, you *chickenshit*!"

". . . you *need* love, you *need* love, love will get you in the end, my friend!"

get me in the End?

Big Ramrod Death, yeah.

he began laughing. then he stopped. heaved again. more blood this time. almost all blood.

he forgot about the phone and made it back to the couch.

". . . you *need* love, you *need* love . . ."

well, thank god, he thought, they've switched records anyhow.

the dying didn't come as easy as he thought it would. there was blood everywhere and the shades were down. people were getting ready to go to work. once, rolling over, he seemed to see the bookcase, all his books of poems and he knew then that he'd failed, it didn't even go back to Eliot, not even to yesterday morning, he'd blew it, he was just another monkey in a tree dropping into the tiger's mouth, and it was sad for a moment but only for a moment.

it was all right and it didn't matter about blowing the blues. Satchmo, go home. Shostakovitch, in your Fifth, forget it. Peter III. Chike, because you'd married a nutty soprano with wrinkles showing under her eyes, and a lesbian when you were not even a man, forget it. we've all been tempted with the fire and we've all failed as cocksuckers, artists, painters, doctors, pimps, green berets, dishwashers, dentists, trapeze artists and pear-pickers.

each man nailed to his own special cross.

blow the blues.

"you *need* love, you *need* love . . ."

then he got up and pulled up all the shades. god damned shades were rotten. they snapped at the touch, fell apart, zipped a bitch-spurt of sound, fell to the floor.

god damned sun was rotten. bringing forth the same old flowers, the same old young girls of everywhere.

he watched the people going to work. he knew no more than he ever knew.

the unsecurity of knowledge was the same as the security of no-knowledge.

neither was superior; neither was anything.

he put himself flat along the landlord's couch. his couch, for a moment.

after all that trouble there was nothing to it.

he died.

———

the little tailor was quite happy. he just sat there sewing. it was when the woman came to the door, rang the bell, that he became disturbed. "sour cream, I have sour cream for sale," she told him. "get away, you stink," he told her, "I don't want your god damned sour cream!" "*eewwww!*" she said, "your place *stinks*! why don't you throw out the garbage?" she ran off.

it was then that the tailor remembered the three dead bodies. one was in the kitchen, stretched along in front of the stove. another one was upright, hung by its collar in the closet, stiffened, standing there. and the third was in the bathtub, sitting upright, well, not exactly upright, for the head could just be seen above the rim of the tub. the flies were beginning to come around and that was bad. the flies seemed very happy with the bodies, they were drunk on the bodies, and when he swatted at them they became very angry. he'd never heard flies buzz in such anger. they even attacked and bit him, so he let them be.

he sat down to sew again and the bell rang again. looks like I'll never get any sewing done, he thought.

it was his pal, Harry.

"hello, Harry."

"hello, Jack."

Harry came in. "what's the stink?"

"dead bodies."

"dead bodies? you kiddin'?"

"no, look around."

Harry found them with his nose. he found the one in the kitchen, then the one in the closet, then the one in the bathtub. "why'd you kill 'em? you gone crazy? what are you going to do? why don't you hide the bodies, get rid of them? are you crazy? why'd you kill them? why don't you call the police? are you out of your mind? god, it STINKS! listen, man, don't get NEAR me! what are you going to do? what's going on? ARRRG! THE STINK! I'M GETTING SICK!"

Jack just kept on sewing. he just sewed and sewed and sewed. it was like he was trying to hide.

"Jack, I'm going to call the police."

Harry went toward the phone but then he got sick. he went to the bathroom and vomited in the crapper while the head of the dead body in the tub stuck out just over the rim.

he came out and made the phone. he found that by taking out the mouthpiece he could slip his penis into the phone. he slid it back and forth and it felt good. very good. soon he completed his act, hung up the phone, zipped up and sat down across from Jack.

"Jack, are you insane?"

"Becky says she thinks that I'm crazy. she threatens to have me committed."

Becky was Jack's daughter.

"does she know about all these dead bodies?"

"not yet. she's on a trip to New York. she's a buyer for one of the large department stores. got herself a good job. I'm proud of that girl."

"does Maria know?"

Maria was Jack's wife.

"Maria don't know. she don't come around no more. since she got that job at the bakery she thinks she's something. she's living with another woman. sometimes I think she's turned into a dyke."

"well, man, I can't call the police on you. you're my friend. you'll have to settle it yourself. but do you mind telling me why you killed these people?"

"I disliked them."

"but you don't go around killing people you dislike."

"I disliked them very much."

"Jack?"

"eh?"

"you want to use the phone?"

"if you don't mind."

"it's your phone, Jack."

Jack got up and unzipped. he slipped his penis into the phone. he slid it back and forth and it felt good. he completed the act, zipped up, sat down and began sewing again. then the phone rang. he went back to the phone.

"oh, Hello, Becky! nice of you to call! I feel all right. oh yeah, we took the mouthpiece out of the phone, that's why. Harry and I. Harry's here now. Harry's what? you really think so? I think he's all right. nothing. I'm just sewing. Harry's sitting here. a kind of a dark afternoon. really gloomy when you think about it. no sun. people walking by the window with ugly faces. yes, I'm all right. I feel all right. no, not yet. but I have a frozen lobster in the refrigerator.

I just love lobster. no, I haven't seen her. she thinks she's hot shit now. yes, I'll tell her. don't worry. Goodbye, Becky."

Jack hung up and sat down again, began sewing again.

"you know," said Harry, "that reminds me. when I was a young man – god *damn* these flies! I'm not DEAD! – when I was a young man I used to have this job, me and this other kid. the job was washing down these dead bodies. we got some good-looking women in there sometimes. I came in one time and Mickey, that was the other kid, had mounted one of these women. 'Mickey!' I said, 'what are you DOING? SHAME!' he just looked at me sideways and kept going. when he got down he said, 'Harry, I've screwed at least a dozen of them. it's good! try her. you'll see!' 'oh, no!' I said. one time when I was washing down a real good one, I fingered her. but I never could do more than that."

Jack kept sewing.

"you think you would have tried one, Jack?"

"hell, I don't know! I have no way of knowing."

he kept sewing. then he said, "listen, Harry, I've had a hard week. I want to eat something and get some sleep. I've got some lobster. but I'm funny. I like to eat alone. I don't enjoy eating with people. so?"

"so? you want me to leave? you're a bit upset. so, o.k., I'll leave."

Harry stood up.

"don't go away mad, Harry. we're still friends. let's keep it that way. we've been friends a long time."

"sure, since '33. those were the days! FDR. the NRA. the WPA. but we made it. these kids today just don't know."

"they sure don't."

"well, goodbye, Jack."

"goodbye, Harry."

Jack walked Harry to the door, opened the door, watched him walk away. still the same old baggy pants. the guy always did dress like a schmuck.

then Jack walked into the kitchen, got the lobster out of the freezer and read the instructions. they always had fucked-up instructions. then he noticed the body in front of the stove. he'd have to get rid of the body. the blood had long ago dried underneath it. the blood had long ago hardened on the floor. the sun finally came out from behind a cloud and it was very late afternoon, almost evening and the sky became pink and some of the pink came through the kitchen window. you could almost see it come through, slowly, like the giant feeler of a snail. the body was face downward, face turned toward the stove, and under the body the right arm was twisted with the open upturned hand sticking just outside of the left side of the body. the pink feeler of the snail lit on the hand. it made the hand pink. Jack noticed the hand. so pink. it looked so innocent. just a hand, a pink hand by itself. it was like a flower. for a moment Jack thought it had moved. no, it hadn't moved. a pink hand. just a hand. an innocent hand. Jack stood there looking at the hand. then he sat down with the lobster and looked at the hand. then he began to cry. he put the lobster down and put his head in his arms there at the table and began to cry. he cried for a very long time. he cried like a woman. he cried like a child. he cried like anything. then he walked into the other room and picked up the phone.

"operator, I want the police department. yes, I know that it sounds funny; the mouthpiece is missing, but I want the police department."

Jack waited.

"yes? well, listen, I've killed a man! three men! I'm serious, *yes*, I'm serious! I want you to come get me. and bring a wagon to take the bodies. I'm insane. I've lost my mind. I don't know how it happened. what?"

Jack gave them the address.

"what? that's because the mouthpiece is missing. I did. I screwed the phone."

the man kept on talking but Jack hung up. he walked back to the kitchen and sat down at the table and put his head back in his arms. he didn't cry anymore. he just sat there with the sun now no longer pink; the sun was gone and it was getting dark, and then he thought about Becky and then he thought about killing himself and then he didn't think about anything. the packaged South African lobster sat by his left elbow. he never got to eat that lobster.

————

I had gotten a bit drunk one night when this guy who had published a couple of my books said to me, "Bukowski, you want to go see L?"

L – was a famous writer. had been a famous writer for some time. works translated into everything, dog turds even. grants, mistresses, wives, prizes, novels, poems, short stories, paintings . . . stays in Europe. acquainted with the great. all that.

"no, shit, no," I said to Jensen, "his stuff bores me."

"but you say that about everybody."

"well, it's true."

Jensen sat and looked at me. Jensen liked to sit and look at me. he couldn't understand why I was so stupid. I was stupid. but so was the moon.

"he wants to meet you. he's *heard* of you."

"he has? and I've heard of him."

"you'd be surprised how many people have heard of you. I was over at N.A.'s the other night and she said she wanted you to come to dinner. you know, she knew L. in Europe."

"she did?"

"and they both knew Artaud."

"yeah, and she wouldn't give Artaud a piece of ass."

"that's right."

"I don't blame her. I wouldn't either."

"do me a favor. let's go see him."

"Artaud?"

"no, L."

I finished my drink.

"let's go."

it was a long drive from skid row to L's place. and L. had a place. Jensen ran the car up the driveway and the driveway was as long as an ordinary freeway off-ramp.

"is this the guy who is always hollering POVERTY?" I asked.

"it's said he owes the government 85 grand in back taxes."

"poor devil."

we got out of the car. it was a three-story house. there was a swing on the front porch and a $250 guitar laying in the swing. a big ass German shepherd ran up, snarling, foaming and I held him off with the guitar and I don't mean by playing it, I mean by swinging it while Jensen rang the bell.

this yellow wrinkled face opened a peephole and said,

"who's there?"

"Bukowski and Jensen."

"who?"

"Bukowski and Jensen."

"I don't know you."

the German shepherd leaped, his teeth just clicking past my jugular as he flew by. I banged him good when he landed but he just shook himself and coiled to leap again, hair raising, showing me those dirty yellow teeth.

"Bukowski. he wrote, *ALL THE DAMN TIME, SCREAMING IN THE RAIN.* I'm Hilliard Jensen, *NEW MOUNTAIN PRESS.*"

the shepherd gave a last pissed-off snarl before readying to leap when L. said, "oh, Poopoo, stop that!"

Poopoo uncoiled a bit.

"nice Poopoo," I said, "nice Poopoo!"

Poopoo looked at me knowing that I was lying. finally old man L. opened the door. "well, come in," he said.

I threw the broken guitar into the swing and we walked in. the front room was like an underground parking lot.

"sit down," said L. I had a choice of three or four chairs, took the closest one.

"I give the establishment one more year," said L. "the people have awakened. we are going to burn the whole fucking thing down."

L. snapped his finger – "it will be gone" (snap) "like that! a new and better life for all of us!"

"got anything to drink?" I asked.

L. rang a little bell by his chair. "MARLOWE!" he screamed.

then he looked at me: "I read your last book, Mr. Meade."

"no, I'm Bukowski," I said.

he turned to Jensen, "then *you're* Taylor Meade! forgive me!"

"no, no, I'm Jensen. Hilliard Jensen. NEW MOUNTAIN."

just then a Japanese, black shiny pants, white jacket, trotted into the room, bowed just a bit, smiling, like some day he would kill us all.

"Marlowe, you stupid fuck, these gentlemen want some drinks; take their orders, posthaste, and return quickly or I'll have your ass!"

curiously, L's face looked as if all pain had been removed. although there were wrinkles, the wrinkles seemed more or less rivulets, sewed on or painted on, or *thrown* on. an odd face. yellow. bald. tiny eyes. a hopeless and insignificant face, at first glance. but *then*, how could he have written all *that*? "Oh, Mack had a big dick! Oh, Mack had the biggest dick! what a dick Mack had! Mack had the biggest dick in town. biggest West of the Mississippi. everybody talked about Mack's dick. oh, Mack had a big dick . . ." etc. when it came to style, L. had them all beat, even tho' I did find it dull.

Marlowe came back with the drinks and I'll say something for Marlowe: he poured them tall and he poured them strong. he left them and trotted off. I watched his haunches bobbing in his tight pants as he ran back into the kitchen where he belonged.

L. had already looked drunk. he drained half his glass. a scotch and water man. "I'll always remember that hotel in Paris. we were all there. kaja, Hal Norse, Burroughs . . . the greatest literary minds of our generation."

"do you think it helped your writing, Mr. L.?" I asked.

it was a stupid question. he looked at me sternly, then allowed me to watch him smile, "everything helps my writing."

we all just sat there then, drinking and looking at each other. L. rang the bell again and Marlowe trotted in for the refueling process.

"Marlowe," said L., "is translating Edna St. Vincent Millay into the Japanese."

"wonderful," said Jensen of NEW MOUNTAIN.

I don't see a damn thing wonderful about translating Edna St. Vincent Millay into the Japanese, I thought.

"I don't see a damn thing wonderful about translating Edna St. Vincent Millay into the Japanese," said L.

"well, Millay is dated, but what's wrong with modern poetry?" asked the NEW MOUNTAIN.

too young, too quick and they quit too soon, I thought.

"no lasting qualities," said the old man.

I don't know. everybody stopped talking. we really didn't like each other. Marlowe trotted in and out with the drinks. I got the feeling that I was in a terrible underground cave or a movie without meaning. just unattached scenes. toward the end, L. got up once and slapped Marlowe, hard. I didn't know what it meant. sex? boredom? play? Marlowe grinned and ran back to Millay's cunt.

"let no man enter my home who cannot bear all shadow and bear all light," said L.

"look, man," I said, "I think you're full of shit. I never did like your stuff."

"and I never liked your stuff either, Meade," said the old man, "all that stuff about sucking-off movie stars. anybody can suck-off a movie star. that's no big thing."

"it *can* be," I said, "and I'm not Meade!"

the old man got up and wobbled toward my chair, translated into eighteen languages.

"you want to fight or fuck?" he asked.

"I want to fuck," I said.

"MARLOWE!" screamed L.

Marlowe trotted in and L. screamed, "DRINKS!"

I had REALLY expected him to ask M. to drop his pants so I could have my wish, but it didn't happen. I simply watched M.'s haunches wobble as he ran back into the kitchen.

we began on the new rounds. "like that" (snap!) said L., "the establishment is finished! we burn them down!"

then the old man's head fell forward and he dozed, he was finished.

"let's go," said Jensen.

"wait a minute," I said. I walked over to the old man and ran my arm down the back of his rocker, down toward his ass.

"what are you doing?" asked Jensen.

"everything helps my writing," I said, "and this bastard is loaded."

I got down and got the wallet and said, "let's go!"

"you shouldn't," said Jensen and we walked toward the front door.

something had my right arm and then it was hammer-locked behind my back.

"we leave ALL MONIES HERE BEFORE LEAVING IN HONOR OF MR. L!" said the translator of E. V. Millay.

"you're breaking my god damned arm, you slant-eyed chicken-shit!"

"WE LEAVE ALL MONIES HERE! HONOR MR. L!" he screamed it.

"CLUB HIM, JENSEN! CLUB HIM ONE! GET THIS FUCKER OFF ME!"

"your friend touch me, your arm is BROKEN!"

"all right, take the wallet. to hell with it! I've got a check coming from GROVE PRESS."

he took L.'s wallet, dropped it to the floor. then he took *mine*, dropped it to the floor.

"hey, wait a MINUTE! what are you? some kinda god damned crook?"

"WE LEAVE ALL MONIES HERE! HONOR MR. L!"

"I don't believe it. this is worse than a whorehouse."

"now, tell your friend to drop his wallet on floor or I break your arm!"

Marlowe added a little pressure to show me that it could be done.

"Jensen! your wallet! DROP IT!"

Jensen dropped his wallet. Marlowe let go of my arm. I turned on him. I only had the left one to work with.

"Jensen?" I asked.

he looked at Marlowe.

"no," he said.

I looked at the old man as he dozed. there seemed to be a little tender smile upon his lips.

we opened the door, went outside.

"nice Poopoo," I said.

"nice Poopoo," said Jensen.

we got into the car.

"any more people you want me to visit tonight?" I asked.

"well, I was thinking of Anaïs Nin."

"stop thinking. I don't think I could handle her."

Jensen backed it out the drive. it was just another warm Southern California night. soon we found Pico Blvd. and Jensen headed East. the Revolution couldn't come too fucking fast for me.

———

"'Red,'" I told the kid, "to the female I no longer exist. much of it is my fault. I don't go to dances, church bazaars, poetry readings, love-ins, all that shit, and this is where the whores hustle. I used to make it in the bars or on the train back from Del Mar, anywhere drinking was going on. now I can't stand the bars anymore. those guys just sitting there, lonely, passing the hours, hoping some syphed-up hole will drop in. the whole scene is disgraceful to the human race."

'Red' flipped a beerbottle through the air, caught it, broke off the cap on the end of my coffee table.

"it's all in the mind, Bukowski. you don't need it."

"it's all in the end of my pecker, 'Red.' I need it."

"once we got hold of this old wino gal. we tied her to a bed with rope. charged 50 cents a piece. every cripple, madman and freak on the row must have got a piece of ass. in three days and three nights we must have passed through 500 patrons."

"jesus christ, 'Red,' you're making me sick!"

"I thought you were the Dirty Old Man."

"it's just that I don't change my stockings every day. did you let her up to urinate or defecate?"

"what's 'defecate'?"

"oh shit. did you feed her?"

"winos don't eat. we gave her wine."

"I'm sick."

"why?"

"it was beastly cruel, beastly inhuman. come to think of it, the beasts wouldn't do it."

"we made $250."

"what'd you give her?"

"nothing. we left her in there, two more days on the rent."

"did you untie her?"

"sure, we didn't want a murder rap."

"very nice of you."

"you talk like a preacher."

"have another beer."

"I can get you some pussy."

"how much? 50 cents?"

"no, a little more than that."

"no, thanks."

"see, you don't really want it."

"I guess you're right."

we each went for another beer. he put it down pretty good. then he stood up. "see, I always carry a little razor, right here, under my belt. most bums have problems shaving. not me. I'm ready.

and when I'm on the road I wear two pair of pants – see – and I take off the outside pair when I hit town, shave, got a wash and wear white shirt on under my navy blue, I rinse it out in the sink, got a strip necktie, I buff my shoes, pick up a matching coat to the pants at a 2nd hand store and two days later I got me a white collar job among the shits. they don't know I just got off a boxcar. but I can't stand them jobs. next thing I know I'm back on the road."

I didn't know what to say about that, so I maintained a silence and kept drinking.

"and I always carry this little ice pick just up my sleeve in this elastic strap halfway up my arm, see?"

"yeah, I see. a friend of mine says a beer can opener is a great weapon."

"your friend's right. now when the cops stop me I always flip the ice pick out, I throw up my arms, holler, DON'T SHOOT!

('Red' went through the act on the rug)

"– and I flip the ice pick out. they never find it on me. I don't know how many ice picks I've flipped off. countless."

"have you ever used the ice pick, 'Red'?"

he gave me a very strange look.

"o.k.," I said, "forget the question."

so we sat there again sucking at the beer.

"I came across your column once in this rooming house. I think you're a great writer."

"thanks," I said.

"I've tried to be a writer but it doesn't come out. I sit down and it doesn't come out."

"how old are you?"

"twenty-one."

"give it time."

he sat there thinking about being a writer. then he reached into his back pocket.

"they gave me this to keep me quiet."

it was a leather wallet woven into fine strips.

"who?"

"I saw these two guys kill a guy and they gave me this to keep me quiet."

"why'd they kill him?"

"he had this wallet with seven dollars in it."

"how'd they kill him?"

"with a rock. he was drinking wine and when he got drunk they cracked his head with a rock. and took the wallet. I was watching.

"what'd they do with the body?"

"early in the morning the train made a water stop. they carried his body out and dumped it just below one of those cattle runways, down in the grass. then they got back in the car and the train moved on."

"ummmm," I said.

"the cops find a body like that later, look at the clothes, the wino-face, no 'ident.' they just erase the case from the books. just another bum. it don't matter."

we sat there a few more hours drinking and I told a few, not nearly as good. then we both got silent. kept thinking.

then 'Red' stood up.

"well, listen, man, I gotta get rolling. but it's been a good night."

I stood up.

"it sure has, 'Red.'"

"well, shit, see you around."

"shit, yes, 'Red.'"

there was some kind of hesitancy in leaving. in a sense, it had been a good night.

"see you, kid."

"o.k., Bukowski."

I watched him go around the bush to the left, out toward Normandie, out toward Vermont where he had a room with three or four days rent left, and then he was gone and what was left of the moon shone in, she did, and I closed the door, drained a last tired beer, lights out, I made it to the bed, got the clothes off, dropped in as down in the railroad yards they moved across the tracks picking cars, places, hoped destinations – better towns, better times, better love, better luck, better something. they'd never find it, they'd never stop looking.

I slept.

———

his name was Henry Beckett and it was a Monday morning, he had just gotten up, looked out the window at a woman in a very short mini-skirt, thinking, I am almost getting used to it, that's too bad. yet a woman has to have something on or there's nothing to take off. raw meat is only raw meat.

he was already in his shorts and moved to the bathroom to shave. when he looked into the mirror he saw that his face was gold-colored with green polka dots. he looked again, still holding the shaving brush in his hand. then the brush dropped to the floor. the face stayed in the mirror: gold-colored with green polka dots. the walls began to move. Henry held to the wash basin. then, somehow, he moved back to the bedroom, threw himself belly down on the bed. he stayed there five minutes, his mind flupping, throbbing, probing, puking. then he got up and walked to the bathroom and looked into the mirror again: gold-face with green polka dots. bright gold face with bright green polka dots.

he went to the phone. "yes, hello. this is Henry Beckett. I won't be able to get in today. I'm sick. what? oh, a terribly upset stomach. terribly upset."

he hung up.

walked to the bathroom again. it was useless. the face was still there. he filled the bathtub with water, then went to the phone. the nurse wanted to give him an appointment for next *Wednesday*.

"listen, this is an *emergency*! I've got to see the doctor *today*! it's life and death! I can't tell you, no, I can't tell you, but *please*, squeeze me in today! you've got to!"

she gave him a 3:30 appointment.

he took off his shorts and got into the tub. he noticed that his body was also gold with green polka dots. everywhere. it covered his belly, his back, his testicles, his penis. it wouldn't rub off with soap. he got out, toweled himself, put his shorts back on.

the phone rang. it was Gloria. his girl friend. she worked down there.

"Gloria, I can't tell you what's wrong. it's awful. no, I

don't have the syph. it's worse than that. I can't tell you. you wouldn't believe it."

she said she was coming over on her lunch hour.

"please don't, baby, I'll kill myself."

"I'm coming over right *now*!" she said.

"please, PLEASE don't . . ."

she had hung up. he looked at the phone, put it down, walked into the bathroom again. no change. he went back to the bedroom, stretched out, looked at the cracks in the ceiling. it was the first time he had noticed the cracks in the ceiling. they looked very warm, charming, friendly. he could hear the traffic, an occasional bird-chirp, voices in the street – a woman telling a child, "well, walk *faster*, please," and every now and then the sound of a motor-driven airplane.

the doorbell rang. he went into the front room and peeked through the curtains. it was Gloria in a white blouse with light blue summer skirt. she looked better than he had ever seen her. a strawberry blonde booming with life; nose a little too ugly, a little too fat, but after you got used to the nose you loved that too. he could feel his heart ticking like a bomb in an empty closet. it was as if his guts had been scooped out and just the heart was in there, whaling hollow. wailing hollow.

"I can't let you in, Gloria!"

"open this goddamned door, you silly ass!"

he could see her trying to look at him through the curtains.

"Gloria, you don't understand . . ."

"I said, 'OPEN THIS DOOR!'"

"all right," he said, "goddamn it, all right!"

he could feel the sweat circling his head, dripping behind his ears, running down his neck.

he threw the door open.

"JESUS!" she half-screamed, putting her hand to her mouth.

"I TOLD you, I tried to TELL you, I TOLD you!"

he backed up. she closed the door and moved toward him.

"what is it?"

"I dunno. christ, I dunno. don't touch me, don't touch. it might be contagious."

"poor Henry, oh, my poor boy . . ."

she kept coming toward him. he tripped over a wastebasket.

"god damn it, I told you to stay away!"

"why, you're almost pretty!"

"ALMOST!" he screamed, "BUT I CAN'T SELL INSURANCE THIS WAY, CAN I?"

they both began laughing then. then he was on the couch and he was crying. he had his gold and green face in his hands and he was crying.

"god, why can't it be cancer, heart attack, something nice and clean? God has shitted on me, that's all, God has shitted on me!"

she was kissing him along the neck and through his hands that covered his face. he pushed her away, "stop it, stop it!"

"I love you, Henry, I don't care about all this."

"you goddamned women are crazy."

"sure. now, when do you see the doctor?"

"3:30."

"I've got to get back to the office. phone me when you find something out. I'll be by tonight."

"o.k., o.k.," then she was gone.

at 3:10 he had a hat pulled low over his eyes and a scarf around his throat. he had dark shades on. he drove to the doctor's looking straight ahead, trying to appear invisible. nobody seemed to notice him.

in the doctor's office they were all reading *LIFE, LOOK, NEWSWEEK* and so forth. there were hardly enough chairs and sofas and it was hot in there. the pages turned. he looked down at his magazine, trying not to be seen. it went all right for fifteen or twenty minutes and then a little girl who had been running around bouncing a balloon, bounced it near him, it bounced off his shoe and when it bounced off his shoe she caught it and looked at him. then she went back to a very ugly-looking woman with ears like small pancakes and eyes like the insides of spiders' souls and she said, "Mommy, what's wrong with that man's FACE?"

and Mommy said, "sssssssshhhh!"

"BUT IT'S ALL YELLOW WITH BIG PURPLE SPOTS ALL OVER IT!"

"*Mary Ann*, I TOLD you to be QUIET! now you just SIT here by me for a while and stop that runnin' around! NOW, I said SIT DOWN HERE!"

"ah, *Mommy*!"

the little girl sat down, sniffling, looking at his face, sniffling and looking at his face.

the little girl and Mommy were called in. others were called in, others entered, left. finally the doctor called him.

"Mr. Beckett."

he followed the Dr. in. "how are you, Mr. Beckett?"

"look at me and you'll see."

the doctor turned around. "Good God!" he said.

"yeah," said Mr. Beckett.

"I've never seen *anything* like it! please disrobe and sit on the table. when did this first occur?"

"this morning when I woke up."

"how do you feel?"

"like I'm smeared with shit that won't come off."

"I mean, physically."

"I felt fine until I saw the mirror."

the doctor wrapped the tube around his arm.

"blood pressure, normal."

"let's cut the horseshit, Dr. you'll be asking me to step on the scales next. you don't know what it is, do you?"

"no, never have I seen anything like it."

"your grammar is bad, Dr. where are you from?"

"Austria."

"Austria. what are you going to do with me?"

"I do not know. maybe a skin specialist, hospitalization, tests."

"I'm sure they'd find me very interesting. but it won't go away."

"what won't go away?"

"what I've got. I can feel it inside. it won't go away, ever."

the doctor began to listen to his heart. Beckett knocked the stethoscope away. he began to get dressed.

"don't be hasty, Mr. Beckett. please!"

then he was dressed and out of there. he left the hat, scarf, dark shades. he made it to his place and got his hunting rifle and enough rounds of ammunition to kill a batallion. he found the cutoff on the freeway that led to the knoll. the knoll overlooked a slow turn that cut the speed of the cars down. why he'd ever noticed the knoll he never knew. he got out of the car and climbed to the top of the highest hill. he dusted the telescopic sight, loaded, took off the safety catch and flattened out.

at first he didn't get it right. each time he fired the shot appeared to hit behind the car. then he practiced leading the cars into the bullet. the speeds of each of the cars were practically the same, but instinctively he varied the lead to the changing speed of each car. the first one he got was very strange. the bullet entered the right forehead and the man seemed to look right up at him, and then the car flipped, it hit the fence, flipped on its side and he shot at the next one coming by, a woman, missed, hit her engine, there was fire, and she just sat in the car screaming and waving her arms and burning. he didn't want to see her burn. he shot her. the traffic stopped. people got out of their cars. he decided not to shoot any more women. bad taste. or children. bad taste. a doctor from Austria. why didn't they stay in Austria? weren't there any sick in Austria? he got four or five more men before they knew a shooting was going on. then the patrol cars came and the ambulances. they blocked off the freeway. he let them load the dead and wounded into the ambulance. he didn't shoot at the attendants. he shot at the cops. he got one cop. a real bulky one. he lost sense of time. it got dark. he sensed they were moving up the knoll toward him. he didn't stay in the same position. he moved toward them. he caught two of them in ambush from the left flank. then some firing from his right drove him toward the knoll. they were backing him up. an established position was the worst thing. he tried to make one more break but the fire was too heavy. he slowly backed toward the knoll, saving what ground he could. he could hear them talking and cursing. there were many of them. he stopped firing and waited. he got one more, seeing a pantleg through the brush, he aimed where he thought the trunk of the body would be, heard a scream, then moved further up the knoll. it was getting darker. Gloria would have dumped him. he would have dumped Gloria with a paint job like that. can you imagine taking a purple and gold girl to a concert of Brahms?

then they had him on top of the knoll but there wasn't any brush coverage for them. jut small-sized boulders. and all of them wanted to go home alive. he decided he could hold for quite a while. they began to shoot flares up on the knoll. he shot some of them off but parts of others remained and soon there were too many flares burning to knock out. they were potting at him, getting closer . . . shit. shit. well.

a flare lit particularly close and Henry could see his hands on the rifle. he looked again. his hands were WHITE.

WHITE!

it was *gone*!

he was WHITE, WHITE, WHITE!

"HEY!" he screamed, "I QUIT! I GIVE UP! I QUIT!"

Henry ripped at his shirt, looked at his chest: WHITE.

he took his shirt off, tied it to the end of his rifle, waved it. they stopped firing. the ridiculous mad dream was over, the polka-dot man was finished, the clown gone; what a joke, what shit, had it happened? it couldn't have happened. it must have been his mind. or had it happened? had Hiroshima happened? had anything ever really happened?

he threw his rifle down toward them, he threw it hard. then he walked slowly down toward them, his hands high over his head, hollering, "I QUIT! I SURRENDER! SURRENDER! I SURRENDER!"

he could hear voices as he moved toward them.

"what are we going to do, man?"

"I don't know. watch for tricks."

"he killed Eddie and Weaver. I hate his guts."

"he's getting closer."

"I QUIT! I SURRENDER!"

one of the cops fired five shots. three in the belly, two in the lungs. they left him out there a good minute before anybody moved. then they came out. the one who shot him got there first. he turned the body over with his boot, from the front to the back. he was a black cop, Adrian Thompson, 236 pounds, a home almost paid for near the west side, and he grinned down in the moonlight.

the traffic on the freeway was moving again, as usual.

———————

everywhere we hang onto the walls of the world, and in the darkest part of hangover, I think of two friends who advise me on various methods of suicide. what better proof of loving camaraderie? one of my friends has razor scars running all along his left arm. the other jams pills by the bucketloads into a mass of black beard. they both write poetry. there is something about writing poetry that brings a man close to the cliff's edge. probably, though, all three of us will live into our nineties. can you imagine the world of 2010 a.d.? of course, the way it will look will depend a lot on what is done with the Bomb. I suppose men will still eat eggs for breakfast, have sex problems. write poetry. commit suicide.

I think that it was in 1954 that I last tried suicide. I was living on the third floor in an apartment building on N. Mariposa Avenue. I closed all the windows and turned on the oven and the gas jets, without lighting them, of course. then I stretched out on the bed. escaping unlit gas has this very soothing hiss. I went to sleep. it would have worked too, only inhaling the gas gave me such a headache that the headache awakened me. I got up off the bed, laughing, and saying, "You damn fool, you don't want to kill yourself!" I turned off the gas and opened up the windows. I kept laughing. it seemed a very funny joke. then too, the automatic pilot on the stove wasn't working or that little flame would have blasted me right out of my precious little season in Hell.

a few years earlier I awakened from a week's drunk and pretty determined to kill myself. I was shacked with a sweet little thing at the time and not working. the money was gone, the rent was due, and even if I had been able to find a flunk's job of some sort, that would have only seemed like another kind of death. I decided to kill myself when she left the room the first time. meanwhile, I went outside on the street, slightly curious, just slightly, as to what day it was. on our drunks, days and nights ran together. we just drank and made love continually. it was about noon and I walked down the hill to check the corner newspaper for the day. Friday, the paper said. well, Friday seemed as good a day as any. then I saw the headline. MILTON BERLE'S COUSIN HIT ON HEAD BY FALLING ROCK. now how the hell are you going to kill yourself when they write headlines like that? I stole a paper and brought it back to the room. "guess what?" I asked. "what?" she said. "Milton Berle's cousin was hit on the head by a falling rock." "no SHIT?" "yeah." "I wonder what kind of rock it was?" "I think it was a kind of round smooth yellow one." "yeah, I think so too." "I wonder what color eyes Milton Berle's cousin has?" "I'd guess they're a kind of brown, a very pale brown." "pale brown eyes, light yellow rock." "CLUNK!" "yeah, CLUNK!" I went out and cuffed a couple of bottles and we had a fairly nice day after all. I think the paper with that headline that day was something called "The Express" or "The Evening Herald." I'm not sure. anyway, I wish to thank whatever paper it was and also Milton Berle's cousin and that round smooth yellow rock.

well, since the subject seems to be suicide, I remember once I was working on the docks, we used to eat our lunch on those Frisco docks with our feet hanging over the edge of the pier. well, one day I am sitting there when this guy next to me takes off his shoes and stockings, piles them very neatly by his side. he was sitting next to me. then I heard the splash and he was down in there. it was very strange, he screamed "HELP!" just before his head hit the water. then there was just this little whirling puddle and not feeling very much at all, just watching those air bubbles come up. then a man ran up to me and started screaming at me, "DO SOMETHING! HE'S TRYING TO TRY TO COMMIT SUICIDE!" "hell, what'll I do?" "get a rope, throw him a rope or something!" I jumped up and ran to a shack where an old man wrapped packages and cartons. "GIMME SOME ROPE!" he just looked at me. "GODDAMN IT, GIVE ME SOME ROPE, A MAN'S DROWNING, I GOTTA THROW HIM ROPE!" the old man turned around and got something. then he held it out to me. he held it out between his two fingers – it was a little piece of shriveled white string. "YOU ROTTEN SON OF A BITCH!" I screamed at him.

by then a young man had peeled down to his shorts and dived in and brought our suicide up. the young man was given the rest of the day off with pay. our suicide claimed he had fallen in by accident but he couldn't explain away the taking off of the shoes and stockings bit. I never saw him again. maybe he finished the job that night. you can never tell what is troubling a man. even trivial things can become terrible when you get into a certain mind-state. and the worst worry/fear/agony tiredness of them all is the one you can't explain or understand or even think out. it just lays on you like a slab of sheet metal and there's no getting it off. not even for $25 an hour. I know. suicide? suicide seems incomprehensible unless you yourself are thinking about it. you don't have to belong to the Poet's Union in order to join the club. I was living in this cheap hotel when I was a younger man and my friend was an older man, an ex-con, who had a job scrubbing out the insides of candy-making machines. it doesn't seem like much to live for, does it? anyhow we drank together some nights and he seemed a good sort, a kind of big 45-year-old kid, loose and easy, not vicious at all. Lou was his name. x-hard rock miner. nose like a hawk. big, mangled hands, scuffed shoes, uncombed hair, not as good with the ladies as I was – at that time. anyhow, he missed a day's work because of drinking and the big rock candy boys let him go. he came in and told me about it. I told him to forget it – a job just ate up a man's good hours anyhow. I didn't seem to impress him very much with my home-spun stuff and he left. I went down to his door a couple of hours later to bum a couple of smokes. he didn't answer my knock so I figured he was in there drunk. I tried the door and it opened. there he was on the bed with the gas jets going. I guess the Southern California Gas Co. just doesn't realize how many people they serve. anyhow, I opened the windows and turned off the gas hotplate and his gas heater. he didn't have a stove. just an icon who had lost his candy-machine scrubbing job because he had missed one day's work. "the boss tells me I'm the best worker he ever had. the thing is I miss too many days – 2 last month. he tells me if I miss another I'm finished."

I walked over to the bed and shook him. "you rotten mother!"

"wha'?"

"you rotten mother, you ever do that again I'm going to kick your ass all over this rotten town!"

"hey, Ski, you SAVED MY LIFE! I OWE YOU MY LIFE! YOU SAVED MY LIFE!"

he kept on this "you-saved-my-life" bit all through a couple of weeks of drunks. he'd lean toward my girl friend with that hawknose, put his big mangled hand on her hand or, worse, her knee, and say, "Hey, this rotten son of a bee saved my LIFE! YA KNOW THAT?"

"you've told me many times, Lou."

"YEAH, HE SAVED MY LIFE!"

a couple of days later he left, two weeks behind in the rent. I never saw him again.

this has been some hangover but talking about suicide beats doing it. or does it? I am down to my last beer and my radio on the floor plays music from Japan. the phone just rang. some drunk. long distance. from New York. "listen, man, as long as they trot out one Bukowski every fifty years, I'm gonna make it." I allow myself to enjoy this, to manipulate it in my favor because I have the deep blue skies, the honed-edge fever. "remember those drunks we used to go on, man?" he asks. "yeah, I remember." "whatcha doin' now, ya still writing?" "yeah, right now I'm writing about suicide." "suicide?" "yeah, I have this column, kind of, in a new paper that's starting, OPEN CITY." "they'll print the suicide thing?" "I dunno." we talk awhile and then he hangs up. some hangover. some column. I remember when I was a kid, they used to have a song BLUE MONDAY. they played it in Hungary, I believe. and everytime they played BLUE MONDAY somebody took the suicide way. they finally barred the song from being played. but they are playing something from the floor on my radio that sounds just as bad. if you don't see this column next week it may not be because of subject matter. meanwhile, I doubt if I put Coates or Weinstock out of business.

———

it was last Monday a.m. I had worked all Sunday until midnight and then drove to this place with the lights on. I brought in a 6-pack and this tended to get them started. somebody went out and got some more.

"you shoulda seen Bukowski last week," this one guy said. "he was dancing with the ironing board. then he said he was going to screw the ironing board."

"yeah?"

"yeah. then he read us his poems. we had to snatch the book from his hands or he would have read us his poems all night."

I told them there was this virgin-eyed woman sitting there looking at me – woman, hell, girl, girl she was – and it was hard to stop.

"lemme see," I told them, "now this is mid-July and I haven't had a piece of ass this year."

they laughed. they thought it was funny. people who are getting ass always think it is funny when somebody else isn't.

then they talked about the young blond god guy who was now shacking with three chicks at the same time. I warned them that when this kid got to be 33 years old he'd have to go find himself a job. this seemed like a kind of flat and vengeful warning. nothing for me to do but drain the beer can and wait for the bomb to drop.

I took a little piece of paper from somewhere and when nobody was looking I wrote down:

love is a way with some meaning; sex is meaning enough.

soon all the young ones got tired and had to go to sleep. I was left with an old-timer, a man about my age. we are bred to go on all night – drinking, that is. after the beer was gone he found a fifth of whiskey. he was an old newspaper man, now an editor on some big city rag back east. the talk was pleasant – two old dogs agreeing on too much. morning came fast. around 6:15 a.m. I said I had to leave. I decided not to drive my car. the walk in was about 8 blocks. old-timer walked with me down to Hollywood Blvd. by the bowling alley. then an old-fashioned handshake and we parted.

As I got about two blocks from my place, I noticed a woman in a car trying to get it started, trying to get it away from the curbing. she was having her troubles. it would leap forward a few feet, then stall. she would start it immediately in what I sensed to be a rather erratic and panicky fashion. it was a late model car. I stood on the corner and watched her. soon the car stalled right next to me, right where I was standing on the curbing. I looked in. there sat this woman. she had on high heels, long dark stockings, blouse, earrings, wedding ring and panties. no skirt, just these light pink panties. I inhaled the morning air. she had this old woman's face and these young big unwrinkled girl's legs and thighs.

the car jumped forward again, stalled again. I walked on down and stuck my head in the window:

"lady, you'd better park that thing. the police are pretty busy this time of the morning. you might get into trouble."

"all right."

she maneuvered it into the curbing, then climbed out. under the blouse were young girl's breasts too. there she stood in her pink panties and long dark stockings and highheels at 6:25 a.m. on a Los Angeles morning. a 55 year-old face with an 18 year-old body.

"are you sure you're all right?" I said.

"sure I'm all right," she said.

"are you *really* sure?" I asked.

"sure I'm sure," she said. then she turned and walked away from me. and I stood there watching the whirling of the buttocks under that pink tight sheen. it was walking away from me, down the street between rows of houses, and nobody in sight, no police, no humans, not even a bird. just those whirling pink young buttocks walking away from me. I was too high to groan; I just felt the eating and wild sadness of another good thing lost forever. I hadn't said the right words. I hadn't said the right combination of words, I hadn't even tried. I deserved an ironing board, so what the hell, just some nut running around in pink panties at 6 a.m. in the morning.

I stood there watching it walk off. the boys would never believe this one – the one that got away. then, as I watched, she turned around and walked back toward me. she looked pretty good from the front too. in fact, the closer she got the better she looked – throwing out the face. but you had to throw out my face too. the face is the first thing you throw out when the luck gets bad. the remaining decay follows in slower order.

she got right up to me. there still wasn't anybody around. there are times when insanity becomes so real that it isn't insanity anymore. here was pink panties back breathing against me, and not a cruise car anywhere, and nobody anywhere between Venice Italy and Venice California, between the sniffboards of hell and the last vacant lot in Palos Verdes.

"good, you came back," I said.

"I just wanted to see if the back of the car was sticking into the driveway."

then she bent over. I couldn't bear up anymore. I grabbed her arm.

"come on, we're going to my place. it's just around the corner. let's catch a few drinks and get off the street."

she looked at me with that fallen-apart face. I still couldn't place the head upon the body. I was throbbing like a stinking beast. then she said, "o.k., let's go."

so we walked around the corner. I didn't touch her. I offered her a cigarette I found in my shirt pocket. we stood outside a church as I lit it for her. I expected, at any moment, a voice from one of the neighboring houses: "HEY, WOMAN, GET OFF THE STREETS WITH YOUR GOD-DAMNED PANTIES OR I'M GONNA CALL THE FUZZ!" maybe it paid to live on the outskirts of Hollywood. there were probably three or four guys peeking through the curtains as the wife got breakfast ready. meanwhile giving themselves whiplash handjobs.

we got inside and I sat her down and got out a half-jug of mountain red some hippy had left. we drank quietly. she seemed more sensible than most. she didn't bring out the photos of her family from her purse – the children, I mean. of course, the husband always comes out.

"Frank makes me sick. Frank doesn't want me to have any fun."

"yeh?"

"he keeps me locked up. I'm sick of being locked up. he hid all my skirts, all my dresses. he always does that when I'm drinking. when we're drinkin'."

"yeh?"

"he wants to keep me like some kind of slave. do you think a woman ought to be a slave to a man?"

"oh, hell no!"

"so I had stockings and heels and panties and blouse but no skirt and when Frank passed out, I escaped!"

"Frank's probably a good guy, tho," I said, "don't knock Frank too much, you know what I mean?"

this is the old pro's line. always pretend to be understanding, even when you are not. women never want sensibility, all they want is a kind of emotional vindictiveness toward somebody else they care for too much. women are basically stupid animals but they concentrate so much and entirely upon the male that they often defeat him while he is thinking of other things.

"I think Frank's a bastard. but aren't you glad I'm here?"

it sure beat ironing boards. I finished my drink and reached around and grabbed that old face and, keeping the body in mind, I kissed it, tongued it down good, her tongue finally grabbing my round tongue and sucking at it, sucking at it, as I played with those young girl's nylon legs and mother-miracle breasts. Frank was a good guy, especially when he snored.

we took a breather and had another drink. "what do you do?" she asked.

"I'm an interior decorator," I said.

"don't get filthy," she said.

"hey, you're pretty sharp."

"I been to college."

I didn't ask her where. the old pro knows how it works.

"you been to college?"

"not too much."

"you've got beautiful hands. you've got hands like a woman."

"I've heard that too much. you say that once more and I'm gonna knock your teeth out."

"what are you, some kind of artist or painter or something. you seem kind of mixed up. and I notice you don't like to look a person in the EYES. I don't like people who CAN'T LOOK ME IN THE EYE. are you a coward?"

"yes. but the eyes are different. I don't like people's eyes."

"I like you."

she reached around and grabbed me in front. I wasn't expecting it; I was ready to walk her back to her car. or worse, just let her walk away alone.

it was good. I mean, her holding me. forgetting the words.

we drank down a couple of tall fast ones and then I worked her toward the bedroom, or she worked me toward there. it didn't matter. there is no time like the first time. I don't care what anybody says. I make her leave on her stockings and high heels. I am a freak. I cannot bear the human being in present state, I must be fooled. the psychiatrists must have a word for it, and I have a word for the psychiatrists.

it is just like riding a bicycle: once you get back into the seat the balance and wonderment is there again.

it was good. after getting through with the bathroom we went out front again and killed the jug, I don't remember going back to bed but I awakened with this 55-year-old face leering at me, really a dementia kind of look. the eyes were insane. I had to laugh. she had worked up my string while I was asleep. the same thing had happened to me once with a plump young negress on Irolo Street.

"go, baby, go!" I told her.

I reached up and in and spread her cheeks wide apart. that 55-year-old face came down and kissed me. it was horrible but the 18-year-old body was tit tight, tilting, rippling; snake of a thing as mad as wallpaper come alive. we made it.

then I really slept. I was awakened by something. I looked up and pink panties had pink panties on again and was working her way into one of my ragged old pair of pants. it was sad – seeing her ass not properly fitted into my wallowing pants. it was sad and ridiculous and ornery and a tear-hurling jerker, but the old pro narrowed his eyes, pretended to be asleep.

Frankie, here comes your LOVE!

when she can.

I watched her look through an empty cigarette pack, I watched her look down at me – it may seem terrible ego but I sensed that she admired me. fuck that, I had my own troubles, still, I did feel bad as I saw what had given something to me walking out of my bedroom door with a torn ripped lousy pair of my workman's pants on. but the pros can tell a pre-supposed mechanical future based upon chance vs. the real thing which never shows up – except in the shape of an ironing board. she walked out of the bedroom. I let them go; they let me go. everything is horrible really, and I add to it. they will never let us sleep until we are dead and then they will think up another trick. balls, yes, I almost cried, but then orientated by centuries, Christ's fuck-up, every sad and ripping thing, stupid, I leaped up and checked my only unripped pants not yet ripped from falling down at the knees while drunk. I checked for wallet, I checked for $$$$ and finding $7, I figured I had not been robbed. and giving a little ashamed smile in the mirror, I fell back upon the x-love bed and . . . slept.

———

"the squirs came to my house."
  "they did?"
  "yes."
  "squirrels?"
  "*squirs!*"
  "were there many of them?"
  "many of them."
  "what happened?"
  "they talked to me."
  "they did?"
  "yes, they talked to me."
  "what did they say?"
  "they asked me if I wanted . . ."
  "what did they say?"
  "they asked me if I wanted a fix."
  "what? what did you say?"
  "I *said* – 'they asked me if I wanted a fix.'"
  "and what did *you* say?"
  "I said, 'no.'"
  "and what did the squirs say?"
  "they said, 'WELL, ALL RIGHT!'"
          *   *   *
"mama saw Bill, mama saw Gene, mama saw Danny."
  "she did?"
  "yaeah."
          *   *   *
"can I touch your thing?"

"no."

"I got tits. you got tits."

"that's right."

"look! I can make your bellybutton disappear. does it hurt when I make your bellybutton disappear?"

"no, that's just fat."

"what's fat?"

"too much of me where I shouldn't be."

"oh."

* * *

"what time is it?"

"it's 5:25."

"what time is it now?"

"it's still 5:25."

"now what time is it?"

"listen, time doesn't change very fast. it's still 5:25."

"what time is it NOW?"

"I told you – 'it's 5:25.'"

"now what time is it?"

"5:25 and 20 seconds."

"I'm gonna throw you my ball."

"good."

* * *

"what are you *doing*?"

"I'm *climbing*!"

"don't fall! if you fall from there you're finished!"

"I won't fall!"

"don't."

"I won't! I won't! look at me *now*!"

"o, jesus!"

"I'm coming down! I'm coming down now!"

"o.k., now you *stay* down there!"

"oh, FARK!"

"what did you say?"

"I said, 'FARK!'"

"that's what I thought you said."

"mama saw Nick, mama saw Andy, mama saw Rueben."

"she did?"
"yaeah!"
"you goin' to work?"
"yes."
"but I don't *like* for you to go to work!"
"I don't like to go either."
"then don't go."
"it's the only way I can get money."
"oh."
"that's right."
"you got your pen?"
"yes."
"you got your keys?"
"yes."
"you got your badge?"
"yes."
"go to work, go to work, go to work, go to work, go to work . . ."

* * *

"we went to workshop last night."
"yeah?"
"yeah."
"what'd the people do?"
"they talked. all the people talked and talked. and talked."
"and what'd you do?"
"I went to sleep."

* * *

"where did you get those big, beautiful blue eyes?"
"I made them myself!"
"you made them yourself?"
"yaeah!"
"I see."
"*your* eyes are blue."
"no, they're green."
"no, they're *blue*!"
"well, maybe it's the light. the light is bad in here."
"did you make your eyes yourself?"

"I think I had a little help."

"I made my *own* eyes, and my hands and my nose and my feet and my elbows. all that."

"sometimes I think you're right."

"and your eyes are *blue*!"

"o.k., my eyes are blue."

* * *

"I *farted*! ha, ha, ha! I *farted*!"

"you did?"

"yaeah!"

"you wanna crap?"

"NO!"

"you ain't pee-pee'd in hours. is something wrong with you?"

"no. is something wrong with you?"

"I don't know."

"why?"

"I don't know why."

"what time is it?"

"it's 6:35."

"now what time is it?"

"it's still 6:35."

"what time is it now?"

"6:35."

"oh, FARK!"

"what?"

"I said, 'oh, FARK! FARK! FARK! FARK!'"

"listen – go get me a beer."

"o.k. . . ."

"mama saw Danny, mama saw Bill, mama saw Gene."

"o.k., let me drink my beer."

she runs over and starts stuffing blocks, paper clips, rubber bands, extension cords, blue chip stamps, envelopes, advertisements and a small statue of Boris Karloff into her purse. I drink my beer.

———

in Philly, I had the end seat and ran errands for sandwiches, so forth. Jim, the early bartender, would let me in at 5:30 a.m. while he was mopping and I'd have free drinks until the crowd came in at 7:00 a.m. I'd close the bar at 2:00 a.m., which didn't give me much time for sleep. but I wasn't doing much those days – sleeping, eating or anything else. the bar was so run down, old, smelled of urine and death, that when a whore came in to make a catch we felt particularly honored. how I paid the rent for my room or what I was thinking about I am not sure. about this time a short story of mine appeared in *PORTFOLIO III*, along with Henry Miller, Lorca, Sartre, many others. the Portfolio sold for $10. a huge thing of separate pages, each printed in different type on colored expensive paper, and drawings mad with exploration. Caresse Crosby the editoress wrote me: "a most unusual and wonderful story. who ARE you?" and I wrote back, "Dear Mrs. Crosby: I don't know who I am. sincerely yours, Charles Bukowski." it was right after that that I quit writing for ten years. but first a night in the rain with *PORTFOLIO*, a very strong wind, the pages flying down the street, people running after them, myself standing drunk watching; a big window washer who always ate six eggs for breakfast put a big foot in the center of one of the pages: "here! hey! I got one!" "fuck it, let it go, let all the pages go!" I told them, and we went back inside. I had won some sort of bet. that was enough.

about 11 a.m. every morning Jim would tell me I had enough, I was 86'd, to go take a walk. I would go around to the back of the bar and lay down in the alley there. I liked to do this because trucks ran up and down the alley and I felt that anytime might be mine. but my luck ran bad. and every day little negro children would poke sticks in my back, and then I'd hear the mother's voice, "all right now, all right, leave that man alone!" after a while I would get up, go back in and continue drinking. the lime in the alley was the problem. somebody always brushed the lime off of me and made too much of it.

I was sitting there one day when I asked somebody, "how come nobody here ever goes into the bar down the street?" and I was told, "that's a gangster bar. you go in there, you get killed." I finished my drink, got up and walked on down.

it was much cleaner in that bar. a lot of big young guys sitting around, kind of sullen. it got very quiet. "I'll take a scotch and water," I told the barkeep.

he pretended not to hear me.

I touched up the volume: "bartender, I said I wanted a scotch and water!"

he waited a long time, then turned, came over with the bottle and set me up. I drained it down.

"now I'll have another one."

I noticed a young lady sitting alone. she looked lonely. she looked good, she looked good and lonely. I had some money. I don't remember where I got the money. I took my drink and went down and sat next to her.

"whatya wanna hear on the juke?" I asked.

"anything. anything you like."

I loaded the thing. I didn't know who I was but I could load a juke box. she looked good. how could she look so good and sit alone?

"bartender! bartender! 2 more drinks! one for the lady and one for myself!"

I could smell death in the air. and now that I smelled it I wasn't so sure whether it smelled any good or not.

"whatch havin', honey? tell the man!"

we'd been drinking about a half an hour when one of the two big guys sitting down at the end of the bar got up, slowly walked down to me. he stood behind, leaned over. she'd gone to the crapper. "listen, buddy, I wanna TELL you something."

"go ahead. my pleasure."

"that's the boss's girl. keep messing and you're going to get yourself killed."

that's what he said: "killed." it was just like a movie. he went back and sat down. she came out of the crapper, sat down next to me.

"bartender," I said, "two more drinks."

I kept loading the juke and talking. then I had to go to the crapper. I went to where it said MEN and I noticed there was a long stairway down. they had the men's crapper down below. how odd. I took the first steps down and then I noticed that I was being followed down by the two big boys who had been at the end of the bar. it was not so much the fear of the thing as it was the strangeness. there was nothing I could do but keep walking on down the steps. I walked up to the urinal, unzipped my fly and started to piss. vaguely drunk, I saw the blackjack coming down. I moved my head just a little and instead of taking it over the ear I caught it straight on the back of my head. the lights went in circles and flashes but it was not too bad. I finished pissing, put it back in and zipped my fly. I turned around. they were standing there waiting for me to drop. "pardon me," I said and then I walked between them and walked up the steps and sat down. I had neglected to wash my hands.

"bartender," I said, "two more drinks."

the blood was coming. I took out my hanky and held it to the back of my head. then the two big boys came up out of the crapper and sat down.

"bartender," I nodded toward them, "two drinks for those gentlemen there."

more juke, more talk. the girl didn't move away from me. I didn't make out most of what she was saying. then I had to piss again. I got up and made for the MEN'S room again. one of the big boys said to the other as I passed, "you can't kill that son of a bitch. he's crazy."

they didn't come down again, but when I came back up I didn't sit by the girl again. I had proved some kind of point and was no longer interested. I drank there the rest of the night and when the bar closed we all went outside and talked and laughed and sang. I had done some drinking with a black-haired kid for the last couple of hours. he came up to me: "listen, we want you in the gang. you've got guts. we need a guy like you."

"thanks, pal. appreciate it but I can't do it. thanks anyhow."

then I walked off. always the old sense of drama.

I hailed a cop car a few blocks down, told them I had been blackjacked and robbed by a couple of sailors. they took me to emergency and I sat under a bright electric light with a doc and a nurse. "now this is gonna hurt," he told me. the needle started working. I couldn't feel a thing. I felt like I had myself and everything under pretty good control. they were putting some kind of bandage on me when I reached out and grabbed the nurse's leg. I squeezed her knee. it felt good to me.

"hey! what the hell's the matter with you?"

"nothing. just joking," I told the doc.

"you want us to run this guy in?" one of the cops asked.

"no, take him home. he's had a rough night."

the cops rode me on in. it was good service. if I had been in L.A. I would have made the tank. when I got to my room I drank a bottle of wine and went to sleep.

I didn't make the 5:30 a.m. opening at the old bar. I sometimes did that. I sometimes stayed in bed all day. about 2 p.m. I heard a couple of women talking outside the window. "I don't know about that new roomer. sometimes he just stays in his room all day with the shades down just listening to his radio. that's all he does."

"I've seen him," said the other, "drunk most of the time, a horrible man."

"I think I'll have to ask him to move," said the first one.

ah, shit, I thought. ah, shit, shit shit shit shit.

I turned Stravinsky off, put on my clothes and walked on down to the bar. I went on in.

"hey, there he is!!!"

"we thought ya got killed!"

"did ya hit that gang bar?"

"yeah."

"tell us about it."

"I'll need a drink first."

"sure, sure."

the scotch and water arrived. I sat down at the end stool. the dirty sunshine around 16th and Fairmount worked its way in. my day had begun.

"the rumors," I began, "about it being a very tough joint are definitely true . . ." then I told them roughly about what I have told you.

the rest of the story is that I couldn't comb my hair for two months, went back to the gang bar once or twice more, was nicely treated and left Philly not much later looking for more trouble or whatever I was looking for. I found trouble, but the rest of what I was looking for, I haven't found that yet. maybe we find it when we die. maybe we don't. you've got your books of philosophy, your priest, your preacher, your scientist, so don't ask me. and stay out of bars with MEN's crapper downstairs.

---

when Henry's mother died it wasn't bad. nice Catholic funeral. the priest waved some smoking sticks and it was all over. the coffin remained closed. Henry went right from that funeral to the racetrack. had a good day. found a light yellow girl there and they went to her apartment. she cooked steaks and they made it. when his father died it was more complicated. they left the coffin open and he had the last look. before that, the old man's girl friend, somebody he'd never met, a Shirley, this Shirley reached into the coffin, moaning and crying and grabbed that dead head and kissed it. they had to pull her off. then when Henry came down the steps this Shirley grabbed him and started kissing him. "oh, you look just like your father?" he got hot as she kissed him and when he shoved her off something was showing through his pants. he hoped the people didn't notice. he made a note to check Shirley out. she wasn't much older than he. he went from the funeral to the track, but no high yellow this time. and he also lost some money. the old man had left his stigma on him.

the lawyer said no will had been left. there was no money but there was a house and a car. Henry wasn't working so he moved right in. and drank. drank with his old girl friend Maggy. he got up about noon and watered the damn lawn, and the flowers. the old man liked flowers. he watered the flowers. he stood there hung over, remembering how the old man hated him because Henry didn't like to work. just drink and lay up with women. now he had the damn house and the car and the old man was down in the dirt. he got to know the neighbors especially the guy on the north. some guy who was manager of a laundry. Harry. this Harry had a yard full of birds. 5,000 dollars full of birds. all kinds. from everywhere. they were strangely colored and strangely shaped and some of them talked one of them kept saying over and over again, "go to hell go to hell" Henry squirted water on the thing but it was no use. the bird said "got a match?" and then it would say "go to hell" five or six times, real fast. the whole yard was full of these wire cages. Harry lived for the birds. Henry lived for the booze, and the gash. maybe he'd try one of those birds. how do you screw a bird?

Maggy was good on the springs but she was Irish-Indian and had one hell of a temper when she drank. once in a while he had to hit her. he got Shirley's phone number and asked to come over. she started to kiss him again, saying he looked just like her father. he let her and kissed back. he didn't make it that night, choosing to wait and make sure. he didn't want to scare her.

Harry came over almost every night with his wife and they drank. Harry talked about the laundry and the birds. the birds hated Harry's wife. Harry's wife crossed her legs real high while talking about how she hated the birds and Henry got something working under his pants. god damned women kept teasing him. then Shirley started coming over and they all drank together. Maggy didn't like Shirley there and Henry kept looking from Shirley to Harry's wife and wondering which one was best. so it all happened the same night. Harry's wife got drunk and let all the birds out. 5,000 dollars worth of birds, and Harry sat in shock, drunk, and then he started screaming and hitting his wife. every time he hit his wife she fell down and Henry peeked up her dress. he saw her panties several times. he started to get hot as hell. Maggy ran outside trying to catch the birds and put them in their cages, but she couldn't seem to catch them. they were running all up and down the street, sitting in trees, standing on roof tops, 5,000 dollars worth of crazy birds, all different shapes and colors, tasting the confusion of freedom. Henry couldn't stand it anymore and grabbed Shirley and took her into the bedroom. he stripped her down and got on top. he was almost too drunk to operate. each time Harry hit his wife, his wife screamed and he gave an extra little thrust. then Maggy came in with a bird, a bird with an orange tuft on its head and an orange tuft on its chest and two orange tufts at the top of the feet. the rest of the bird was gray skin and stupid. he'd cost Harry $300. Maggy hollered, "I caught a bird!" and when she didn't see Henry she went into the bedroom and when she saw what was happening she just sat in a chair with the bird in her lap, watching and screaming, and Harry kept knocking his wife down and she kept screaming, and when the police came in that's the way it was. two young cops. the cops pulled Henry off, made everybody put on their clothes and took them down to the station. another patrol car came with two other young cops. Maggy got vicious and hit one of the cops and they took her along in one of the patrol cars. the cop drove the car into the hills and they each screwed Maggy in the back seat. they had to handcuff her. the other cop took Henry, Harry, Shirley, Harry's wife down to the station, booked them and jailed them, and the birds ran all up and down the street.

that Sunday the preacher spoke of the "lecherous alcoholics who bring sin and shame to our community." Maggy was the only one who was out of jail. she was very religious. she sat in the front row with her legs crossed high. from the pulpit the preacher could look right up her legs. he could almost see her panties. he started to get something under his pants, the pulpit, luckily, hid this section of him from view.

he had to look out the window and keep talking until the thing under his pants went away.

Harry lost his job. Henry sold the house. the preacher made it with Maggy. Shirley married a tv repairman. Harry sat around looking at the empty cages and the birds starved and died in the streets. every time he saw another dead bird in the streets he beat his wife again. Henry gambled and drank away the money in six months.

my name is Henry. Charles is my middle name. when my mother died it wasn't bad. nice catholic funeral. smocking sticks. closed coffin. when my father died it was complicated. they left the coffin open and the old man's girl friend reached into the coffin . . . kissed that dead head, and that started the whole thing.

P.S. – you can't screw a bird if you can't catch one.

---

the best thing about a modern gas dryer, of course, is the way it treats clothes, and the King kicked me in the ass five times, one two three four five, and there I was in Atlanta, worse off than in New York, broker, crazier, sicker, thinner; no more chance than a 53-year-old whore or a spider in a forest fire, anyway, I walked down the street, it was night and cold, and God didn't care, and the women didn't care, and the dizzy editor didn't care. the spiders didn't care, couldn't sing, didn't know my name, but the cold did and the streets licked my belly cool and empty, haha, the streets knew plenty, and I walked along in a calif. white shirt cold and it was freezing and I knocked on a door, it was around 9 p.m., nearly two thousand years after Christ gave it up, and the door opened and a man without a face stood in the doorway. I said, I need a room, I see you have a sign Room For Rent. and he said, you don't dig me. so I don't want to be bothered.

all I want is a room, I said. it's very cold. I'll pay you. I may not have enough for a week but I just want to get out of the cold. it's not dying that's bad, it's being lost that's bad.

*   *   *

fuck off, he said. The door closed.

I walked along the streets I didn't know the name of. didn't know which way to walk. the sadness was that something was wrong. and I could not formulate it. it hung in my head like a bible. what shit nonsense. what a way to be strung out. no map. no people. no sound, just wasps. stones. walls. wind. my pecker and balls dangling without feeling. I could scream out anything in the street and nobody would hear, nobody would care a tit. not that they should. I wasn't asking for love. but something was *very* odd. the books never spoke about it. the parents never spoke about it. but the spiders knew. fuck off.

I noticed for the first time that everything OWNED BY ANYBODY had a LOCK on it. everything was locked. a lesson for thieves and bums and madmen, America the beautiful.

then I saw a church. I didn't particularly like churches, especially when they were filled with people. but I didn't figure it to be that way at 9 p.m. I walked up the steps.

hey hey, woman, come see what's left of your man.

I could sit there a while and breathe in the stink, maybe make something out of God, maybe give him a chance. I pulled at the door.

the motherfucker was locked.

I walked on back down the steps.

I kept on walking down the streets, turning corners without reason, kept walking. now it was upon me. the wall. this is what men were afraid of. not only being shut out forever. but also not having a friend. so, no wonder, I thought, this CAN scare the shit out of you. can KILL you. their cheap trick is to get in and hang in. have all kinds of cards in your wallet. money. insurance. automobile. bed. window. toilet. cat. dog. plant. musical instrument. birth certificate. things to get angry about. enemies. backers. flour sacks. toothpicks. undiseased ass. bathtub. camera. mouthwash o my god, oooo. locks (sink in it, swim in it, rub its back) (everything you have – jam it into you like a couple of fins, rubber wings, spare dick in medicine cabinet.)

I walked over a little bridge and then I saw another sign: ROOM FOR RENT. I walked up to the house, knocked. of course I knocked. what do you think I'd do? tap dance in that calif. white shirt with my kool cold ass??

yes, the door opened. old woman, it was too cold to notice if she had a face or not. I guess she did not. I worked on percentages. hell of a mathematician with a cold ass. I rubbed my lips for a while and then spoke.

I see ya gotta room for rent.

at's right. so?

I have reason to believe that I might need a room.

you'll need a buck and a quarter.

for the night?

for the week

for the week?

at's right.

jesus.

I got up the buck and a quarter. that left me two or three dollars. I looked into the house. jesus. they had a big fire going. five feet wide, three feet tall. I don't mean the house was on fire, I mean they had it going where it counted. a magic fireplace. you could get your life back just staring into that fire. you could gain two pounds without eating, just looking at that fire. there was an old man sitting by the fire. I could see him bathed in the red glory of fire shadow. mother. his mouth hung open, he didn't seem to know where he was, he shook all over. he couldn't stop shaking. the poor devil. the poor old devil. I moved forward a step inside.

fuck off, said the old woman.

whatcha mean? I paid my rent. a whole WEEK'S worth.

at's right. your room's outside. foller me.

the old woman closed the door on that poor devil in there and I followed her down the pathway toward the front. pathway, hell. the whole front yard was dirt. hard cold dirt. I hadn't noticed but there was a cardboard shack in the front yard. my power of observation was always shitty. she pushed open the cardboard door that was hanging on one hinge.

ain't no lock. but nobody's gonna bother ya in there.

I do believe you're right.

she left. I had been right. I had seen her face, she didn't have a face. just flesh hung on bone like crumpled meat on a chicken back.

there wasn't any light. just a cord hanging there from the ceiling. the floor was dirt. but there was newspaper on the floor, kind of ruglike, a bed, no sheets, thin blanket. one. thin blanket. then I found a kerosene lamp! grace! luck! charm!! I had a match and lit the thing. A FLAME APPEARED!

it was a beauty fire, it contained soul, the sides of sunshine mountains, hot streams of smiling fish, warm stockings smelling a bit like toast. I held my hand over the little flame. I had beautiful hands. that one thing I had. I had beautiful hands.

the little flame went out.

I played with the kerosene lamp but being born in the 20th century I didn't know too much about it. but it didn't take me a lifetime to figure that I needed more liquid, fuel, kerosene, whatever you call it.

I pushed open my cardboard door and went out into God's starlit night. I knocked on the door of the house with my beautiful hands.

yeah. the door opened. the old woman stood there. who else? Mickey Rooney? I sneaked an other peek at that poor devil of an old man shaking by the glorious fire. goddamned idiot.

whatzit? the old woman asked from her chickenback head.

well I don't like to bother you, but you know that little kerosene lamp?

yeh.

well, it went out.

yeh?

yeh. I wondered if I could borrow some fuel?

you crazy, boy, thet shit costs MONEY!

she didn't slam the door. she had the ancient Kool. she closed it with a kind of slob unthinking gentility, the training of centuries. nice ancestors. all with chickenback faces. the chickenback faces shall inherit the earth.

I went back to my room (?) and sat on the bed. then a very embarrassing thing happened: even tho I hadn't eaten for a long time, suddenly I had to shit. I had to get up and walk into god's world again and knock on that door again. It wasn't Mickey Rooney this time either.

yeh.

sorry to bother you again. but there's no toilet in my room. is there a toilet anywhere?

right thar! she pointed.

there??

THAR! and lissen . . .

yeh?

fuck off, boy. you all come here poundin' with your crazy head. yo let all the COL' AIR frum out THERE in HEEYAH!

sorry.

she slammed the thing this time. I could feel the warm air along my ears, between the balls a moment. it was sweet. then I moved toward the structure that served as a crapper.

the toilet didn't have a lid.

I looked down into the toilet. it seemed to go miles into the earth. and it stank like no toilet ever stank, and that's some statement. in the moonlight I could see a spider sitting in the middle of its web. a black, fat spider. very knowing. the web was spun across the mouth of the bowl. suddenly all desire to shit left me.

I walked back to my room. I sat on the bed and swung my beautiful hand as close as I could come to that hanging electric wire. I could come closer. I sat there half nutty, full of dried shit, swinging at that wire. then I got up and walked outside. I walked down about a block and stood under a frozen tree. a great frozen tree. with all that dried shit in me. I stood outside a grocery store. there was a fat woman standing in there talking to the grocer. they just stood there under that yellow light, talking. and all that FOOD in there. they didn't give a damn about the arts, or the short story, or

Plato, or even Captain Kidd. they cared for Mickey Rooney. they were dead but in a way they had more sense than me. the insensitive sense of bugs and wild dogs. I wasn't shit. I couldn't.

I went back to my room. in the morning I wrote a long letter to my father on the edges of newspapers. I bought an envelope and a stamp and mailed the thing. I told him I was starving and would like bus fare to L.A., and as far as I was concerned the short story could go to hell. look at DeMass, I wrote, he caught the syph and went crazy rowing a rowboat. send money.

I don't remember if I ever crapped while waiting. but the answer came. I ripped the envelope open. I shook the pages. there were ten or twelve pages of writing, both sides, but no money. the first words were: THE PINCH IS OFF!

. . . you still owe me TEN DOLLARS which you haven't PAID BACK TO ME! I work hard for my money. I can't afford to support you while you write your silly short stories. if you had EVER sold a story or had some TRAINING it would be different, but I read your stories, they're UGLY. people don't want to read UGLY things. you ought to write like Mark Twain. he was a great man. he could make people laugh. in all your stories your people kill themselves or go insane or murder somebody. most of life isn't the way you imagine it. get a good job, MAKE something of yourself . . .

the letter went on and on. I couldn't finish it. all I wanted was money. I shook the pages again. I was too sick to feel the cold. later that day as I was walking along I saw a sign – Help wanted. and sure enough, they needed a man for a track gang somewhere west of Sacramento. I signed on in. I had some trouble there and with the track gang. I was not popular with the boys, the train was one hundred years old with dust. one of the guys got under my seat while I was trying to sleep and blew dust into my face while the others giggled. SHITS! well it was better than Atlanta. finally I got angry and sat up. the guy walked up front and stood with his gang.

that guys nuts, he said. if he comes up here I want you guys to help me.

I didn't go up there. Mark Twain probably could have squeezed some laughs out of the thing, he'd probably be up there drinking out of a bottle with the shits and singing songs. a real man. Sam Clem. I wasn't much, but I was out of Atlanta, not quite dead yet, had beautiful hands and a way to go.

the train ran on.

———

I don't know if it was those Chinese snails with the little round assholes or if it was the Turk with the purple stickpin or if it was simply that I had to go to bed with her seven or eight or nine or eleven times a week, or something else and something else, and something, but I was once married to a woman, a girl, who was coming into a million dollars, all somebody had to do was die, but there isn't any smog in that part of Texas and they eat well, drink the finest booze and go to the doctor for a scratch or a sneeze. she was a nympho, there was something wrong with her neck, and to get it down close and fast, it was my poems, she thought my poems were the greatest thing since Black, no I mean Blake – Blake. and some of them are. or something else. she kept writing. I didn't know she had a million. I'm just sitting in a room on N. Kingsley Dr., out of the hospital with hemorrhages, stomach and ass, my blood all over the county general hospital, and they telling me after nine pints of blood and nine pints of glucose, "one more drink and you're dead." this is no way to talk to a suicide head. I sat in that room every night surrounded by full and empty beer cans, writing poems, smoking cheap cigars, very white and weak, waiting for the final wall to fall.

meanwhile, the letters. I answered them. after telling me how great my poems were she would enclose a few of her own (not too bad) and then came the same thing: "no man will every marry me. it's my neck. I can't turn it." I kept hearing this: "no man will ever marry me, no man will ever marry me, no man will ever marry me." so I did it while drunk one night: "for Christ's sake I'll marry you! relax."

I mailed the letter and forgot about it, but she didn't. she had been sending photos that looked very good, then after I told her the thing, came some horrible looking photos. I looked at these photos and I REALLY got drunk on them. I'd get down on my knees in the center of the rug, I was terrified, I'd say, "I hereby sacrifice myself. if a man can make just one person happy in a lifetime, then his life has been justified." hell, I had to come up with some type of balm. I'd look at one of those photographs and my whole soul would shake and scream and down would go a whole beer can worth.

or maybe it wasn't those Chinese snails with the little round assholes, maybe it was the Art class. where am I?

well, she came out on a bus, mama didn't know, papa didn't know, grandpa didn't know, they were on vacation somewhere and she only had a little change. I met her at the bus station, that is, I sat there drunk waiting for a woman I had never seen to get off a bus, waiting for a woman I had never spoken to, to marry. I was insane. I didn't belong on the streets. the call came. it was her bus. I watched the people swing through the door. and here comes this cute sexy blonde on high heels, all ass and bounce and young, young, 23, and the neck wasn't bad at all. could that be the one? maybe she'd missed her bus? I walked up.

"are you Barbara?" I asked.

"yes," she said, "I guess you're Bukowski?"

"I guess I am. should we go?"

"alright."

we got into the old car and drove to my place.

"I almost got off the bus and went back."

"I don't blame you."

we got on in and I drank some more but she said she wouldn't go to bed with me until we got married. so we got some sleep and I drove all the way to Vegas and back, we were married. I drove all the way to Vegas and back without rest, and then we got into bed and it was worth it ... the FIRST time. she had told me she was a nymph but I hadn't believed it. after the third or fourth round I began to believe it. I knew that I was in trouble. every man believes that he can tame a nymph but it only leads to the grave – for the man.

I quit my job as shipping clerk and we took the bus to Texas. it was then that I found out that she was a millionairess, but the fact didn't particularly elate me. I was always a little crazy. it was a very small town, voted the last town in America by the experts that anyone would care to atom bomb and the experts were right. when I took my little walks between my trips to the bedroom, feeble pale, blase, the people would all stare, of course. I was the city slicker who had hooked the rich girl. I MUST have something, surely. and I did: a very tired cock and a suitcase full of poems. she had an easy job at city hall, a desk and nothing to do, and I would sit by the window in the sun and brush off the flies. papa hated my guts but grandpa seemed to like me but papa had most of the money. I sat and brushed flies. a big cowboy walked in. boots. tall cowboy hat. the works. "Hell Barbara." he said then he looked at me . . .

"tell me" he asked, "what do you do?"

"DO?"

"yes, JUST WHAT DO YOU DO?"

I let a long time go by. I looked out the window. I brushed a fly away. then I turned to him. he was leaning across the counter, all 6′ 5″ of him, red-faced Texas American hero. man.

"Me? oh I just kinda . . . well, kinda DRIFT around and luck it."

he ripped his head back around the counter, was around the corner and gone.

"you know who that was?" she asked.

"naw."

"that was the town bully. he beats people up. he's my cousin."

"well he didn't DO anything, DID he?" I drawled.

she looked at me strangely for the first time. she saw the soiled beast creature. the sensitive-poet thing was just a rose in my mouth at Christmastime. on blue jean day I put on my only suit and walked up and down the town all day. it was like a Hollywood movie. anybody not wearing blue jeans was supposed to be thrown in the lake, but it wasn't as easy as I make it. I had a few drinks in me as I walked around, but I never saw the lake. the town was mine. the town doctor wanted to go hunting and fishing with me. her relatives came around and stared at me as I flipped beer cans into the wastebasket and told jokes. they mistook my suicide carelessness for bravery. the joke was mine.

but she wanted to go to Los Angeles. she never lived in a big city. I tried to talk her out of it. I liked loafing around the town, but no, she had to go, so gramps wrote us a nice check, and we got back on the bus and rode right on back to L.A. potential millionaires slumming on a greyhound. worse, she insisted that we support ourselves. so I got another job as a shipping clerk, and she sat around wishing SHE could get a job. I'd get drunk every night after work. "good lord," I would say, "look what I've done. I've married a real country hick." this would piss her tremendously. I couldn't kiss ass to that million bucks, it wasn't in me. we lived in a house on top of a hill, a small house, rented, and there was long grass in the back yard and the flies hid in the long grass and then came out and they were all over the yard, 40,000 flies, they'd drive me crazy. I'd go out with a big can of spray and kill a thousand a day but they fucked too fast, and so did we. the crazy people up front who had once lived there had put these shelves all around the bed and on these shelves were pots and pots of geraniums. big pots, little pots. all geraniums. when we fucked the bed would shake the walls and the walls would shake the shelves, and then I'd hear it: the slow volcano sound of the shelves giving away and then I'd stop. "no NO, DON'T STOP, OH JESUS, DON'T STOP!" and I'd catch the stroke again and down those shelves would come, down on my back and ass and head and legs and arms, and she'd laugh and scream and MAKE IT. she loved those pots. I'm gonna rip those shelves off the wall," I would tell her. "oh, no," she'd say. "OH, PLEASE PLEASE DON'T!" she said it so nicely that I couldn't. so I'd hammer the shelves back, put the pots back on and we'd wait for next time.

she bought a little black subnormal dog and named him Bruegel. Peter Bruegel was a painter, used to be or something. but after a few days she was no longer interested. she kicked the dog when he got in the way, hard, with that pointed toe, hissing "outa the way, you bastard!" so Bruegel and I would roll on the floor and fight when I drank my beer. that's all he could do – fight, and his teeth were better than mine. somehow I sensed the million going, and I didn't care.

she bought us a new car, a '57 Plymouth which I am still driving, and I told her she could get on with the county. she took an exam and went to work for the Sheriff's Dept. I told her I had been fired from my job as shipping clerk and I used to wash the car everyday and then go down and pick her up after work. one day as we were driving off, all these kids in flowered shirts, t-shirts, pasty-faced, slump-shouldered, with silly grins and high-school strides came out of her building.

"who are those punks?" I asked her.

"those are police officers," she said in her haughty little bitch tone.

"ah, come on! they look like subnormals! those aren't cops! what? come on, THOSE aren't cops!"

"those are police officers and they are all VERY nice fellows."

"AH SHIT!" I said.

she was very angry. we only fucked once that night. the next day it was something else.

"there goes José," she said, "he's a Spaniard."

"a Spaniard?"

"yes, he was born in Spain."

"half the Mexicans I have worked with in factories have claimed they were born in Spain. it's an act; Spain is the father, the ace-bullfighter, the Big Dream of old."

"José was born in Spain, I know he was."

"how do you know?"

"he told me."

"AH, SHIT!"

then at night she decided to go to Art Class. she painted all the time. she was the genius of her town. maybe her state. maybe not.

"I'll go to class with you," I told her.

"YOU? what FOR?"

"so you'll have somebody to drink coffee with on your coffee breaks, and I can drive you back and forth to class."

"well, all right."

we got in the same class and after three or four sessions she began to get very angry, ripping up paper and throwing it on the floor. I just sat there and tried not to watch her. they were all very busy, immersed, yet tittering as if it were a big joke or as if they were ashamed to paint.

the Art instructor came back. "listen, Bukowski, you are supposed to paint something. why are you just sitting here looking at the paper?"

"I forgot to buy brushes."

"very well. I will lend you a brush, Mr. Bukowski, but please return it at the end of class."

"yeah."

"now, you paint that bowl with the flowers sticking out of it."

I decided to get it done with. I worked fast and finished, but everybody else was still at it, holding their fingers in the air, testing for shadow or distance or some damn thing. I walked out and got a coffee, smoked a cigarette. when I walked back in there was a big crowd around my desk. a blonde with nothing but breasts (well, you know) turned to me and put those breasts up against me and said, "ah, you've painted BEFORE, haven't you?" "no, this is my first thing." she wiggled the breasts and drilled them into me, "ah, you're KIDDING!" "ummmmmmmm," was all I could say.

the prof took the painting and hung it up front. "now THIS is what I WANT!" he said, "see the FEELING, THE FLOW, THE NATURALNESS!"

oh lord, I thought.

she got up angry and took her stuff into the tiny room where they cut paper and went in there and tore up paper and threw paint around. she even tore down a collage some poor idiot had created.

"mr. Bukowski," the prof came up to me, "is that woman your . . . wife?"

"ah yes."

"well, we don't tolerate these prima donnas around here. you might as well tell her. and could we use your work in the Art Show?"

"sure."

"ah, thank you, thank you, thank you!"

the prof was crazy. everything I did he wanted for the Art Show. I didn't even know how to mix paints. I'd failed to make a color wheel. I'd mixed purple with orange, brown with black, white with black, anywhere the brush fell. most of the stuff looked like a huge splotch of smeared dogshit but the prof thought I was . . . the cockprint of God. well. she quit class. so I quit class and left the paintings there.

then she started coming home from work and telling me what a gentleman the Turk was. "a purple stickpin, he wears a purple stickpin, and today he kissed me on the forehead, ever so lightly and said I was BEAUTIFUL."

"listen, sweetheart, you've got to learn, these things go on all the time in the offices of America. sometimes something happens. but most of the time nothing happens. most of these guys jack off in the closet and see too many Charles Boyer movies. the guys who are really getting it are very quiet about it, not out front. I'll give you a hundred-to-one your boy has seen too many movies. squeeze his balls and he'll run."

"at LEAST, he's a GENTLEMAN! and he's SO tired! I'm sorry for him."

"tired from WHAT? working for the L.A. County?"

"he owns a drive-in movie and operates it at night. he doesn't get his rest."

"well, I'm a pig's ass!" I said.

"you sure are," she said sweetly. but that night the pots fell twice more.

then came the night of the Chinese snail dinner. or they might have been Japanese snails. anyhow, I went to the market and for the first time I saw this special rack. I bought the whole rack: tiny octopi, snails, snakes, lizards, slugs, bugs, grasshoppers . . . I cooked the snails first. put them on the table.

"I cooked them in butter," I told her. "jam 'em in your craw. this is what the poor shits eat, by the way," I asked, jamming two or three snails into my mouth, "how was old Purple Stickpin today?"

"they taste like rubber . . ."

"rubber, slubber . . . EAT 'em!"

"they have those tiny assholes . . . I see their tiny assholes . . . oh. . ."

"everything you eat has an asshole. you have an asshole, I have an asshole, we all have assholes. Purple Stickpin has an asshole . . ."

"oooooh . . ."

she got up from the table and ran to the bathroom and started heaving.

"those tiny assholes . . . ooooh . . ."

I laughed, blubber slubber and jammed the tiny assholes into my mouth and drained them down with beer and laughed.

I wasn't too surprised when one morning a couple of days later somebody knocked on my door, her door, and served me with a divorce summons.

"baby, what's this?" I showed her the paper. "don't you love me, baby?"

she began to cry. she cried and cried and cried.

"there, there, don't you worry, maybe Purple Stickpin will be the guy. I don't think he jacks off in the closet. he might well be the one."

"ooooooh, ooooooh, ooooooh."

"he probably jacks off in the bathtub."

"oh, you rotten shit!"

she stopped crying. then we brought the flowerpots down for one last good time. she went to the bathroom and started humming and singing, getting ready for work. that night I helped her find a new place and pack, and moved her out. she said she didn't want to stay in the old place, it would break her heart. rotten cunt. I got a paper on the way back and opened it to the classified ads looking for: shipping clerk, stockboy, janitor, warehouse man, aide to the crippled, telephone book deliveryman. then I threw the paper down, went out and got a fifth and drank my million goodbye. I saw her once or twice – casually, no flower-pots – and she said she only made it once with Purple Stickpin and then quit her job. she said she was going to begin painting and writing "seriously."

later she went to Alaska and married an Eskimo, a Japanese fisherman, and my joke is when drunk, to now and then tell somebody, "I once lost a million dollars to a Japanese fisherman."

"oh, come on now, you never HAD a million dollars."

and I guess they were right: I never did have it.

I get a letter once or twice a year, a long letter, one usually before Christmas. "write," she says. there are now two or three children with Eskimo names. and she says she has written a book, it is on the shelves up there, it is a children's book but she is "proud" and she is now going to write a "serious" novel about "character disintegration!" she is going to write TWO NOVELS ABOUT CHARACTER DISINTEGRATION. ah, I think, one is about me. and the other is about the Eskimo, who is, by now, fucking up. or fucking out. or maybe the other is about Purple Stickpin?

maybe I should have followed up that girl with tits in Art Class. but it's hard to please a woman. and she might not have liked the tiny assholes either. but you ought to try the octopi. like baby fingers in melted butter. the spiders of the sea, dirty rats. and while you are sucking at those fingers you get revenge, kiss off a million, knock off a beer, and to hell with the light co., Fuller Brush, tape machines and the

underbelly of Texas and her crazy women with nicks that
won't turn who cry and fuck you, leave you, write homey
letters every Christmas, even tho you are now a stranger,
won't let you forget, Bruegel, the flies, the '57 Plymouth
outside your window, the waste and the terror, the sadness
and the failure, the stage play the horseplay, all our lives,
falling down, getting up, pretending it's ok, grinning, sob-
bing, we wipe our tiny assholes, and the other kind.

To Funky Bukowski

I call you funky Bukowski, because
I think you're nasty
don't get mad, cause, I like your
nasty – it makes me hot to read
about; you looking up ladies dresses
or jacking-off in elevators or sniffing drawers – to get
   high;
now I know you're wondering who
this is writing you. Well I'll tell
you who I am, nice and clear
so there'll be no mistake
in pointing me out. I'm the clean
smooth cunt you think about
when you fuck those discharging wrinkled
pussies, I'm the lady who sits
down the row from you in the all night
movies, and watches you cum and cum
in your jacket pocket, and I slowly hike
my skirt up, hoping you'll look at my thighs
as you – get up to go wipe your hands, I call
it long dis-stance sex. but I love it
I love the feel of your heavy breathing on the
back of my neck as you try to poke your
fingers in my asshole through the crack
in the seat; now you're thinking, (it sounds

nice, but I don't remember you.) but from
now on you will/think of me/and after all –
that's what I wanted any way. my nasty
   man –

unsigned

the public takes from a writer, or a writing, what it needs
and lets the remainder go. but what they take is usually what
they need least and what they let go is what they need most.
however, all this allows me to execute my little holy turns
unmolested if they understood these, then there wouldn't be
any more creators, we'd all be in the same pot of shit. as it
is now, I am in my pot of shit and they are in theirs, and I
think mine stinks better.

sex is interesting but not totally important. I mean, it's not
even as important (physically) as excretion. a man can go 70
years without a piece of ass but he can die in a week without
a bowel movement.

here in the United States, especially, sex is inflated far
beyond its simplest importance. a woman with a sexy body
immediately turns it into a weapon for MATERIAL advance-
ment. and I am not speaking of the whorehouse whore, I am
speaking of your mother and your sister and your wife and
your daughter. and the American male is the sucker (bad
term, yes) who perpetuates the extremism of the hoax. but
the American male has had his brains beaten out by the
American formal education and the American prenumbed
parent and the American monster Advertising long before
he was twelve years old. he is ready and the female is
ready to make him beg and get up the M. this is why a
professional whore with a towel under the springs is so
hated by her counter-female professional whore (the near
remainder of womanhood; there are a FEW good women,
thank the Lord!) and the law. the openly professional whore
poses a breakdown threat to the whole American society
of Strive and Hustle all the way to the grave. she devaluates
the pussy.

yes, sex has gone completely beyond its value. notice sometime, in your newspaper (you ain't gonna find it here in "Open City" except off laughs), a group of entrants in bathing suits posing for a photo for some beauty contest or other, for the queen of this or that. see those legs, those long flanks, the breasts – some magic there, indeed. and these girlies know this, plus the bargaining price attached. THEN look at the eight or ten faces, smiling. the smiles are not smiling, they are carved onto paper faces, onto carbons of death. the noses and ears and mouths and chins are properly shaped within our concepts, but the faces are ugly beyond all essence of brutality. there is no thought there, no force, no density. no kindness . . . nothing, nothing. flat murdered flares of skin. eyeless. but show these faces of horror to the average American male and he will say, "yeah, real CLASS broads. I can't rate those."

you see these same beauty contest winners years later, grown old, in supermarkets; they are fussy, insane, bitter, demeaned – they put their stock in something unlasting, they were tricked; beware the sharp knives of their shopping carts – they are the madwomen of the Universe.

so, to some writers, including the gloriously impertinent Bukowski, sex is obviously the tragicomedy. I don't write about it as an instrument of obsession. I write about it as a stage play laugh where you have to cry about it, a bit, between acts. Giovanni Boccaccio wrote it much better. he had the distance and the style. I am still too near the target to effect total grace. people simply think I'm dirty. if you haven't read Boccaccio, do. you might begin with "The Decameron."

yet, I still have a little distance and after 2,000 pieces of ass, most of them not very good, I am still able to laugh at myself and my trap.

I remember once in the cellar of a lady's dress shop, I was a flunky shipping clerk, and my boss (the foreman, that is) was a fairly young but little balding snip and this little snip was being drafted into World War II. was he worried about being killed? the meaning of war? the non-meaning of war? what it meant to be split into pieces by a lob of mortar?

he confided in me. he thought I was a nice guy. we were both alone in this big basement room – the other packers were sweating a floor above – were down in the sub-basement, dank and dusty there, and we were scrambling along over the tops of cardboard packing cases that stood six feet high oblong. we were looking for a number, a certain type of cloth or dress to be shipped out, and there were only three or four small electric light bulbs to light the whole basement area, and there we were leaping along like spider-monkeys on our fours, leaping from case to case, peering for some magic number, a special type of cloth to be cut into a lady's dress.

oh god, mercy, I thought, what a hell of a way to make a living, what a hell of a way to survive and die just for pennies. surely suicide was the kindest out?

and the little snip would holler at me, "SEEN THE NUMBER YET?"

and I'd say, "naw." barely getting the word out.

shit, I wasn't even looking. what interest did I have in finding the number? every now and then when he would look back, I would leap from the top of one cardboard carton to another. finally he came leaping back toward me, sat on the carton next to mine and lit a cigarette.

"Bukowski, you're a nice guy."

I didn't answer.

"I'm being drafted. this is my last week here."

all during my short employee-tenure there I had done everything I could to keep from slugging the guy and now he was giving me some wearisome confessional.

"you know what worries me about the Army?" he asked.

"no."

"I won't be able to fuck my wife. now most of these guys don't get any. but I can tell by looking at you that you're getting some . . ."

(I wasn't getting any.)

". . . so I tell my wife this say, 'honey, what I am going to do, I won't be able to fuck you.' and you know what she says?"

"she says, 'for Christ's sake, go into the army and be a man. I'll be here when you get back,' but damn, I'm going to miss it; I'm going to miss it; most of these guys don't know what it is but you and I know what it is, yeah."

(I didn't tell him that somebody would fuck his wife for him while he was gone. and that if he didn't come back, she would adjust to the next position of Body for Sale with whatever she had left.)

he was a little mole of a man who would suffer a two-bit job or the suicide charge of the BANZAI! Jap, or even worse, the determined checkboard advance of the beaten, Snow-Hun, coming through the falling whiteness looking for HIS number. the Snow-Hun, bitter and trained and brave, a last shot of madness in the Bulge, looking for his number. ah, the mole! he would SUFFER these, almost like an itch or a yawn or a bit of the flu, just to remain on in, on the right side of the social structure, hoping to luck it through so he might come back to fuck his wife.

there's your sex: it concerns assholes and the entire movements of armies. men are decorated for Valor who only have pussies for brains. but bravery? the bravery of an imbecile hardly counts; it's the thinking man's bravery that counts – it takes a bit of work and a lucky stomach.

and you mix sex in with the rest of us and you've got something very difficult, and the more you study it the less you know. one theory replaces another, and in almost every case, the insult is to the human being. maybe it should be. with all our potential, the fiercest growth is downward.

the sex thing even confuses the great Bukowski. I remember one night sitting in a bar just west of one of those downtown tunnels. at the time, I lived in a room just around the corner in a place halfway up the hill. anyhow, I am sitting there, well on the way, and I g.d. figure I am young and tough and can take anybody who wants trouble. I even want people who want trouble, but still life is just new enough to me, say at 22, 23, that I am some kind of asshole Romantic; I find life vaguely interesting instead of actually terrifying. so the night wears on a little and then I look around – I am mixing drinks – I mean buying straight shots, wine, beer – I am trying to knock myself out but nothing works and God has not arrived.

then I kind of look around and here is a very sad beautiful type of little girl (around seventeen) sitting next to me. she has this long blonde hair (I've always been soft on these longhair types, I mean where the hair goes down to the asshole and you keep grabbing hair, the strands of it as you work, and it makes it rather symphonic instead of the same old drag) and she's quiet, very quiet, almost holy, ah, but she's a WHORE, and next to her is the protector, the madam-lesbian, and they'd rather NOT, you know, but they need the money. I engaged them in conversation rather out of my left brain lobe. I'm sure it was senseless to them but that didn't matter, you know: they needed the $$$. I ordered the drinks.

the bartender set them down in front of the seventeen year old like she was thirty five. where was the law? thank god, the law was bypassed for some reason or another.

for each drink they drank I drank three. this encouraged them. I was the "mark." I had the chalkmarked "X" on my back. what they damn sure didn't know was that I had won drinking contests all through the city with some of the toughest drinkers of the time, free booze and pick up the chips. I don't know why it took so much to knock me out. it might have been my extreme anger or sorrow, or it might have been a part of the brain-soul missing. probably both are true.

anyhow, not to bore you with these damn side remarks, forgive me; we finally went up the hill toward my room, together.

I have forgotten to tell you that the madam-lesbian was a fat hunk of human shit with cardboard eyes and senseless hunks of haunch, plus one of her hands was missing and instead of a hand there was this very very SHINY and thick interesting steel CLAW.

so we went up the hill.

then we got into my room and I looked at them both. my pure and beautiful slim and magic little girl glorious fuck with the hair dangling down to the asshole, and next to her the tragedy of the ages: slime and horror, the machine gone wrong, frogs tortured by little boys and head-on car collisions and the spider taking in the ball-less buzzing fly and the landscape brain of Primo Carnera going down under the dull playboy guns of cocksure Maxie Baer – new heavyweight champ of America – I, I rushed at the Tragedy of the Ages – that fat slob of accumulated shit.

I grabbed her and tried to throw her onto my dirty bed but she was too strong and too sober for me. with one arm she worked me free. she shoved me off with her pure lesbian hatred, and then getting me off, she began SWINGING THAT ARM WITH THAT BIG INTERESTING SHINY STEEL CLAW.

I could not as one man, change the course of sexual history, I just didn't have it.

she swung that CLAW in wide and wonderful swift arcs and by the time I had ducked and raised my head to see where the CLAW was at, here it came again. but, during iron claw's whole attempt to murder me, I, being note taker by instinct, had taken very quick and timed glance at the beautiful and holy and young whore and I do think that of the three of us that she did suffer the most. I could see it in her face. truly, she could not fathom why I wanted that ugly accumulation of all things zero and dead as compared to what she had. but I guess mama lesbian knew the answer, for each time she swung that thing at me, she'd turn to her little one and say "this guy's crazy, this guy's crazy, this guy's crazy." – and under one of her "this guy's crazy" iron claw swings I swung out and free and under to the other side of the room near the door. I pointed at the dresser and shouted, "THE MONEY'S IN THE TOP DRAWER!" and mama L., being a true shit, was taken in and turned. by the time she turned around I was nearly up to the top of the hill, up at Bunker Hill heaven, looking around and breathing heavy, checking for my parts, then wondering where the nearest liquor store was.

when I came back with my bottle, the door was still open, but they were gone. I bolted the door, sat down and poured a quiet drink. to sex and madness. then I had another, went to bed alone and let the world go by.

to my nasty man
I've wrote you once
before
or was it three
times
I breathe in your ear
licking my tongue out
so you'd feel what I meant
and you felt,
yeh, baby, you felt good.
you'd say, "Hey! what are you doing,
who are you???"
I could hear you getting a glass
pouring a big one I bet.
"you sound good to me, tell me your name."
you said, then . . . I would breathe deep
and hard, and you began to speak softer
to me, you'd whisper to me, then breathe
with me
I heard your zipper
slowly being pulled down
I caught my breath
then, "Flip . . . Flap, Plook,"
"I love you." you said, "Slip, Slap."
as you put down the glass, to
use both hands, "Flop, Flap, Blipp"
Faster and Faster, and I knew you had your
hands on it, it's dry now but not for
long.
AHHHHH-oh-AHHHHH, I hissed

"Slip, Flap."
he's doing it – I thought, I closed my eyes
ugh – AHHHHHH-OHOO!!!
"Flip-Flip" getting wet, "Slap, Bloop, Flap."
very very slippery; "AHHH-OHO-YEAAA!"
"that's it baby." you said. "Flip, Flap."
"say something!" you screamed.
OOOOOOH – GOOD GOD I cried, then
my knees felt something – stroke of love juice –
    shot up my slender thighs – I slammed my legs
shut, I hung up.

                       unsigned

Dear Unsigned:
    oh my god, baby, I can hardly wait!

                      yours truly,
                   Charles Bukowski

---

it all begins and ends with the mailbox, and when they find a way to remove mailboxes, much of our suffering will end. right now our only hope is in the hydrogen bomb, and dispirited as I may seem, this does not quite seem the proper remedy.

well, the mailbox: after a sleepless night I walked out onto my rented porch, and looked at that great gut-gray mindless thing with a subnormal spider hung there below it sucking the last love chance out of a butterfly. well, so I stand, thinking, ah, maybe the Pulitzer Prize or a grant from the humanities or my copy of "Turf Digest" so I reach in and there it is, one letter in the mailbox, I know the writing, I know the address, I know the mood, the form of each hand written letter, the female insane slanting crossfire of bungled image two-bit soul:

dear bongo:
    I watered the plants today. my plants are dying. how are you? it will soon be christmas. my friend Lana

teaches poetry at the in insane asylum. they have a magazine. could you submit something of yours. must go now. I'm sure they would be happy to print something of yours. the children will be home soon. saw your last poem in Oct. issue of the *BLUE STARDUST JACK-OFF*. it was lovely. you are the world's greatest living writer. the children are coming home soon must go. must go.

Love,
meggy

———————

meggy keeps on writing these letters. I have never met meggy, as I told you, but she does send photos, and she looks like a big healthy fuck, and she has also sent poems, her poems, and they are a bit on the comfortable side, tho they speak of agony and death and eternity and the sea, it's a great big yawning comfortable thing – almost as if one stuck in a pin in order to scream and then could not scream, just another female disappointment in the aging process and in her lessening husband; just another female dulled by her OWN easy sellout from the beginning and now piddling with the vacuum cleaner days and little troubles with junior who is also rapidly working towards zero times nothing.

it is their own minds that women ingest into a man's work – either willfully misreading the intent or either sensing tired prey upon the bloody cross. either way they screw it up good. whether they want to or have to, it doesn't matter to the victim. which is the man, of course.

if meggy had lived close enough I could have ended the whole torture easily enough, herself at my place breathing in the fine lilting flare of my poets eyes, the pantherpiss stride, pants torn at the knees with 2:30 a.m. falls – comparing me with, say, Stephen Spender – I would turn and say in not very articulate English:

"baby, in a couple of minutes I'm going to rip off your god-damned panties and show you some turkey neck you'll remember all the way to the graveside. I have a vast and curved penis, like a sickle, and many a gutted pussy has gasped come upon my callous and roach-smeared rug. first let me finish this drink."

then you drink down a tall water glass of straight whiskey, smash the glass against the wall, muttering "Villon ate fried titty for breakfast," pause to light a cigarette and when you turn your problems will be solved – it will leave out the front door. if it remains it deserves what it gets. and so do you.

but meggy lives in a state quite far north of here and so that was out. but I answered the letters for several years thinking that she might get close enough to fuck or scare off some day.

finally the seemingly endless hard-on wore off. the letters kept coming but I simply didn't answer them. her letters were as usual, excellently dull and pointedly depressing, but the fact that I had decided not to answer them DID take some of the poison out of them. it was a great plan, a plan that a simple mind like mine would need all that time to plot out – don't answer the letters and you are free.

there was a pause in the mail. I felt that it was over; I had used the last trick of the kind: be cruel to the cruel, be stupid to the stupid. the cruel and the stupid were the same: there was nothing you could do to them; there were only things they could, and would do to you. I had defeated a problem of the centuries; the elimination of the unwanted. it doesn't take a number of men and women to smother and dismember the life of any individual, it only takes one. and it usually is one. even when armies face armies, ants face ants, any way you want to work it.

I began to see things again with my EYES. I noticed a sign over a cleaning shop, some joker had placed; TIME WOUNDS ALL HEELS. I never would have seen the sign before. I began, at last, to be freer. I saw almost everything. I saw the strange and crazy things I used to notice, upside down, romantic, explosive things that seemed to give chance to no chance. that seemed to show magic forces where before there was nothing.

KILLS INVENTOR

Monterey, Nov. 18 (UPI)

A Carmel Valley man has been killed by a device he invented to unwrinkle prunes.

that's all the dispatch said. perfect. I was alive again. then one morning I went out to the mailbox. a letter. along with the gas bills, threats from the dentist. a letter from an ex-wife I could hardly remember, and an ad for a poetry reading of talentless poets.

dear bongo:

this is the LAST letter. god damn you to hell. you are not the ONLY one who has abandoned me. I'll see all of you who have abandoned me – I'LL SEE ALL OF YOU IN THE GRAVE FIRST!

meggy

my grandmother used to talk that way to me and she never gave me any pussy either.

well a couple of days later, shaking of the hangover of joy. I went to the mailbox. some letters. I opened them. the first

dear mr. b:

your application for an individual grant from the National Endowment for the Arts has been considered by the National Council on the Arts. with the advice of an independent panel of literary experts, we regret to inform you . . .

another letter:

hello bongo:

crouched in the corner of this evil smelling hotel room the only thing that breaks the silence is the click of wine bottles on teeth . . . I'm rheumy, legs covered w/sores; 51 aces turned up blank, 52nd. in the mail . . . I covered all corners y'know? and it turned out to be a bloody dog damn circle . . . fired from lemon groves for being gone too long. (hog farm wedding: 4 days) and pickin' too little. came back to s.f. & missed sure xmas job at post office by one day . . . sit in the corner of this room lites out waitin' for peace and gladness baptist church to turn in its red neon sign so I can start crying . . . dog in the street gets runned over by a runaway bus . . . wish I was that dog, cause I don't know how to do it myself . . . even that requires decisions . . . where's them cigarettes . . . walked out of the mission this morning. unnameable food attacking my hog-maw guts. looked around on market street at all them pretty girls hair like clear winter san frisco sunshine . . . well. what the hell.

M.

and another:

dear bongo:
  forgive me. I get this way. try to love me a little. I got a new sprinkle today. the other was rusty. I enclose a poem from "Poetry Chicago." I thought . . . of myself . . . as I read it. must go now. the children are on the way home.

love me,
meggy

the enclosed poem is carefully typed. not an error. double-spaced the words she typed are engraved into the paper with the same pressure the same measured . . . love. – it's a horrible poem.

it speaks of the wind and some undersized comfortable tragedy. it is 18th century. bad 18th century.

but still I do not answer. I go to my garbage job. they know me down there. they are my superiors. I like it. they allow me to flow. they don't know T. S. Eliot from Lawrence of Arabia. I am drunk for two or three days. still make the job.

I have a special ring-system that must work before I will pick up my phone. I am not a snob; it is simply that I am not interested with what most people have to say, or what they want to do – mostly with my time. but one night, steadying myself to make it on in to the garbage job, the phone rang. since I was leaving in a couple of minutes I figured there wasn't much they could do with me. it wasn't the signal but I picked up the phone anyway.

"bongo?"

"eh? yeh?"

"this is . . . meggy."

"oh, hello, meggy."

"listen I don't mean to impose myself. I just get haywire."

"oh yeh. we all do."

"just don't HATE my letters."

"well, meggy, it's like this. I really don't hate your letters. they are really so comfortable that –"

"oh I'm SO glad!"

she hadn't let me finish. I had meant to say that her letters were so comfortable that they terrified me with their vacuum cleaner yawns. but she never let me finish.

"I'm really glad."

"yeh," I said.

"but you haven't sent any poems for our class at the institution."

"I am trying to find some that will fit."

"I'm sure that any of yours will do."

"the torturer is sometimes good at the innuendo."

"what do you mean?"

"forget it."

"bongo, aren't you writing anymore? I remember when you used to make every issue of *Blue Stardust*. Lilly writes that you haven't submitted in years. have you forgotten the 'littles?'"

"I'll never forget those motherfuckers."

"you're funny. but I mean, don't you SUBMIT your WORK anymore?"

"well, there's *Evergreen*."

"you mean, they've ACCEPTED YOU?"

"once or twice. but, *Evergreen* isn't a little magazine, please remember that. write Lilly. tell her I have deserted from the barricades."

"oh bongo, I knew from the first moment I read your lines that you were destined. I still have your first collection, 'Christ Creeps Backwards.' Oh, bongo, bongo."

I got rid of her telling her I had to go collect some garbage. meanwhile I was thinking, now who would WANT to unwrinkle a prune? they surely don't taste good: perhaps a little like dried chilled turds. their only charm is the WRINKLES THEMSELVES, the cold wrinkles and that slippery iced seed that slips from your tongue onto the plate like a living thing itself.

I went over and opened a beer. decided that I couldn't make work that day. it was good to sit in a chair. tilt the bottle up and let everything go to hell. I knew one who claimed she slept with Pound at St. Liz. I got well rid of her after a lengthy correspondence by foolishly insisting that I also knew how to write and that I found the "Cantos" dull.

I had meggy's letters everywhere. there was an old one on the floor near the typewriter. I got up walked over and picked it up:

dear bongo,

all my poems are coming back. well, if they don't know good poetry, that's their fault. sometimes I still read your first volume *CHRIST CREEPS BACK-WARDS*. and all your other volumes. so long as I know that I can bear up under ALL their terrible stupidity. the children will be home soon.

love me
meggy

p.s. – my husband jokes with me – "bongo hasn't written in a long time. what has happened to bongo?"

I empty the beer bottle. throw it into the wastebasket.

I could see it now, her husband mounting her thrice a week. her hair like a fan on the pillow. like the sex writers like to say. she really imagines that he is bongo. he imagines that he is bongo.

"oh bongo! bongo!" she says.

"coming, mother." he says.

I open another beer and walk to the window. it is the usual dark sterile senseless Los Angeles day. I am still alive, in a sense. it has been a long time since the first volume of poems; it has been a long time since the Watts riots. we have wasted ourselves. John Bryan wants a column. I could tell him about meggy. but the meggy story is unfinished. she will be in my mailbox tomorrow morning. if I were in the movies I could handle it:

"look little john, there's this broad see? she's bugging me, see? you know what to do. don't mess it up. give her that fourteen inch dick and get her off my back, see? you'll find her. she's in this room with a vacuum cleaner lookin' sad eyed, see? room full of poetry magazines, she's unhappy. she thinks she's been crucified by life but she really don't know what life is, see? put her straight: give her the fourteen."

"aw right."

"and little john . . ."

"yeh."

"don't make any stops on the way."

"aw right."

I go back and sit down, suck up my beer. I ought to get drunk, fly up there, appear at her door in rags, drunk, beating on the wood, buttons all across my torn shirt: "IMPEACH JOHNSON." "STOP THE WAR." "UN-BURY TOM MIX." anything.

but nothing will work. I just have to sit and wait. the "Humanities" are out. I have stopped writing poems for *Evergreen.* there will be only one thing in that box:

dear bongo
　　blah blah blab blah blab blab blah. I have watered the
pots. the children are coming home soon. blah blah blah.
　　　　　　　　　　　　　　　　　　　　love me
　　　　　　　　　　　　　　　　　　　　　meggy

did this ever happen to Balzac or Shakespeare or Cervantes? I hope not. man's worse invention has three heads:
the mailbox the mailman, and the letter-writer. I have a blue
coffee can on the shelf full of unanswered letters. I have a
large paper box in the closet full of unanswered letters. when
do these people get drunk, fuck, earn money, sleep, bathe,
crap, eat, cut their toenails? and meggy leads the pack: love
me, love me, love me.
　　a fourteen inch dick might get me out, or in, or make it
worse. with what I have, there has been trouble enough
already.

----

in those days there was usually somebody in my room
whether I was there or not. you usually didn't know who was
going to be there or who wasn't. it was just somebody. a big
human and not too holy. there was always a party. party
meaning: an extension of luck and the ways: two dollars and
some change bought a roomful of talk and electric light
sound for six or seven.
　　all right, one night, lights all out, I awakened in bed drunk,
but clear, you know, suddenly clear the unclean walls. the no
purpose at all, the sadness the everything. and I got up on one
elbow and looked around and everybody seemed gone. just
those empty wine bottles on their moonlit sides. gross tough
morning waiting, and I looked around me in the bed and
there's this human form. some cunt had decided to stay with
me – that was love, that was bravery. shit, who could really
stand me? anyone who could stand me had a lot of forgiveness
of soul. I just had to REWARD this sweet, little dear deer for
having the guts and insight and courage to stay with me.

what better reward than to fuck her in the ass?

I had run into a strange breed of woman, a strange line of women and none of them had wanted it in the tail and so I had never done it that way and it was working on my mind. it used to be all I could talk about when I got drunk. I'd say to some woman,

"I'm gonna get you in the ass, and I'm gonna get your mama in the ass, and I'm gonna get your daughter in the ass." and the answer would always be, "oh no you don't!" they'd do anything and everything but that. maybe it was just the time and the weather, or just mathematical, because much later after that there was nothing but women sitting around and saying, "Bukowski, why don't you screw me up the stovepipe? I've got a big round soft butt." and I'd answer, "you sure have, dearie, but I'd rather not."

but then in those days, I'd just never given it that way, and I was feeling a little crazy, as usual, and I had this strange idea that a good fuck in THEIR ass would solve a lot of MY spiritual and mental problems.

I found the last glass of wine mixed with cigar ashes and sadness. then I got back into bed, winked at the moon and slipped my little weenie into that bulging snoring immaculate backside. a sneak thief does not precious the prize so much as the stealing. I loved both. my little stick raised to the top of its insanity. my god, ugly and perfect. vengeance, some-how, upon all manner of things, upon old icecream men with mad pigeon eyes, upon my dead mother living and smearing cream across her impartial and tasteless iron face.

she's still asleep, I thought. which made it better. it's probably Mitzi. maybe Betty. what's the difference? my victory – sad, unemployed and starving cock slipping into doorways of things forever forbidden! GLORIOUS! I felt very dramatic really – the top side of DRAMA, like Jesse James catching the slug, like Christ at the cross under klieg lights and rockets, I worked away.

she moaned and went AARRG UG, HO AR, HA ... I knew then she was only pretending to be asleep. trying to save her wine-head honor which was just as terrible and just as real as all the honored. I was just jamming the guts out of her with my demented and falsified glory.

she is just PRETENDING to be asleep and I am a MAN AND NOTHING, O, NOTHING CAN WHIP ME!

I seemed to have a lot of string for a change and the glory of it and the magic-horse violence of me, of it, of everything obsessed me. I poked and rammed and jammed and everything was pure.

then in the excitement the blanket fell back. I saw more clearly the head. the back of the head and the shoulders – it was one Baldy M. American MALE! all went limp. I fell back in indecent horror. I fell back sick, staring at the ceiling, and not a drink in the place. Baldy M. did not move or speak I finally decided to sleep and wait for morning.

in the morning we awakened and nothing was mentioned. somebody came in and we got up a little money for wine.

and the days went on and I kept waiting for him to leave. the girls began looking at me strangely. he stayed two weeks, three weeks. and he didn't run a tight ship, as they say. one evening after unloading crates of frozen fish from boxcars, my hand cut and bleeding, one foot numbed and almost broken from a falling crate, I limped on into a party in my room. the party was all right, I never bitch on wine drinking. but the sink in my place had been getting bad. they had eaten all my canned food, used up all the glasses and dishes and silverware, and it was all in the sink in the water, the stinking water, and the sink was clogged and that was all right, that was almost normal, but when I looked into the sink and found they had also found my paper plates and used them and threw them into the sink, floating there, that was bad, but then on top of that, somebody had VOMITED into the sink, and when I saw that, I poured a water glass full of wine, drank it down, and crashed the glass against the wall and screamed, "THAT'S IT! EVERYBODY OUT! NOW!"

they filed on out, the whores and the men, and the scrub-woman Helen, I had once screwed her too, white hair and all, and out they went solemnly, sadly. everybody left but Baldy M.

he just sat on the edge of the bed saying, "Hank, Hank, whatza matta? whatza matta, Hank?"

"shut up or I'll k.o. you, so help me christ!"

I went out to the hall phone. I found the number of his mother. he was one of those pure and brilliant, stupid, high eye-Q bastards who lives with his mother forever.

"listen, Mrs. M., please come and get your son. this is Hank."

"oh, that's where he has BEEN! I thought so, but I didn't know where you lived. we turned in a missing person report on him. you're bad for him, Hank. Listen Henry, why don't you leave my boy alone?" (her "boy" was 32 years old.)

"I'll try, Mrs. M. now why don't you come get him?"

"I just can't understand why he stayed so LONG this time. he usually likes to come home after a day or two out."

"just come and get him."

I gave her the address, then went back to the room.

"your mother is coming to get you," I told him.

"no, I don't want to go. no! listen, Hank, is there any more wine? I need a drink, Hank."

I poured him a wine and poured myself one.

he drank some of the wine. "I don't want to go," he said.

"listen, I kept asking you to leave. you wouldn't leave. I had one of two choices. either to beat hell out of you and throw you out into the street or phone your mother. I've phoned your mother."

"but I'm a MAN! I'M A MAN, DON'T YOU SEE? I WAS IN THE CHINA THEATRE! I LED THE CHINESE TROOPS THROUGH THE FIELDS! I WAS A FIRST LT. IN THE AMERICAN ARMY IN MOMENTS OF DANGER!"

and it was true. he had done that. and had been honorably discharged. I refilled our glasses.

"to the China theatre," I toasted.

"to the China theatre," he said.

we drank them down.

then he began again: "I'm a MAN! god damn it. can't you see that I am a MAN? jesus christ, can't you see THAT I AM A MAN?"

she arrived about 15 minutes later, only said one word: "WILLIAM!" then she reached over on the bed and took him by the ear. she was a bent old lady, surely nearing 60. she tools him by the EAR and lifted him from the bed and still holding his ear she took him down the hall and stood and pushed the elevator button, him bent almost double and crying, him crying all the time. those big REAL tears running dripping sliding down his face. and she took him into the elevator by his ear and as they went down I could hear him crying, "I AM A MAN, I AM A MAN, I AM A MAN!" and then I went to the window and watched as they walked down the sidewalk. she was still holding him by the EAR, this old woman of 60. and then and there she threw him into the car and got into the other side while he was lying on the car seat. and then and there she drove off with my only piece of round-eye crying, "I AM A MAN! I AM A MAN!"

I never saw him again nor did I ever make any particular effort to look for him.

---

the night the 300 pound whore came in I was ready. nobody else was ready but I was ready. she was god awful fat all around and not very clean either. where the hell she had come from and what she wanted and how she had survived up to now was a question you could ask about any human being. and so we drank drank and laughed and I sat next to her, pressed next to her, sniffing and laughing and goading.

"baby, baby, I could reach you with something that could make you cry instead of laugh!"

"ah hahahahaha, ha" she laughed.

"when I put it in, my head will reach your head, all the way through the stomach, esophagus, up through the trachea. yeah!"

"ah hahahahaha, ha!"

"god damn, I bet when you shit that the cheeks of your ass hang down to the floor, eh? and when you shit, baby, you clog the plumbing for a month. eh?"

"ah hahahahaha, ha!"

at closing time we left together – me 6 feet tall and 165 pounds and she 5 feet and 300 pounds. the lonely and ridiculous world was walking down the sidewalk together. I finally got me a piece of ass better than a knothole.

we made it to the outside of my rooming house. I reached for my key.

"jesus christ." I heard her say, "what's that?"

I looked around us. behind us was a very simple and small building with a very simple sign: STOMACH HOSPITAL.

"oh, that? laugh now baby, I like your laugh, let me hear you laugh now, baby!"

"it's a dead body, they're bringing out a dead body!"

"a friend of mine, old time football player, used to block for Red Grange. I saw him this afternoon. he looked fine. I gave him a pack of smokes. they sneak the dead out at night. I see them drag one or two stiffs out each night. bad business to do it in daylight."

"how do you know it's your friend?"

"bone structure, shape of the head under the sheet. one night when I was high I almost decided to snatch a body when they went back in. I don't know what I would have done with the damn thing. stood it up in a closet I guess."

"where they going now?"

"to get another body. how's your stomach?"

"fine, fine!"

we got upstairs, somehow, although one time she lurched and I thought she was going to take out the whole west wall. we stripped and I got on top.

"jesus christ!" I said, "show me some MOVEMENT!"

"don't just LAY there like a giant pot of putty! lift those vast and giant redwood legs . . . mother I can't FIND you!"

she started giggling, "oh, hehehehehe, oh, hehehehehehehehe."

"oh what the fuck!" I snarled. "MOVE IT! SHAKE IT!"

then she really started to bounce and whirl. I hung on and tried to find the rhythm: she rotated pretty good, but it was rotate and then up and down and then back to rotate. I got the rhythm of the rotate, but on the up and down I got thrown out of the saddle several times. I mean the deck would be coming up as I hit it, which is all right under ordinary conditions, but with her as I hit the deck coming on it simply caromed me completely out of the saddle and oftentime almost out of the bed onto the floor. I remember one time almost grabbing at a giant tit of a breast thing, but it was a most horrible and indecent looking thing and I simply hung to the side of the mattress like a hungry bedbug, lurched forward again and flung myself like some dog back into the center of that 300 pounds, sinking again into the center of "oh, hehehehehe, oh, hehehehehe," and riding and hanging on, not knowing whether I was fucking or being fucked, but then, one seldom does.

"may the good Lord be with us." I whispered into one of her fat hot dirty ears.

both being very drunk, we worked on and on, myself being thrown off again and again, but leaping back to battle. I'm sure we both wanted to quit but that somehow there was no way out. sex can sometimes become the most horrible of tasks. even once, in desperation, I grabbed one of those enormous breasts and lifted it like a flabby pancake thing and jammed a nipple into my mouth. it tasted of sadness, of rubber and agony and spoiled yogurt. I flung the thing out of my mouth with disgust, then dug back in.

finally I wore her down. I mean, she was still working, she did not lay back like dead, I've got to give her that, but I wore her down, got inside the rhythm, found it, hit it, hit it proper a score of times and finally like a house of resistance that doesn't want to give, it gave, she gave, I had her hooked. finally, she moaned and cried like a small child, and I smoked it out. it was beautiful. then we slept.

in the morning when we awakened, I found that the bed was flat on the floor. we had broken all four legs down to the floor in our crazy freakfuck.

"oh lord!" I said. "Oh lord! Lord!"

"whatza matta, Hank?"

"we broke the bed."

"I thought we might."

"yeah, but I don't have any money. I can't pay for a new bed."

"I don't have any money either."

"I guess I ought to give you some money, Ann."

"no please don't you're the first man who has made me feel anything in years."

"well, thanks, but I've got this goddamned bed on my mind now."

"you want me to leave?"

"no hard feelings, but do. it's the bed. I'm worried."

"sure Hank. can I use the bathroom first?"

"of course."

she got dressed and went down the hall to the crapper. when she came back she stood in the doorway.

"goodbye, Hank."

"goodbye, Ann."

I felt lousy letting her go like that, but it was the bed, then I remembered the rope I had bought to hang myself with. it was good sturdy rope. I found that all the bed legs were cracked along a central grain. it was only a matter of binding them like broken human legs. I tied them back together. then I got dressed and went downstairs.

the landlady was waiting. "I saw that woman leaving. she was a woman of the streets, mr. Bukowski. I do believe she was up in your room. I know all my other roomers too well."

"Mother," I said, "few men can do without."

then I hit the streets. made for the bar. the drinks came along all right, but I had the bed on my mind. it's screwy, I thought, for a man who wants to kill himself to be worried about a bed, but I was. so I had a few more and went on back. the landlady was waiting.

"mr. Bukowski, you can't fool me with all that rope! you busted that bed! my lands, there must have been some goings on up there last night to bust all FOUR legs on that bed!"

"I'm sorry," I said, "I can't pay for that bed. I lost my job as a busboy and all my short stories are coming back from *Harpers* and the *Atlantic Monthly*."

"well, we've got you a new bed!"

"a new bed?"

"yes, Lila is putting it together now."

Lila was a beautiful little colored maid. I had only seen her once or twice because she worked days, and days I was usually down at the bar, drinking it up.

"well," I said, "I'm tired, maybe I ought to go on up."

"yes, I should think you would be tired."

we walked up the stairway together. we passed a cloth sign on the wall: GOD BLESS THIS HOUSE.

"Lila!" the landlady said as we got near the top of the stairway near my room.

"yes?"

"how you comin' with the bed?"

"oh man, this god damned thing knocks me out! I can't seem to get the last laig in! thing just din't seem to fit nohow!"

we both stood outside my door.

"listen ladies," I said, "please pardon me, I have to go to the bathroom for a while ..."

I went down to the bathroom and had a good slow but steady beer – vodka – wine – whiskey shit. what a stink! I flushed it away and walked back toward my room. as I got near, I heard a final pounding then my landlady began to laugh and then they were both laughing together. then I walked in. their laughter stopped. their faces got very stern, I might say, even angry. my beautiful colored maid ran out and down the stairway and then I began to hear her laughing again. then the landlady stood in the doorway and looked at me.

"please try to behave yourself Mr. Bukowski. we have only the finest tenants in here."

then she slowly closed the door and then it was shut.

I looked at the bed. it was made of steel.

then I undressed and climbed naked between the new sheets of my new bed, Philadelphia, one p.m. in the afternoon the sky spreading all over the place outside, I pulled the clean white sheet and the cover up to my chin and then I slept, alone, easy, gracious and touched by the miracle. it was o.k.

———

"Dear Mr. Bukowski:
    You say you began writing at 35. what were you doing before then?

                                                            E.R."

"Dear E.R.
    Not writing."

Mary tried all the tricks. she really didn't want to leave that night. she came out of the bathroom with her hair all piled to one side. "look!" I'd just pour another wine "whore, you god damned whore . . ." then she came out with big lips on, big fat lipstick. "look! ya ever see Mrs. Johnson?"
    "whore, whore ya god damned whore . . ."
    I went over and lay on the bed, cigarette in one hand, wine-glass half tottering on the nightstand. barefoot, in shorts and undershirt a week dirty. she came over and stood over me.
    "YOU'RE THE NUMBER ONE RAT OF ALL TIMES!"
    "ah, hahahahaha," I snickered.
    "well, I'm leaving!"
    "that doesn't concern me. just one thing I'm warning you about!"
    "what's that?"
    "don't slam that door when you leave. I'm getting tired of slamming doors. if you slam that door I'm going to have to deck you."
    "you wouldn't have the GUTS!"
    she really slammed that door when she left. it was so loud it put me in a state of shock. when the wall stopped trembling I leaped up, drained the wineglass and opened the door. there

was no time to dress. she heard me open the door and started running, but she had on high heels. I ran down the hall in my shorts and caught her at the top of the stairway. I spun her and gave her a fair open hand slap along the cheek. she screamed and went down. as she fell her legs went down last and I looked up her dress at those long fine legs spun in nylon, I saw way up, and I thought, god damn, I must be Crazy! but there was no way out and I turned and walked slowly back to the door, opened it, closed it, sat down and poured a wine. I could hear her crying out there. then I heard another door open.

"whatza matta, honey?" it was another woman.

"he HIT me! my husband HIT me!"

(HUSBAND?)

"oh you poor dear, let me help you up."

"thank you."

"what are you going to do now?"

"I don't know. I don't have any place to stay."

(lying bitch)

"well listen, get yourself a room overnight, then when he goes to work you can come back here."

"WORK!" she screamed, "WORK! WHY THAT SON OF A BITCH HAS NEVER WORKED A DAY IN HIS LIFE!!"

I thought that was very funny. I thought that was so funny that I couldn't stop laughing. I had to turn and put my face into the pillow so that Mary couldn't hear me. when I finally stopped laughing and pulled my face out of the pillow and got up and looked down the hall, everybody was gone.

she was back a couple days later and it was the same old thing me in my shorts getting sour and Mary getting all dressed up fine getting ready to leave, trying to show me what I was going to lose.

"this time I'm not coming back! I've had it truly! I've had it! I'm sorry, I can't stand you anymore. you're just damn rotten through and through and that's all there is to it."

"you're a whore, you're nothing but a god damned whore . . ."

"sure I'm a whore or else I wouldn't be living with you."

"hmmm, I never thought of it that way."

"think of it."

I drained a wineglass. "this time I'm going to WALK you to the door, open it and close it MYSELF and wish you well. are you ready dear?"

I walked to the door and stood there in my shorts, refilled wineglass in my hand, waiting. "come come, I don't have all night. let's get to the crux of this thing, shall we? Ummmm?"

she didn't like it. she walked out the door, turned, stood facing me.

"well, come come now, toddle off into the night. maybe you can sell some of that syphed-up snatch for a buck and a quarter to that newsboy with the right thumb missing and the face like a rubber mask. toodle-ooh, dear."

I started to close the door and she raised her purse over her head, "you ROTTEN son of a bitch!" I saw the purse coming down and just stood there with a little calm smile on my face. I'd been in some fights with some rough boys; a woman's purse was the last thing I was worried about. it came down. I felt it. plenty. she had stuffed the thing and in the front corner, the part that hit me over the head was a white cold cream jar. it was like a rock.

"baby." I said. I was still grinning and holding onto the door-knob, but I couldn't move, I was Frozen.

she came down with the purse again.

"listen, baby,"

again.

"oh, baby."

the legs began to go. as I folded slowly down she had more leverage for the top of the head. she really went to it, faster and faster as if she was trying to crack my skull. it was my third k.o. in a rather spotted career, but the first by a woman.

when I awakened the door was closed and I was alone. I looked around and the floor was an inch thick in my blood. luckily the whole apartment was covered with linoleum. I splashed through the stuff and headed for the kitchen.

I'd saved a bottle of whiskey for a special occasion. this was it. I opened it and poured a good bit of it over my head, then I poured a glassful and drank it straight down. rotten bitch had tried to KILL me! unbelievable. I thought of turning her in to the police, but that wasn't any good. they'd probably get their charge out of it and throw me in too.

we were on the fourth floor. I had a little more whiskey and walked over to the closet. I got her dresses, shoes, pants, slips, brassieres, slippers, hankies, garterbelts, all that crap and piled it in front of the window, one by one sipping at my whiskey. "god damned whore tried to kill me . . ." sailed them out the window. there was a large vacant lot below next to a small house. the apartment was built next to an excavation so we were really about eight stories high. I tried for the electric wires with the panties, but I missed. then I got angry and started throwing things out without aiming. shoes and panties and dresses were all over the place . . . on bushes, in trees, across the fence or just flat in the lot. then I felt better, began to work on the whiskey, found a mop and mopped the place up.

in the morning my head really hurt. I couldn't comb my hair but wet it back with my hands. a huge three inch scab had formed on my head. it was about 11 a.m. I walked down the steps and got down to the first floor and went out the back to pick up the clothes and stuff. it was all gone. I couldn't understand. there was an old fart working in the backyard of the small house, poking around with a trowel.

"listen," I asked the old fart, "did you happen to see any clothes lying around here?"

"what kinda clothes?"

"women's clothes."

"they were all around here. I gathered them up for the salvation army. I phoned the salvation army to come get them."

"those were my wife's clothes."

"looked like somebody threw them away."

"a mistake."

"well, I still got them in a box."

"you have? listen, can I have them back?"

"sure, only it looked like somebody threw them away."

the old fart went into the house and came back with the box. he handed it over the fence to me. "thanks," I said.

"it's all right." he turned around, dropped to his knees and plunged the trowel into the ground. I took the clothes back upstairs.

she came back that night with Eddie and the Duchess. they had wine. I poured it all around. "the place sure looks clean." said Eddie.

"listen, Hank. let's not fight anymore. I get sick of this fighting! and you know I love you, I really do." said Mary.

"yeah."

the Duchess sat there with the hair all down in her face, her stockings all torn, and little rolls of spit coming down the side of her mouth. I made a note to get into her. she had that sick sexy look. I sent Mary and Eddie out for more wine and the minute the door closed I grabbed the Duchess and threw her on the bed. she was all bones and looked very dramatic. the poor thing probably hadn't eaten food for two weeks. I dropped it in. it wasn't bad. a fasty. we were sitting in the chair when they got back.

we'd been drinking about another hour when the Duchess looked up out of that hair and pointed that bony death finger at me. there had been a lull in the conversation. the finger kept pointing at me, then she said "he raped me, he raped me while you were out getting the wine."

"listen Eddie, you're not going to believe that are you?"

"sure, I'm going to believe it."

"listen if you can't trust a friend then get the hell out of here!"

"the Duchess doesn't lie. if the Duchess said that you . . ."

"GET THE HELL OUT OF HERE! GOD DAMN YOU SONS OF BITCHES!"

I stood up and threw a full glass of wine smashing it against the north wall.

"me too?" asked Mary.

"YOU TOO!" I pointed my own finger at her.

"oh Hank, I thought we were through with all this, I'm so tired of breakups . . ."

they filed on out. Eddie in front, the Duchess next, followed by Mary. the Duchess kept saying "he raped me, I tell you he raped me. he raped me, I tell you, he raped me . . ." she was crazy.

they were just outside the door when I grabbed Mary's wrist.

"come in here, bitch!"

I pulled her back into the room and put the chain on the door. then I grabbed her and gave her a big sexy kiss, ripping at a whole haunch of her butt with one hand.

"oh, Hank . . ."

she liked it.

"Hank, Hank, you didn't screw that bag of bones did you?"

I didn't answer. I just kept working on her. I heard her purse fall to the floor. one of her hands went to my balls and squeezed them. I was getting in deep, I needed a rest, about an hour or so.

"I threw all your clothes out of the window," I said.

"WHAT?" the hand dropped away from my balls, the eyes were very wide.

"but I went out and picked them up, let me tell you about it." I walked over and poured two more drinks. "you know you almost killed me, don't you?"

"what?"

"you mean you don't remember?"

I sat down with my drink in a chair and she came over and looked at the top of my head. "oh you poor baby. god, I'm sorry."

she leaned down and kissed that bloody scab very tenderly. then I reached up and under her skirt and then we tangled again. I needed about forty-five minutes. there we stood in the middle of the room wrestling amidst poverty and broken glass. there would be no fight that night, there were no whores or bums anywhere. love had taken over. and the clean linoleum tossed with our shadows.

———————

it was New Orleans, the French Quarter, and I stood on the sidewalk and watched a drunk leaning against a wall and the drunk was crying, and the Italian was asking him "are you a Frenchman?" and the Frenchman said, "yes I'm a French-man." and the Italian hit him in his face hard, knocking his head against the wall, and then he asked the drunk again, "are you a Frenchman?" and the frog would say yes, and the wop would hit him again, meanwhile saying over and over again, "I'm your friend, I'm your friend, I'm only trying to help you. don't you understand that?" and the Frenchman would say yes and the Italian would hit him again. there was another Italian sitting in his car shaving with a flashlight hung up and shining in his face. it seemed very odd. there he sat with shaving cream all over his face and shaving with his long open razor. he just ignored the action and sat there shaving away in the night. that was all right until the Frenchman fell away from the wall and staggered toward the car. the Frenchman grabbed at the car door and said "help!" and the Italian hit him again. "I'm your friend. I'm your FRIEND!" and the Frenchman fell against the car and joggled the whole car and the Italian inside evidently cut himself and he leaped out of the car with all of the shaving cream on and the cut growing on his face and he said "you sona bitch!" and he began slicing at the Frenchman's face and when the Frenchman held up his hands he sliced at the hands. "you sona bitch, you dirty sona bitch!"

it was my second night in town and very hard to take, so I went inside the bar there and sat down and the guy next to me turned and asked, "are you a Frenchman or an Italian?" and I said, "actually I was born in China. my father was a missionary and was killed by a tiger when I was a very little boy."

just then somebody behind me began to play on a violin and that saved me from further questions. I worked at my beer. when the violin stopped somebody came up on the other side of me and sat down. "my name's Sunderson. you look like you need a job."

"I need money. work I'm not crazy about."

"all you have to do is sit in this chair a few more hours a night."

"what's the catch?"

"eighteen bucks a week and keep your hands out of the cash register."

"how you gonna keep me from doing that?"

"I'm paying another guy eighteen bucks a week to watch you."

"are you a Frenchman?"

"Sunderson. Scotch – English. distant relative of Winston Churchill."

"I thought there was something wrong with you."

———————

it was a place where the cabbies from this cab co. would come in for gas. I would pump the gas, take the money and throw it into the register. most of the night I sat in a chair. the job went all right the first 2 or 3 nights. a little argument with the cabbies who wanted me to change flats for them. some Italian boy got on the phone and raised shit with the boss because I wouldn't do anything but I knew why I was there – to protect the money, the old man had shown me where the gun was, how to use it and be sure to make the cabbies pay for all the gas and oil they used. but I had no desire to protect the $$$$$$ for eighteen bucks a week and that was where Sunderson's thinking was wrong. I would have taken the money myself, but the morals were all fucked up: somebody had jobbed me with the crazy idea one time that stealing was wrong, and I was having a hard time over-coming my preconceptions. meanwhile I worked on them, against them, with them, you know.

about the fourth night a little negress stood in the doorway. she just stood there smiling at me. we must have been looking at each other for about 3 minutes. "how you doing?" she asked. "my name's Elsie."

"I'm not doing very good. my name's Hank."

she came in and leaned against a little old desk in there. she seemed to have on a little girl's dress. she had little girl movements and the fun in her eyes, but she was a woman, throbbing and miraculous electric woman in a brown and clean little girl's dress. "can I buy a soft drink?"

"sure."

she gave me the money and I watched her open the cover of the soft drink box and, with much serious deliberation, she selected a drink. then she sat on the little stool and I watched her drink it down. the little bubbles of air floating through electric light, through the bottle. I looked at her body, I looked at her legs, I was filled with the warm brown kindness of her. it was lonely in that place just sitting in that chair night after night for eighteen bucks a week.

she handed me the empty bottle.

"thanks."

"yeh."

"mind if I bring some of my girl friends over tomorrow night?"

"if they're anything like you sweetie, bring them all."

"they're all like me."

"bring them all."

the next night there were three or four of them, talking and laughing and buying and drinking soft drinks. jesus, I mean they were sweet, young, full of the thing, all young colored little girls, everything was funny and beautiful, and I mean it was, they made me feel that way. the next night there were eight or ten of them, the next night thirteen or fourteen. they began bringing in gin or whiskey and mixing it with the soft drinks. I brought my own. but Elsie, the first one was the finest of them all. she'd sit on my lap and then leap up and scream, "hey, Jesus Christ, you gonna shove my TESTINES out of the top of my head with that there FISHPOLE!" she'd act angry, real angry, and the other girls would laugh. and I'd just sit there confused, smiling, but in a sense I was happy. they had too much for me but it was a good show. I began to loosen up a bit myself. when a driver would honk, I'd stand up a bit leery, finish my drink, go find the gun, hand it to Elsie and say, "now look Elsie baby, you guard that god damned register for me, and if any of them girls makes a move toward it, you go on and shoot a hole in her pussy for me, eh?"

and I'd leave Elsie in there staring down at that big luger. it was a strange combo, the both of them, they could kill a man, or save him, depending upon which way it went. the history of man, woman and the world. and I'd walk out to pump the gas.

then the Italian cabbie, Pinelli, came in one night for a soft drink. I liked his name, but I didn't like him. he was the guy that bitched most about me not changing flats. I was not anti-Italian at all but it was strange that since I had landed in town that the Italian Faction was at the forefront of my misery. but I knew it was a mathematical, rather than a racial thing. in Frisco an old Italian woman had probably saved my life. but that was another story. Pinelli stalked in. and I mean STALKED. the girls were all around the place, talking and laughing. he walked over and lifted the lid of the soft drink container.

"GOD DAMN IT, ALL THE SOFT DRINKS ARE GONE AND I'M THIRSTY! WHO DRANK ALL THE SOFT DRINKS?"

"I did," I told him.

it was very quiet. all the girls were watching. Elsie was standing right by me watching him. Pinelli was handsome if you didn't look too long or too deep. the hawk nose, the black hair, the Prussian officer swagger, the tight pants, the little boy fury.

"THESE GIRLS DRANK ALL THOSE SOFT DRINKS, AND THESE GIRLS AREN'T SUPPOSED TO BE IN HERE, THESE DRINKS ARE FOR TAXI DRIVERS ONLY!"

then he came close to me, stood there, spreading his legs like a chicken does, a bit, before it craps:

"YOU KNOW WHAT THESE GIRLS ARE, WISE GUY?"
"sure, these girls are my friends."
"NO, THESE GIRLS ARE WHORES! THEY WORK IN THREE WHOREHOUSES ACROSS THE STREET! THAT'S WHAT THEY ARE – WHORES!"

nothing was said. we just all sat there looking at the Italian. it seemed like a long look. then he turned and walked out. the rest of the night was hardly the same, I was worried about Elsie. she had the gun. I walked over to her and took the gun.

"I almost gave that son of a bitch a new belly button," she said, "his mother was a whore!"

the next thing I knew the place was empty. I sat and had a long drink. then I got up and looked at the cash register. it was all there.

about 5 a.m. the old man came in.

"Bukowski."

"yes, Mr. Sunderson?"

"I gotta let you go." (familiar words)

"what's wrong?"

"the boys say you ain't been runnin' this place right, place full of whores and you here playin' around. them with their breasts out and snatches out and you suckin' and lickin' and tonguin'. is THAT what goes on around here early in the morning?"

"well, not exactly."

"well I'm gonna take your spot until I can find a more dependable man. got to find out what's going on around here."

"all right it's your circus, Sunderson."

I think it was two nights later that I was coming out of the bar and decided to walk past the old gas station. there were two or three police cars around.

I saw Marty, one of the cab drivers I got along with. I went up to him:

"what's up Marty?"

"they knifed Sunderson, and shot one of the cabbies with Sunderson's gun."

"jesus, just like a movie. the cabbie they shot, was it Pinelli?"

"yeah, how'd you know?"

"get it in the belly?"

"yeah, yeah, how'd you know?"

I was drunk. I walked away back towards my room. It was high New Orleans moon. I kept walking towards my room and soon the tears came, a great wash of tears in the moonlight. and then they stopped and I could feel the tear-water drying on my face, stretching the skin. when I got to my room I didn't bother with the light, got my shoes off, my socks off, and fell back on the bed without Elsie, my beautiful black whore, and then I slept, I slept through the sadness of everything and when I awakened I wondered what the next town would be, the next job. I got up, put on my shoes and socks, and went out for a bottle of wine. the streets didn't look very good, they seldom did. it was a structure planned by rats and men and you had to live within it and die within it. but like a friend of mine once said "nothing was ever promised you, you signed no contract." I walked into the store for my wine.

the son of a bitch leaned forward just a little, waiting for his dirty coins.

---

scribbling on shirt cardboards during two day drunks:

When Love becomes a command, Hatred can become a pleasure.

* * *

if you don't gamble, you'll never win

* * *

Beautiful thoughts, and beautiful women never last

* * *

you can cage a tiger but you're never sure he's broken. Men are easier.

* * *

if you want to know where God is, ask a drunk.

* * *

there aren't any angels in the foxholes.

* * *

no pain means the end of feeling; each of our joys is a bargain with the devil.

* * *

the difference between Art and Life is that Art is more bearable

* * *

I'd rather hear about a live American bum than a dead Greek God.

* * *

there is nothing as boring as the truth

* * *

The well balanced individual is insane

* * *

Almost everybody is born a genius and buried an idiot

* * *

a brave man lacks imagination. Cowardice is usually caused by lack of proper diet.

* * *

sexual intercourse is kicking death in the ass while singing

* * *

when men rule governments, men won't need governments; until then we are screwed

* * *

an intellectual is a man who says a simple thing in a difficult way; an artist is a man who says a difficult thing in a simple way.

* * *

everytime I go to a funeral I feel as if I had eaten puffed wheat germ

* * *

dripping faucets, farts of passion, flat tires – are all sadder than death.

* * *

if you want to know who your friends are, get yourself a jail sentence

*　*　*

hospitals are where they attempt to kill you without explaining why. The cold and measured cruelty of the American Hospital is not caused by doctors who are overworked or who have gotten used to, and bored with death. it is caused by doctors WHO ARE PAID TOO MUCH FOR DOING TOO LITTLE and who are admired by the ignorant, as witchmen with cure, when most of the time they don't know their own arse-hairs from celery shreds.

*　*　*

Before a metropolitan daily exposes an evil, it takes its own pulse.

*　*　*

end of shirt cardboards.

————

well here's your Christmas story, little children – gather round.
　"ah," said my friend Lou, "I think I got it."
　"yeah?"
　"yeah."
　I poured another wine.
　"we work together," he continued.
　"sure."
　"now you're a good talker, you tell a lot of interesting stories. it doesn't matter if they're true or not."
　"they're true."
　"I mean, that doesn't matter, now listen, here's what we do. there's a class bar down the street, you know it – Molino's. now you go in there and all you need is money for the first drink. we'll pool for that. now you sit down and nurse your drink and look around for a guy flashing a roll. they got some fat ones in there. you spot the guy and go over to him. use some pretext. you sit down next to him and turn it on. you turn on the bullshit. he'll like it. you've even got a vocabulary when high. one night you even claimed to me that

you were a surgeon. you explained the complete operation on the mesocolon to me. o.k. so he'll buy you drinks all night, he'll drink all night. keep him drinking.

"now when closing time comes, you lead him west near Alvarado Street, lead him west past the alley. tell him you're going to get him some nice young pussy, tell him anything but lead him west. I'll be waiting in the alley with this."

Lou reached behind the door and came out with a baseball bat. it was a very large bat. I think at least forty-two oz.

"jesus christ Lou, you'll kill him!"

"naw, NAW, you can't kill a drunk, you know that! maybe if he were sober I'd kill him but drunk it'll only knock him out. we take the wallet and split it two ways."

"and the last thing he's gonna remember," I said, "is walking with me."

"that's right."

"I mean, he's gonna REMEMBER me, maybe swinging the bat is the better end of the deal."

"I gotta swing the bat, it's the only way we can work it because I don't have your line of bullshit."

"it's not bullshit."

"then you WERE a surgeon, I mean –"

"forget it, but let's put it this way – I can't do that sort of thing, set up a pigeon, because essentially I'm a nice guy, I'm not like that."

"you're no nice guy. you're the meanest son of a bitch I ever met. that's why I like you. you wanna fight now? I wanna fight you. you get first punch. when I was in the mines I once fought a guy with pick handles. he broke my arm with first swing they thought he had me. I beat him with one arm. he was never the same after that fight. he went goofy talked out the side of his mouth continually, about nothing. you get first punch."

and he pushed that battered crocodile head out at me.

"no, you get first punch." I told him, "SWING, MOTHER!"

he did. he knocked me over backwards in my chair. I got up and put one into his belly. the next one put me up against his sink. a dish fell to the floor and broke. I grabbed an empty wine bottle and threw it at his head. he ducked and it smashed against the door. then the door opened. it was our young blond landlady figure, looks, youth. it was so confusing. we both stood there looking at her.

"that'll be all of that." she said.

then she turned to me, "I saw you last night."

"you didn't see me last night."

"I saw you in the vacant lot next door."

"I wasn't there."

"you were there, you just don't remember. you were there drunk, I saw you in the moonlight."

"all right, what!"

"you were pissing. I saw you pissing in the moonlight in the center of that vacant lot."

"that doesn't sound like me."

"it was you. You do that once more and you're out. we can't have that here."

"baby," said Lou, "I love you, oh I love you so much just let me go to bed with you one time and I'll cut off both of my arms, I swear it!"

"shut up, you silly wino."

she closed the door and we sat down and had a wine.

I found one. a big fat one. I had been fired by fat stupidities like that all my life. from worthless underpaid, dull jobs. it was going to be nice. I got to talking. I didn't quite know what I was talking about. I mean I only sensed that my mouth was moving but he was listening and laughing and nodding his head and buying drinks. he had a wristwatch, a handful of rings, a full stupid wallet. it was hard work yet the drinks made it easy. I told him some stories about prisons, about railroad track gangs, about the whorehouse. he liked the whorehouse stuff. I told him about the guy who got in the bathtub naked, waited around for an hour while the whore took ex-lax, and then the whore came in and drizzled shit all over him and he came on the ceiling.

"oh no, REALLY!"

"oh yeah, really."

then I told him about the guy who came in every two weeks and he paid well. all he wanted was a whore in the room with him. they both took off their clothes and played cards and talked. just sat there. then after two hours he'd get dressed, say goodbye, and walk out. never touch the whore.

"god damn," he said.

"yeah."

I decided that I wouldn't mind Lou's slugger bat to hit a homer on that skull. what a fat whammy. what a useless hunk of shit who sucked the life out of his fellow man and out of himself. he sat there ponderously majestic with nothing but a way to make it easy in an insane society.

"you like young girls?" I asked him.

"oh yeah, yeah, yeah!"

"say around 15½?"

"oh jesus, yes."

"there's one coming in on the one thirty a.m. from Chicago. she'll be at my place around 2:10 a.m. she's clean, hot, intelligent. now I'm taking a big chance, so you got to trust me. I'm asking ten bucks in advance, and ten after you finish. that too high?"

"oh no, that's all right." he went into his pocket and came up with one of his dirty tens.

"o.k. when this place closes you come with me."

"sure, sure."

"now she's got these silver spurs with indented rubies, she can put them on and spur your thighs just as you're cracking your nuts. how'd you like that? but that's five dollars extra."

"no, I'd rather not have the spurs," he said.

2 a.m. finally made it around and I walked him out there, down toward the alley. maybe Lou wouldn't even be there. maybe the wine would get him or he'd just back out. a blow like that could kill a man, or make him addled for the rest of his life. we staggered along in the moonlight, there was nobody around, nobody on the streets.

it was going to be easy.

we crossed into the alley. Lou was there.

but fatso saw him. he threw up an arm and ducked as Lou swung the bat got me right behind the ear.

I fell on down in that rat filled alley (thinking for just a flash: I've got the ten, I've got the ten.), I fell down in that alley full of used rubbers, shreds of old newspapers, lost washers, nails, match-sticks, matchbooks, dried worms, I fell down in that alley of clammy blow jobs and sadistic wet shadows, of starving cats, prowlers, fags – it came to me then – the luck and the way was mine:

the meek shall inherit the earth.

I could barely hear fatso running off, felt Lou reaching for my wallet. then I was out of it.

———

he was a rich bastard in the steam bath, crying. he had all the recordings of J.S. Bach and it still wasn't doing him any good. he had stained glass windows in his place plus a photo of a nun pissing. still: no good. he once had a taxi driver murdered at full moon in the Nevada Desert while he watched. that – wore off in 30 minutes. he tied dogs to crosses and burned out their eyes with his dollar cigars. old stuff. he had screwed so many fine young golden-legged girls that it – wasn't any good anymore.

nothing.

he had exotic ferns burning while he bathed, he threw drinks in the face of his butler.

a rich bastard, insidious paste he was. a real old creep. a spitter into the guts of roses.

he kept crying there on the table as I smoked one of his dollar cigars.

"help me, oh JESUS help me!" he screamed.

it was about time. "wait a minute," I told him.

I went to the locker and got the belt and then he bent over on the table, and all that white mushmeat, that hairy sickening ass, and I swung and laid the belt buckle across hard again and again:

ZAP! ZAP!
ZAP! ZAP! ZAP!
he fell off the table like a crab looking for sea. he crawled on the floor and I followed him with the buckle.
ZAP!
ZAP!
ZAP!
while he screamed again two or three times I leaned down and burned him with the cigar.

then he laid flat, smiling.

I walked into the kitchen where his lawyer sat drinking coffee.

"finished?"

"yeah."

he peeled off five tens, threw them across the table. I poured a coffee and sat down. the cigar was still in my hand. I threw it into the sink.

"jesus," I said, "Jesus Christ."

"yeah," said the lawyer, "the last guy only lasted a month."

we sat there sipping the coffee. it was a nice kitchen.

"come back next wednesday," he said.

"why don't you do it for me?" I asked.

"ME? I'm too sensitive!"

we both laughed and I dropped 2 cubes of sugar.

———

he came down through the laundry shoot and as he slid out, Maxfield hit him with an ax handle, breaking his neck. we went through his pockets. we had the wrong man. "ah, shit," Maxfield said. "ah, shit," I said.

I went upstairs and phoned.

"rabbit ram kay remus. hard," I said.

"shoot bugger damn lame," Steinfelt said.

"spooks," I said, "spooks down tender."

"fuck you," said Steinfelt. he hung up.

as I walked in down there, Maxfield was going down on the dead corpse.

"I always suspected you," I told him.

"bugger bugger reeme," he lifted his mouth to speak.

"what's THAT got to do with it?" I asked.

"gluub," he said.

I sat down on top of a deactivated washing machine. "listen, if we are going to have a better world," I told him, "we are not only going to have to fight in the streets we are going to have to fight in and with our minds. also, if our women can't keep their toenails clean it's a cinch they can't keep their pussies clean. before you pinch a woman's ass, ask her to remove her boots."

"gluub," he said. he got up, satisfied, and removed the corpse's eyeballs. with his jackknife. swastika handle. he looked like Celine at his best. he swallowed the eyeballs.

we both sat and waited.

"have you read *Resistance, Rebellion and Death*?"

"I'm afraid that I have."

"the maximum danger implies the maximum hope."

"you got a smoke?" I asked.

"sure," he said.

as soon as I got the thing good and lit I reached over and pressed the red ash end against his hairy wrist.

"oh, shit," he said. "oh, DO stop that!"

"you're lucky I didn't press the thing into your hairy ass."

"I should be so lucky."

"strip."

he heard me.

"spread your cheeks."

"I pledge allegiance," he said, "to the . . ."

Rimsky Korsakov's cherrazad came on over the overhead wiring, I jammed, no, I jammed the red tip in.

"jesus," he said.

I kept it in there. "why did they raid the Hullabaloo?"

"jesus," he said.

"I asked you a question! why did they?"

"they did," he said. "they did because they did. I am child to my ignorance!"

"let's get to the bottom of this thing," I suggested, placing the burning tip all the way in.

COCKTAILS

"jesus," he said, "oh, sweet jesus!"

"almost every man knows the exactness of his imbecility but who can live the short sweet sheen of his swooning jewning genius?"

"only YOU, Charles Bukowski!"

"you are a brilliant man, Maxfield." I removed the cigarette, sniffed it, no sniffed it and threw it away.

"for cat's asses you take the cake, baby," I told him, "sit down."

"really," he said.

I sat down.

"now, actually," I told him, "it is easy to understand Camus if you follow me. a brukk, a banko, a sestina-vik, like that, a brilliant writer yes, but he sucked in."

"what thevik – fuck are you talking about?" he asked.

"I mean letters to COMBAT. I mean speeches given for L'Amitie Francaise. I mean statements made at the Dominican Monastery of Latour-Maubourg in 1948. I mean the reply to Gabriel Marcel. I mean the speech he gave at the Labor Exchange of Saint-Etienne on 10 May 1958. I mean the speech delivered 7 December 1955 at a banquet in honor of President Eduardo Santos, editor of II Tiempo, driven out of Colombia by the dictatorship. I mean the letter to M. Aziz Kessous. I mean the interview in Demain, issue of 24–30 October 1957."

"I mean, sucked-in, sucked out of position; I mean jacked-off, taken. he died in a car he was no longer driving. it is very fine to be a good guy and enter the field of human affairs; it is something else to see a little shit like you knocking great dead men of human affairs. the large become large targets for small men – small men with rifles, typewriters, unsigned notes under the door, badges, clubs, dogs, these things of small men work too."

"why don't you go fuck yourself?" I asked him.

"trivial angers like trivial pussies will disappear into October's sunlight," he told me.

"sounds good. how about the OTHER kinds?"

"same thing."

"jesus," I said. "jesus," I said.

"sincerely," he said, putting his head, no his hand, on my knee. "I really can't tell you why they raided the hullabaloo."

"could Camus have?" I asked.

"what?"

"raided the Hullabaloo."

"hell no!"

"would he have had an opinion on it?" I asked.

"hell, yes!"

we both stayed in silence a long time.

"whatta we gonna do with this dead body?" I asked.

"I already done it." said Maxwell.

"I mean, NOW."

"your turn now."

"forget it."

we both stayed in silence and looked at the dead body.

"whyant you phone Steinfelt?" asked Maxwell.

" 'whyant'?"

"yeah. 'whyant'?"

"you sure get on my nerves."

I went upstairs and took the phone off the hook. every other phone in America resting in the cradle, all replaced, no more hooks – here was a fucking thing hanging on a hook like a huge resting Negro dong. I picked it up, took it in my hand. It was sweating, of course. and smeared with dry sphagetti, or however you spell it – dried worms who had lost the last race.

"Steinfelt," I spoke.

"who won the 9th?" he asked.

"harness or Del Mar?"

"harness."

"Jonboy Star, entered in 5 grand claimer. ran for 6 at Spokane with Asaphr up, post 8, 6 by 2 and one half. got post

2, switched to Jack Williams. morning line 4. opened 7 to 2.
last minute action brought it down to 2 to one. won easy."
"who'd you have?"
"Smoke Concert."
"so what the hell is it?" he asked.
"rabbit ram kay remus. hard."
"shoot bugger damn lame," Steinfelt said.
"spooks," I said. "spooks down tender. most tender."
"fuck you twice," said Steinfelt.
he hung up.
and I, I walked back in there, I, I, I did. if did, banko
bunko sestina-vink vik. Copeland's Fanfare for the Common
Man was on the overhead wire. Maxfield was back on down
on the buggy dead corpse.
I watched him. I watched him for a while.
"my friend," I told him, "our job is not easy and our
destinies are incomplete. think of Africa, think of Vietnam,
think of Watts, Detroit; think of the Boston Red Sox and the
L.A. Country museum, county, I mean. think of anything.
think of how bad you look in the mirror of life."
"blubb," said Maxfield.
the Decline and Fall of the West was before me. just give
me ten years more, ten more years. dear Spengler. Oswald?
OSWALD???? Oswald Spengler.
I walked over, sat on the washing machine and waited.

———

sit down, Stirkoff.
thank you, sir.
stretch your legs.
most gracious of you, sir.
Stirkoff, I understand you've been writing articles on
justice, equality; also the right to joy and survival. Stirkoff?
yes, sir?
do you think that there will ever be an overwhelming and
sensible justice in the world?
not really, sir.

then why do you write that shit? aren't you feeling well?

I've been feeling strange lately, sir, almost as if I were going mad.

are you drinking a great deal, Stirkoff?

of course, sir.

and do you play with yourself?

constantly, sir.

how?

I don't understand, sir.

I mean, how do you go about it?

four or five raw eggs and a pound of hamburger in a thin-necked flower bowl while listening to Vaughn Williams or Darius Milhaud.

glass?

no, ass, sir.

I mean, the vase, it is glass?

of course not, sir.

have you ever been married?

many times, sir.

what went wrong?

everything, sir.

what was the best piece of ass you ever had?

four or five raw eggs and a pound of hamburger in a . . .

all right, all right!

yes, it is.

do you realize that your yearning for justice and a better world is only a front to hide the decay and shame and failure that reside within you?

yep.

did you have a vicious father?

I don't know sir.

what do you mean, you don't know?

I mean, it's hard to compare. you see, I only had one.

are you getting smart with me, Stirkoff?

oh no, sir; like you say, justice is impossible.

did your father beat you?

they took turns.

I thought you only had one father.

every man has. I mean, my mother got in hers.

did she love you?

only as an extension of herself.

what else can love be?

the common sense to care very much for something very good. it needn't be related by bloodline. it can be a red beachball or a piece of buttered toast.

you mean to say that you can LOVE a piece of buttered toast?

only some, sir. on certain mornings. in certain rays of sunlight. love arrives and departs without notice.

is it possible to love a human being?

of course, especially if you don't know them too well. I like to watch them through my window, walking down the street.

Stirkoff, you're a coward.

of course, sir.

what is your definition of a coward?

a man who would think twice before fighting a lion with his bare hands.

and what is your definition of a brave man?

a man who doesn't know what a lion is.

every man knows what a lion is.

every man assumes that he does.

and what is your definition of a fool?

a man who doesn't realize that Time, Structure and Flesh are being mostly wasted.

who then is a wise man?

there aren't any wise men, sir.

then there can't be any fools. if there isn't any night there can't be any day; if there isn't any white there can't be any black.

I'm sorry, sir. I thought that everything was what it was, not depending on something else.

you've had your cock in too many flower bowls. don't you understand that EVERYTHING is correct, that nothing can go wrong?

I understand, sir, that what happens, happens.

what would you say if I were to have you beheaded?
I wouldn't be able to say anything, sir.
I mean that if I were to have you beheaded I would remain
the Will and you would become Nothing.
I would become something else.
at my CHOICE.
at both our choices, sir.
relax! relax! stretch your legs!
most gracious of you, sir.
no, most gracious of both of us.
of course. sir.
you say you often feel this madness. what do you do when
it comes upon you?
I write poetry.
is poetry madness?
non-poetry is madness.
what is madness?
madness is ugliness.
what is ugly?
to each man, something different.
does ugliness belong?
it's there.
does it belong?
I don't know, sir.
you pretend knowledge. what is knowledge?
knowing as little as possible.
how can that be?
I don't know, sir.
can you build a bridge?
no, sir.
can you make a gun?
no, sir.
these things are the products of knowledge.
these things are bridges and guns.
I am going to have you beheaded.
thank you, sir.
why?

you are my motivation when I have very little.

I am Justice.

perhaps.

I am the Winner. I will have you tortured, I will make you scream. I will make you wish for Death.

of course, sir.

don't you realize that I am your master?

you are my manipulator; but there is nothing you can do to me that cannot be done.

you think that you speak cleverly but through your screams you will say nothing clever.

I doubt it, sir.

by the way, how can you listen to Vaughn Williams and Darius Mihaud? haven't you heard of the Beatles?

oh, sir, everybody has heard of the Beatles.

don't you like them?

I don't dislike them.

do you dislike any singer?

singers can't be disliked.

then, any person who attempts to sing?

Frank Sinatra.

why?

he evokes a sick society upon a sick society.

do you read any newspapers?

only one.

which is?

OPEN CITY.

GUARD! TAKE THIS MAN TO THE TORTURE CHAM-BERS IMMEDIATELY AND BEGIN PROCEEDINGS!

sir, a last request?

yes.

may I take my flower bowl with me?

no, I'm going to use it!

sir?

I mean, I am going to confiscate it. now, guard, take this idiot away! and guard come back with, come back with . . .

yes, sir?

a half dozen raw eggs and a couple of pounds of ground sirloin . . .

exit guard and prisoner. king leans forward, grins evilly as Vaughn Williams comes on over intercom. outside, the world moves forward as a lice-smitten dog pisses against a beautiful lemon tree vibrating in the sun.

Miriam and I had the little shack in the center, not bad, I had grown a run of sweetpeas out front, plus tulips all around. the rent was almost nothing and nobody bothered you on the drunks. you had to find the landlord to pay the rent and if you were a week or two late he'd say, "that's all right," he owned some automobile sales and repair outfit and had all the money he needed. "just don't give the money to my wife, she's a lush and I'm trying to slow her down." it seemed an easy time. Miriam was working. she typed for some big furniture company. I was unable to put her on the bus in the morning because I'd have a hangover, but me and the dog would always be waiting for her at the bus stop when she came on in. we had a car but she couldn't start the thing, and that made it nice for me. I'd wake up around 10:30, put myself together in a very leisurely way, check out sun and rub my belly, then I'd play with the dog, a big monster, bigger than me, and getting tired of that we'd go inside and I'd slowly straighten the place up a bit, make the bed, pick up the bottles, wash the dishes; another beer, check the refrigerator to make sure there was something for her dinner. by then it was time to start the car and make the race track. I could get back just in time to greet her at the bus stop. yes, it was getting good, and never having been much of a lady's man it felt good to be kept, even granted that it wasn't exactly Monte Carlo, and besides being the lover I had to do the dishes and other degrading tasks.

I felt it wasn't going to last, but meanwhile I was feeling better, looking better, talking better, walking better, sitting better, sleeping better, fucking better than ever before. it was nice, truly nice.

then it came about that I got to know the woman in the front, the one who lived in the big front house. I'd be sitting on the steps drinking my beer and throwing the ball for the dog and she'd come out and spread this blanket on the lawn and take a sunbath. she had on a bikini, just a couple of strips of stuff. "hi," I'd say. "hi," she'd say. it went on like that for some mornings. not much conversation. me, I had to be careful. there were neighbors everywhere and Miriam knew them all. but this woman had a BODY, gentlemen, every now and then nature or god or something decides to put together ONE BODY, just ONE for a change. you look at most bodies, you will find that the legs are too short or too long, or the arms; or the neck is too thick or too skinny, or the hips are too high or too low, and most important – the ass. the ass is almost always out of order, a disappointment: too big, too flat, too round, not round, or it hangs like a separate part, something stuck there when it was almost too late.

the ass is the face of the soul of sex.

this woman had an ass to go with all the rest. gradually I found out that her name was Renie and that she was a stripper in one of the small clubs on Western Ave. but her face was Los Angeles hard, world-hard. you got the feeling that she had been taken a few times, lied to and used by the rich boys when she was a bit younger, and now she had the guard up and screw you brother, I'm going to get mine.

one morning she told me, "I've got to sunbathe in back now. that old son of a bitch next door came by one day when I was out front and he pinched me, he copped a feel!"

"he did?"

"yeah, that old freak, he must be seventy years old and he pinched me. he's got money, he can keep his money. there's a guy brings his wife over there every day. he lets the old guy have her every day, they lay around and drink and screw, and then the husband comes and gets his wife in the evening. they think he's going to die and leave her the money. people make me sick. now down where I work, the guy who owns the place, big fat wop, Gregario, he says, 'baby, you work for me, you gotta go all the way, on stage, off stage.' I tell him, "look George, I'm an Artist, you don't like my act the way it is, I quit!' and I called a friend of mine and we packed all that gear out of there and I no sooner got home than the phone started ringing. it was Gregario. he tells me, 'look, honey, I gotta have you back! the place ain't the same, the place is dead. everybody's asking for you tonight. please come back, baby, I respect you as an Artist and a lady, you are a great lady!"

"care for a beer?" I asked her.

"sure."

I went inside and got a couple of beers and Renie got up on the porch steps and we drank.

"what do you do?" she asked.

"nothing right now."

"you've got a nice girl friend."

"she's o.k."

"what'd you do before you did nothing?"

"all bad jobs. nothing to talk about."

"I talked to Miriam. she says you paint and write, you're an artist."

"at rare times I'm an artist; at most other times I'm nothing."

"I'd like you to see my act."

"I don't like the clubs."

"I've got a stage in my bedroom."

"what?"

"come on, I'll show you."

we went in the back door and she sat me down in the bedroom. sure enough, here was this rather circular upraised stage. it took up most of the bedroom. there was a curtained area just off stage. she brought me a whiskey and water and then mounted the stage. she got in behind the curtains. I sat and sipped at my drink. then I heard music. "Slaughter on Tenth Avenue." the curtains parted. out she slank, gliding, gliding.

I finished my drink and decided I wouldn't make the racetrack that day.

the clothing began to detach. she began to bump and grind. she'd left the whiskey by my side. I reached over and poured a bit of a shot, and she got on down to the little string with the beads on it. when she flipped the beads you saw the magic box. she ground it out, down to the last note. she was good.

"bravo! bravo!" I applauded.

she climbed on down and lit a cigarette.

"you really liked it?"

"sure. I know what Gregario means when he says you've got class."

"all right, what's he mean?"

"lemme have another drink."

"sure. I'll join you."

"well, class is something you see, feel, rather than define, you can see it in men too, animals. you see it in some trapeze artists as they walk onto the arena. something in the walk, something in the manner. they have something inside AND outside, but it's mostly inside and it makes the outside work. you do that when you dance; the inside makes the outside work."

"yes, I feel that way too. it's not just a sex-grind with me, it's a feeling. I sing, I talk when I dance."

"you sure as hell do. I caught all that."

"but listen, I want you to criticize me, I want you to make suggestions, I want to improve. that's why I have this stage, that's why I practice. talk to me as I dance, don't be afraid to say things."

"o.k., a few more drinks and I'll loosen up."

"help yourself."

she got back on stage, but behind the curtains. she came out with a different outfit on.

"when a New York baby says goodnight
it's early in the morning
good night sweetheart."

I had to talk loud over the music. I felt like a big-shot director with a sub-normal Hollywood brain.

"DON'T SMILE WHEN YOU COME OUT. THAT'S VULGAR. YOU'RE A LADY. YOU'RE GIVING THEM A

BREAK BY BEING HERE. IF GOD HAD A CUNT YOU'D BE GOD, WITH A LITTLE MORE GENEROSITY. YOU'RE HOLY, YOU'VE GOT CLASS, LET THEM KNOW IT!"

I worked on the whiskey, found some cigarettes on the bed, started chain-smoking.

"THAT'S IT, THAT'S IT. YOU'RE ALONE IN A ROOM! NO AUDIENCE. YOU WANT LOVE THROUGH SEX, LOVE THROUGH AGONY!"

the parts of her costume began to fall away.

"NOW, NOW, SUDDENLY SAY SOMETHING! SAY IT AS YOU ARE WALKING AWAY FROM STAGE FRONT, HISS IT, HURL IT OVER YOUR SHOULDER, SAY ANYTHING THAT COMES TO YOUR HEAD, LIKE 'POTATOS HURL MIDNIGHT ONIONS!' "

"potatoes hurl midnight onions!" she hissed.

"NO, NO! YOU SAY SOMETHING, MAKE IT YOURS!"

"chippy chippy suck nuts!" she hissed.

I almost made my rocks. more whiskey.

"NOW HIT IT, HIT IT! RIP OFF THAT GOD DAMNED STRING! LET ME SEE THE FACE OF ETERNITY!"

she did. the whole bedroom was on fire.

"NOW GET IT GOING FAST, FAST, LIKE YOU'VE LOST YOUR MIND, ABANDONED EVERYTHING!"

she did. for some moments I was speechless. the cigarette burned my fingers.

"BLUSH!" I screamed.

she blushed.

"NOW SLOW, SLOW, SLOW, MOVE IT TOWARD AND TO ME! SLOW, SLOW SLOW, YOU'VE GOT THE WHOLE TURKISH ARMY HARD! TOWARD ME, SLOW, OH JESUS!"

I was just about to leap on stage when she hissed, "chippy chippy suck nuts."

then it was too late.

I had another drink, said goodbye to her, went to my place,

bathed, shaved, washed the dishes, got the dog and just made it down to the bus stop.

Miriam was tired.

"what a day," she said. "one of those damn fool girls went around and oiled all the typewriters. they all stopped working. they had to call in the repair man. 'who the hell oiled these things?' he screamed at us. then Conners was on us to make up lost time, go get out those bills. my fingers are numb from hitting those silly ass keys."

"you're still looking good, baby. you get yourself a nice hot bath, a few drinks, you'll be straight. I've got frenchfries in the oven, plus we'll have cubesteaks and tomatoes, hot french bread with garlic."

"I'm so damned tired!"

she sat in a chair kicked off her shoes and I brought her a drink. she sighed and said, looking out front, "those sweetpea vines are beautiful with the sun coming through like that."

she was just a nice girl from New Mexico.

well, I saw Renie a few times after that but none of the times was like the first time, and we never made it together. first, I was trying to be careful on account of Miriam, and second I had built up such a thing about Renie being an Artist and a Lady that we both almost believed it ourselves. any sexual activity would have impaired the strictly impartial artist-critic relationship, and would have evolved into a possess-or-don't-possess hassle. actually it was a hell of a lot more fun and abnormal the other way. but it wasn't Renie who did me in. it was the little fat housewife of the garage mechanic in the back house. she came over to borrow some coffee or sugar or something about 10 a.m. one morning. she had on this loose dressing gown or whatever it was and she bent over to get the coffee or whatever from a low cupboard and the breasts fell out.

it was gross. she blushed, then stood up. I could feel heat everywhere. it was like being locked in with tons of energy that worked you at their will. the next thing I knew we were embracing as her husband rolled under some car on his little coaster and cursed and turned a greasy wrench. she was a fat little butterdoll. we made the bedroom and it was good. it seemed strange to see her going into the bathroom that Miriam always used. then she left. neither of us had said anything since her opening words, when she had asked to borrow whatever it was she wanted to borrow. me, probably.

it was about three nights later over drinks, Miriam said, "I heard about you screwing fatty out back."

"she's not really fat," I said.

"well, all right, but I can't have that, not when I'm working, anyhow. we're through."

"can I stay tonight?"

"no."

"but where will I go?"

"you can go to hell!"

"after all our times together?"

"after all our times together."

I tried working on her. it wasn't any good. she just got worse.

it was easy for me to pack. what I owned was rags that fit into half a paper suitcase. luckily I had a little money and I found a nice apartment on Kingsley Drive for a very reasonable rate. but I couldn't understand how Miriam had found out about Butterfat without being suspicious of Renie. then I put it together. they were all friends. they communicated, either directly or spiritually or in some way that women communicate to each other that men can't understand. add a little outside information to this and the poor man is finished.

sometimes driving down Western I would check the club bill-board. there it was, Renie Fox. only she wasn't head-lined. there was the name of the main stripper in bold neon and then below, Renie and one or two others. I never went in.

I saw Miriam one more time, outside a Thrifty Drugstore. she had the dog with her. he jumped all over me and I petted him and roughed him up.

"well, anyhow," I told her, "the dog misses me."

"I know he does. I brought him over to see you one night but before I could ring the bell I heard some bitch giggling in there. I didn't want to interrupt anything, so we left."

"you must have imagined the whole thing. there hasn't been anybody around."

"I didn't imagine anything."

"listen, I ought to drop around some night."

"no, don't. I have a nice boyfriend. he has a good job. he works! he's not afraid of WORK!"

and with that, they turned, woman and dog, and walked away from me and my life and my fears, wiggling their asses at me. then I stood and watched the people walking by. there was nobody there. I was at the corner. the signal was red. I watched. when it turned green I crossed the hard street.

––––––

one of my best friends – at least I consider him a friend – one of the finest poets of our Age is afflicted, right now, in London, with it, and the Greeks were aware of it and the Ancients, and it can fall upon a man at any age but the best age for it is the late forties working toward fifty, and I think of it as Immobility – a weakness of movement, an increasing lack of care and wonder; I think of it as The Frozen Man Stance, although it hardly is a STANCE at all, but it might allow us to view the corpse with SOME humor; otherwise the blackness would be too much. all men are afflicted, at times, with the Frozen Man Stance, and it is indicated best by such flat phrases as: "I just can't make it." or: "to hell with it all." or: "give my regards to Broadway." but usually they quickly recover and continue to beat their wives and hit the time-clocks.

but for my friend, The Frozen Man Stance is not to be thrown under the couch like a child's toy. if it only could be! he has tried the doctors of Switzerland, France, Germany, Italy, Greece, Spain and England and they could do nothing. one of them treated him for worms. another stuck tiny needles in his hands and neck and back, thousands of tiny needles. "this might be it," he wrote me, "the needles might damn well do the trick." in the next letter I heard that he was trying some Voodoo freak. in the next I heard that he wasn't trying anything. the Final Frozen Man. one of the finest poets of our time, stuck there on top of his bed in a small and dirty London room, starving, barely kept alive by handouts; staring at his ceiling unable to write or utter a word, and not caring, finally, whether he does or not. his name is known throughout the world.

I could and can well understand this great poet's flop in a barrel of shit, for, strangely, as long as I can remember, I was BORN into the Frozen Man Stance. one of the instances that I can recall is once when my father, a cowardly vicious brute of a man, was beating me in the bathroom with this long leather razor strap, or stop, as some call it. he beat me quite regularly; I was born out of wedlock and I believe he blamed me for all his troubles. he used to walk around singing, "oh when I was single, my pockets did jingle!" but he didn't sing often. he was too busy beating me. for some time say before I reached the age of seven or eight, he almost imposed this sense of guilt upon me. for I could not understand why he beat me. he would search very hard for a reason. I had to cut his grass once a week, once lengthwise, then crosswise, then trim the edges with shears, and if I missed ONE blade of grass anywhere on the front or back lawns he beat the living shit-hell out of me. after the beating I would have to go out and water the lawns. meanwhile the other kids were playing baseball or football and growing up to be normal humans. the big moment would always come when the old man would stretch out on the lawn and put his eye level with the grassblades. he'd always manage to find one. "there, I SEE IT! YOU MISSED ONE! YOU MISSED ONE!" then he'd yell toward the bathroom window where my mother, a fine German lady, always stood about this time of the proceedings. "HE MISSED ONE! I SEE IT! I SEE IT!" then I'd hear my mother's voice: "ah, he MISSED one? ah, shame, SHAME!" I do believe that she blamed me for her troubles too. "INTO THE BATHROOM!" he'd scream. "INTO THE BATHROOM!" so I'd walk into the bathroom and the strap would come out and the beating would begin. but even though the pain was terrible, I, myself, felt quite out of it. I mean, that really, I was disinterested; it didn't mean anything to me. I had no attachment to my parents so I didn't feel any violation of love or trust or warmth. the hardest part was the crying. I didn't want to cry. it was dirty work, like mowing the lawn. like when they gave me the pillow to sit on afterwards, after the beating, after the watering of the lawn, I didn't want the pillow either, so, not wanting to cry, one day I decided not to. all that could be heard was the slashing of the leather strap against my naked ass. it had a curious and meaty and gruesome sound in the silence and I stared at the bathroom tiles. the tears came but I made no sound. he stopped beating. he usually gave me fifteen or twenty lashes. he stopped at a mere seven or eight. he ran out of the bathroom, "Mama, Mama, I think our boy is CRAZY, he don't cry when I whip him!" "you think he's crazy, Henry?" "yes, mama." "ah, too bad!"

it was only the first RECOGNIZABLE appearance of The Frozen Boy. I knew that there was something wrong with me but I did not consider myself insane. it was just that I could not understand how other people could become so easily angry, then just as easily forget their anger and become joyful, and how they could be so interested in EVERY-THING when everything was so dull.

I was not much good at sports or playing with my companions because I had very little practice at it. I was not the true sissy – I had no fear or physical delicacy, and, at times, I did anything and everything better than any of them – but just in spurts – it didn't somehow matter to me. when I got into a fist fight with one of my friends I could never get angry. I only fought as a matter of course. no other out. I was Frozen. I could not understand the ANGER and the FURY of my opponent. I would find myself studying his face and his manner, puzzled with it, rather than trying to beat him. every now and then I would land a good one to see if I could do it, then I would fall back into lethargy.

then, as always, my father would leap out of the house: "That's all! Fight's over. Finish. Kaput! Over!"

the boys were afraid of my father. they would all run away.

"You're not much of a man, Henry. You got beat again!"

I didn't answer.

"Mama, our boy let that Chuck Sloan beat him!"

"our boy?"

"yes, our boy."

"shame!"

I guess my father finally recognized the Frozen Man in me, but he took full advantage of the situation for himself. "Children are to be seen but not heard," he would exclaim. this was fine with me. I had nothing to say. I was not interested. I was Frozen. early, late, and forever.

I began drinking about 17 with older boys who roamed the streets and robbed gas stations and liquor stores. they thought my disgust with everything was a lack of fear, that my non-complaining was a soulful bravado. I was popular and I didn't care whether I was popular or not. I was Frozen. they set great quantities of whiskey and beer and wine in front of me. I drank them down. nothing could get me drunk, really and finally drunk. the others would be falling to the floor, fighting, singing, swaggering, and I would sit quietly at the table draining another glass, feeling less and less with them, feeling lost, but not painfully so. just electric light and sound and bodies and little more.

but I was still living with my parents and it was depression times, 1937, impossible for a 17 year old to get a job. I'd come back off the streets as much out of habit as out of reality. and knock at the door.

one night my mother opened the little window in the door and screamed: "he's drunk! he's drunk again!"

and I heard the great voice back in the room: "he's drunk AGAIN?"

my father came to the little window: "I won't let you in. you are a disgrace to your mother and your country."

"it's cold out here. open the door or I'll break it down. I walked here to get in. that's all there is to it."

"no, my son, you do not deserve my house. you are a disgrace to your mother and your . . ."

I went to the back of the porch, lowered my shoulder and charged. there was no anger in my act or my movement, only a kind of mathematic – that having arrived at a certain figure you continue to work with it. I smashed into the door. it didn't open but a large crack appeared right down the center and the lock appeared to be half-broken. I went back to the end of the porch, lowered my shoulder again.

"all right, come in," said my father.

I walked in, but then the looks upon those faces, sterile blank hideous nightmare cardboard face-looks made my stomach full of booze lurch, I became ill, I unloaded upon their fine rug which was decorated with *The Tree of Life*. I vomited, plenty.

"you know what we do with a dog who shits on the rug?" my father asked.

"no," I said.

"well, we stick his NOSE in IT! so he won't do it NO MORE!"

I didn't answer. my father came up and put his hand behind my neck. "you are a dog," he said.

I didn't answer.

"you know what we do to dogs, don't you?"

he kept pressing my head down, down toward my lake of vomit upon *The Tree of Life*.

"we stick their noses in their shit so they don't shit no more, ever."

there my mother, fine German lady, stood in her night-gown, watching silently. I always got the idea that she wanted to be on my side but it was an entirely false idea gathered from sucking her nipples at one time. besides, I didn't have a side.

"listen, father," I said, "STOP."

"no, no, you know what we do to a DOG!"

"I'm asking you to stop."

he kept pressing my head down, down, down, down. my nose was almost in the vomit. although I was the Frozen Man, Frozen Man also means Frozen and not melted. I simply could see no reason for my nose being pushed into my own vomit. if there had been a reason I would have pushed my nose there myself. it wasn't a matter of CARING or HONOR or ANGER, it was a matter of being pushed out of my particular MATHEMATIC. I was, to use my favorite term, disgusted.

"stop," I said, "I'm asking you, one last time, to stop!"

he pushed my nose almost against the vomit.

I swung from my heels, and I was down by my heels, I caught him with a full flowing and majestic uppercut, I caught him hard and full and very accurate upon the chin and he fell backwards heavily and clumsily, a whole brutal empire shot to shit, finally, and he fell into his sofa, bang, spread-armed, eyes like the eyes of a doped animal. animal? the dog had turned, I walked toward the couch, waiting for him to get up. he didn't get up. he just kept staring up at me. he would not get up. for all his fury, my father had been a coward. I was not surprised. then I thought, since my father is a coward, I am probably a coward. but being a Frozen Man, there wasn't any pain in this. it didn't matter, even as my mother began clawing my face with her fingernails, screaming over and over again, "you hit your FATHER! you hit your FATHER! you hit your FATHER!"

it didn't matter. and finally I turned my face full toward her and let her rip and scream, slashing with her fingernails, tearing the flesh from my face, the fucking blood dripping and jerking an sliding down my neck and my shirt, spotting the fucking *Tree of Life* with flecks and splashes and chunks of meat. I waited, no longer interested. "YOU HIT YOUR FATHER!" and then the slashes came lower. I waited. then they stopped. then started again, one or two, "you . . . hit . . . your . . . father . . . your father . . ."

"have you finished?" I asked. I think the first words I had spoken to her outside of "yes" and "no" in ten years.

"yes," she said.

"you go to the bedroom," my father said from the couch. "I'll see you in the morning. I'll talk to YOU in the morning!"

yet HE was the Frozen Man in the morning, but I imagine, not out of choice.

———————

I have often let shackjobs and whores slash my face as my mother did, and this is a most bad habit; being frozen does not mean let the jackals take control, and, besides, children and old women, and some strong men, now wince, as they see my face. but, to continue, and I do believe these Frozen Man tales interest me more than they do you (interest: a mathematical manner of tabulation), and I will try to cut them short. Christ. I think a very funny one (humor: a mathematical manner of tabulation. and I am serious in these things.) was the time I was in Los Angeles High School, say 1938? 1937?, around there? 1936? I joined the ROTC without any interest in army doings in the least. I had these huge grapefruit boils, immense, slugging out all over me and a boy had one of two choices, at this time, either join the ROTC or take gym. well, really all the decent good guys were in gym. the shits and freaks and madmen, like me, the Frozen Men, what there were of them, were taking ROTC. war was not yet a humane thing. Hitler was just a gibberish Charlie Chaplin doing funny idiot things on RKO-Pathe News.

I went ROTC because in an army uniform they couldn't see my boils; in a tracksuit they could, plenty. now, get me, it wasn't my boils to ME that mattered, it was my BOILS toward THEM. it would upset their glands. with a man in a cave, a Frozen Man such as myself, boils don't matter, what makes them matter are things that don't count – like masses of common people. being Frozen does not mean being unrealistic; being Frozen means to remain Frozen; all else is madness.

be fucked with as little as possible so you may enter wherever you are meant to enter. so I didn't want to be fucked with by the stares of the human eye upon my disjointed boils. so I clothed myself in military uniform to cut down the x-rays. but I didn't want the ROTC. I was FROZEN.

so, here we are, one day, the whole god damned battalion or whatever you call it, and I am still a private and the whole school is in some type of manual of arms competition, the grandstands are packed with fools and here we stand, going through the movements, and it's hot and I'm FROZEN, man, I don't care, and here we follow these orders, and soon only fifty per cent of us are left and soon only twenty-five per cent and soon only ten per cent, and I'm still standing there, these big red ugly boils on my face, no uniform for the face, and it's hot, and I'm trying to get my mind to think, make a mistake make a mistake make a mistake, but I am automatically a master craftsman, there is nothing I can do badly even tho I don't care, but I can't force error and that TOO is because I am FROZEN! and soon there are only two people left, me and my buddy Jimmy. well, Jimmy is a shit and he NEEDS this thing, it will be nice for him. this is what I actually thought. but Jimmy flicked up. it was on the command, "Order Arms!" no, it went like this, "Order . . ." then, pause . . . "Arms!" I don't any longer remember the proper maneuver to this order, being a lousy soldier. it had something to do with the jamming of the bolt into the breech. but Jimmy, who cared and was loved by many or at least liked, Jimmy flicked up with the bolt. and there I was standing alone, boils bulging out over my itchy olive drab woolen collar, boils leaping out all over my skull, even on the top of my head in the hair, and it was hot in the sun and there I stood, disinterested, neither happy or sad, nothing, just nothing. the beautiful girls moaned in the stands for their poor Jimmy and his mother and father put their heads down, not understanding how it could have happened. I too managed to think, poor Jimmy. but that was as far as I could think. the old man running the ROTC was somebody called Col. Muggett, a man who had spent his entire career in the Army. he came up to place the medal upon my itchy shirt, his face was very sad, very. he thought me a misfit, the kid with the empty head, and I thought of him as insane. he pinned the medal on me and then reached to shake my hand. I took his hand and smiled. a good soldier never smiles. the smile meant to tell him that I understood things had gone wrong and that it was beyond me. then I marched back to my company, my squad, my platoon, my whatever the hell. then the Lt. called us to attention. Jimmy's last name was Hadford or something like that. and you ain't gonna believe this but it happened. the Lt. said to the men:

"I wish to congratulate Private Hadford for coming so close in the manual of arms competition."

then: "at ease!"

then: "*fall* out!" or "company dismissed!" or some god damned thing.

I saw the other boys talking to Jimmy. nobody said anything to me. then I saw Jimmy's mother and father come out of the stands and put their arms around him. my parents were not there. I walked off the grounds and into the streets. I took the medal off and walked along holding it in my hand. then without rancor, fear, joy, without anger or direct reason, I threw the medal down a sewer drain outside a drugstore. Jimmy was some years later shot down over the English Channel. his bomber was badly hit and he ordered his men to bail out while he tried to nurse his plane back to England. he never made it. about that time I was living in Philadelphia as a 4-F and I screwed a 300-pound whore who looked like a giant pig and she broke all four legs of my bed, bouncing and sweating and farting during the action.

I might go on and on, giving incidents within The Frozen Man context. it is not quite true that I never CARE or that I never anger or that I never hate or that I never hope or that I never have joy. I do not mean to infer that I am ENTIRELY without passions or feelings or whatever; it is only strange to me that my feelings, my thoughts, my ways are so strangely different and opposite of my fellow man. I can seemingly never get WITH them, hence I am frozen out both by their choice and my way. please stay awake and let me finish this off with a letter, a letter from my poet friend in London who describes his experiences as a Frozen Man. he wrote me:

". . . I'm in this fishbowl, you understand, a vast aquarium & my fins are not strong enough to get around in this big undersea city. i do what i can, tho the magic is surely gone. i just can't seem as yet to pull myself together out of this cold turkey state & get the 'inspiration,' no writing, no fucking, no damn nothing. can't drink, can't eat, can't turn on. just cold turkey. so the gloom, but nothing seems to work just now. it's going to be a long period of hibernation, a long dark night. I'm used to the sun, to the mediterranean brightness & dazzle, to living on the damn edge of the volcano, as in greece, where at least there was light, there were people, was even what is called love. now, nothing. middle-aged faces. young faces that mean nothing, that pass, smile, say hello. oh, cold gray darkness. old poet stuck in the sticks. the styx. the stinks. from doctors to hospitals, with shit specimens, piss specimens, & always the same reports – liver tests & pancreas tests abnormal: but nobody knows what to do, only i know. there is nothing to do but to snap out of this jungle, & meet some mythical young beauty – some sweet domestic thing who will take care of me, make few demands, be warm & quiet, not say too much. where is she? i couldn't damn well give her what she wants, or could i??? it's just possible, of course, that this is all i need. but how, where to find it? i wish i were tough. I'd be able to sit down & begin all over again, from scratch, getting it down on paper, stronger, cleaner, sharper than ever. but something has gone out of me right now, and i'm temporizing, stalling for time. the sky is black & pink and flushed at 4:40 in the afternoon. the city roars outside. the wolves are pacing in the zoo. the tarantulas are squatting beside the scorpions. the queen bee is served by the drones. the mandril snarls viciously, hurling filthy bananas & apples from its crotch at the crazy kids who taunt it. if I'm going to die, i want to come out to california, below l.a., far down the coast, on the beach somewhere, near Mexico. but that's a dream. I'd want to do that somehow. but all the letters I get from the states are from poets & writers who have been here, on this side of the Atlantic, & they tell me how rotten it is back home, what a nasty scene, etc. i don't know, i could never swing it, financially, since my backers are here, and they'd abandon me if i returned, as they more or less like to keep in closer contact with me. yes, the body gives, but hang on, and forgive the deadly dullness of this letter. i can't get inspired, i can't get worked up. i just look at doctor's bills, & other bills, & the black sky, the black sun. maybe something will change, soon . . . that's the way it is. tra la la, let's face it without tears. cheers, friend." Signed "X" (A well-known poet . . . editor).

―――――

well, my friend from London says it much better than I, but how well, how very well I know of what he speaks. and a worldful of energetic hustlers with their minds shaken awry with the pace would only condemn us for sloth or a kind of disgraceful laziness or self-pity. but it isn't any of these things. only the man frozen in the cage can know it. but we'll damn well have to go out of our way and wait. and wait for what? so, cheers, friends. even a dwarf can get a hard-on, and I am Mataeo Platch and Nichlos Combatz at the same time, and only Marina, my small girlchild, can bring light at the highest noon, for the sun will not speak. and up in the plaza between the terminal annex and the union station the old men sit in a circle and watch the pigeons, sit in a circle for hours and watch the pigeons and watch nothing. frozen, but I could cry. and at night we will sweat through senseless dreams. there's only one place to go. tra la la la. la la. la.

―――――

I met her in a bookstore. she was wearing a very short tight skirt, enormous highheels, and her breasts were quite evident even under the loose-fitting blue sweater. her face was very pointed, austere, no make-up, with a lower lip that didn't seem to hang quite right. but with a body like that you could forgive quite a number of things. but it was very odd that she didn't have some great protective bull looming about. then I saw her eyes – christ, they seemed to have no pupils – just this deep deep flash of darkness. I stood there watching her bend over again and again. reaching down for books, or stretching up. the short skirt lifting to show me fat and magic thighs. she was running through books on mysticism. I put down my *How To Beat the Horses* book and walked over. "pardon me," I said, "I am drawn as if my magnet. I fear it is your eyes." I lied.

"fate is God," she said.

"you are God, You are my Fate," I answered. "can I buy you a drink?"

"sure."

we went to the bar next door and stayed there until closing time. I talked her kind of talk, figuring it was the only way. it was. I got her to my place and she was a beautiful lay. our courtship lasted about 3 weeks. when I asked her to marry me she looked at me a long time. she looked at me for so long that I thought she had forgotten the question.

finally she spoke: "well, all right. but I don't love you. I only feel that I must . . . marry you. if it were only love, I would refuse love, only. for you see . . . it . . . wouldn't turn out very well, yet, what must be must be."

"o.k., sweetums," I said.

after we got married all the short skirts and highheels vanished and she went about in this long red corduroy gown down to her ankles. it was not a very clean gown. and she wore torn blue slippers with it. she'd go out in the street this way, to the movies, everywhere. and especially during breakfast she'd like to dangle the arms of the gown into her buttered toast.

"hey!" I'd say, "you're getting butter all over yourself!"

she wouldn't answer. she'd look out the window and say: "OOOOOOOH! a bird! a bird there in the tree! did you SEE the bird?"

"yeh."

or: "OOOOOOOH! a SPIDER! look at the dear God's creature! I just love spiders! I can't understand people who hate spiders! do you hate spiders, Hank?"

"I really don't think much about them."

there were spiders all over the place, and bugs, and flies and roaches. God's creatures. she was a terrible housekeeper. she said housekeeping didn't matter. I thought that she was simply lazy. and, I was beginning to think, a bit goofy. I had to hire a fulltime maid, Felica. my wife's name was Yevonna.

one night I came home and I found them both smearing some kind of ointment on the backs of mirrors, waving their hands over them and saying strange words. they both leaped up with their mirrors, screamed, ran off and hid them.

"Jesus Christ," I said, "what's going on around here?"

"no one's eye must fall upon the magic mirror but one's own," said my wife Yevonna.

"that's right," said the maid, Felica. but Felica had stopped cleaning house. she said it didn't matter. but I had to keep her because she was almost as good on the springs as Yevonna, and, besides, she was a good cook, though I was never quite sure what she was feeding me.

while Yevonna was pregnant with our first child, it was brought to my attention that she was acting odder than ever. she kept having these crazy dreams and she told me that a demon was trying to take up residence. inside her. she described the mother to me. the cat appeared to her in two forms. one of them was a man very much like myself. the other was a creature with a human face, a cat's body and eagle's legs and talons and bat's wings. the thing never spoke to her but she got strange ideas while looking at it. the strange idea she got was that I was responsible for her misery, and created in her an overwhelming urge to destroy. not roaches or flies or ants or filth gathered in corners – but things that had cost me money. she tore up the furniture, ripped down the shades, burned the curtains and couch, threw toilet paper across the room, let the bathtub overflow and swamp the whole place, ran up huge long distance calls to people she barely knew. when she got like that, all I could do was go to bed with Felica, try to forget, go 3 or 4 rounds using all the tricks in the book.

I finally got Yevonna to go to a psychiatrist. she said, "surely, and very well, but it's all nonsense. it's all in your mind: you are both the demon and YOU are insane!"

"all right, baby, but let's go see the man, huh?"

"sit out in the car. I'll be right out."

I waited. when she came out she had on a short skirt, high heels, new nylons, and even makeup. she had combed her hair for the first time since our marriage.

"give me a kiss, baby," I said, "I got rocks."

"no. let's go see the psychiatrist."

with the psychiatrist she couldn't have acted any more normal. she didn't mention the demon. she laughed at stupid jokes and never rambled on, always letting the doctor take the lead. he declared her physically healthy and mentally sound. I knew she was physically healthy. we drove back and then she ran into the house and changed from her short skirt and heels back into her filthy red gown. I went back to bed with Felica.

even after our first child was born (mine and Yevonna's), Y. continued to believe completely in the demon, and he kept on appearing to her. schizophrenia developed. one moment she was quiet and tender; then in another moment she became a slouch, garrulous, dull, inconsiderate and rather mean.

and he'd just start on, rambling and chattering, none of it tying together.

sometimes she would be standing in the kitchen and I would hear this ugly bellow, very loud, it was like a man's voice, very hoarse.

I'd go in and ask her, "whatzup, sweets?"

"well, I'll be a dirty motherfucker," I'd say. then I'd pour myself a big drink, go into the front room and sit down.

one day I managed to sneak a psychiatrist into the house when she was in an off mood. he agreed that she was in a psychotic state and advised me to have her committed to an institution for the insane. I signed the necessary papers and obtained a hearing. once again, out came the short skirt and heels. only this time she didn't play the dull and ordinary broad. she turned on the intellectualism. she spoke brilliantly in defense of her sanity. she made me out as a mean husband who was trying to unload a wife. she managed to discredit the testimony of several witnesses. she confused two court physicians. the judge, after consulting the physicians, said: "The Court does not find the evidence sufficient to commit Mrs. Radowski. This hearing is therefore dismissed."

I drove her on home and waited while she changed back into her filthy red gown. when she came back out I told her, "god damn if you're not going to drive ME nuts!"

"you ARE insane," she said. "now why don't you go to bed with Felica and attempt to rid yourself of your repressions?"

I did just that. this time Y. watched, standing by the bed, smiling, smoking a king-size cigarette out of an ivory holder. maybe she had attained her final cool. I rather enjoyed it.

but the next day, coming home from work, the landlord met me in the driveway: "Mr. Radowski! Mr. Radowski, your wife, your WIFE has been picking quarrels and fights with the neighbors. she's broken every window in your place. I'll have to ask you to move!"

well, we packed up and, myself and Yevonna and Felica, and we went to Yevonna's mother's place in Glendale. the old gal was pretty well fixed but all the incantations and magic mirrors and incense-burning got her down, so she suggested we go to a farm she owned up near Frisco. we left the baby at her mother's and off we went, but when we got there the main house was occupied by a sharecropper, some big guy with a black beard stood in the door, one Final Benson, that's what he said his name was and he said, "I been on this land all my life, and no man moves me off, NO man!" he was six-five and close to 350 pounds and not too old, so we rented a place just off the edge of the land while legal maneuvers began.

it was the very first night, it happened. I was packing it to Felica, trying the new bed, when I heard terrible moans, sobs from the other rooms, and sounds as if the front room couch were breaking. "Yevonna sounds disturbed," I said. I slipped it out. "be right back."

she was disturbed, all right. there was Final Benson riding her, packing it home. it was awesome. he had enough for four men. I went back to the bedroom and did my little bit.

in the morning, I couldn't find Yevonna. "wonder where that dizzy broad's gone?"

it wasn't until Felica and I were having breakfast that I looked out the window and saw Yevonna. she was down on her hands and knees in these blue jeans and a man's olive drab shirt and she was working the land, and Final was right down there with her and they were pulling things up, putting them in baskets. looked like turnips. Final had got himself a woman. "jesus christ," I said, "let's go. let's get out of here, fast!"

Felica and I packed. when we got back to L.A. we took a motel room while we looked for a place. "god damn, sweetie," I said, "my worries are over! you have no idea what I've been through!"

we bought a fifth of whiskey to celebrate, then we made love and stretched out to sleep in peace.

then I was awakened by the sound of Felica's voice: "Thou foul tormenting fiend!" she was saying. "Is there no rest from thee this side of the tomb? Thou has taken away my Yevonna, and now thou has followed me here! Get thee hence, Demon! Get out! Leave us Forever!"

I sat up in bed. I looked where Felica was looking and I think I saw it – this big face, kind of a red glowing with a bit of orange under it, like a hot coal, and green lips, and two long yellow teeth sticking out, a mass of dull glowing hair, and the thing was grinning. the eyes looked down at us like a dirty joke.

"well, I'll be a dirty motherfucker," I said.

"begone!" spoke Felica, "in the Holy Name of Almighty Ja and in the name of Buddha and in the name of a thousand gods I curse and direct and discharge you from our souls forever and ten thousand years hence!"

I switched on the electric light.

"it was just the whiskey, baby. very bad whiskey, plus tiredness from the long drive down here."

I looked at the clock. it was one thirty p.m. and I needed a drink now, pretty bad. I started to get dressed.

"where you going, Hank?"

"liquor store. just time to make it. gotta drink that big face outa my head. too damn much."

I was finished dressing.

"Hank?"

"yeah, sweetzums?"

"something I ought to tell you."

"sure, sweetzums. but snap it up. gotta make the store and get back."

"I'm Yevonna's sister."

"oh yeh?"

"yes."

I leaned over and kissed her. then I went outside and got in my car and started driving. away. I got the bottle at Hollywood and Normandie and just kept driving west. the motel was back east, almost to Vermont Ave. Well, you don't find a Final Benson everyday, not with all that string, sometimes you just have to leave those crazy broads and get yourself back together. there's a certain price on pussy that no man will pay; meanwhile, there's always another fool who will pick up the one you've dropped, so there's really no sense of guilt or desertion.

I stopped at a kind of hotel down near Vine Street and got myself a room. while I was getting my key I saw this thing sitting in the lobby with her skirt pulled up around her ass. too much. she kept looking at the bottle in the bag. I kept looking up her ass. too much. when I got on the elevator she was on there with me. "you gonna drink that bottle all by yourself, mister?" "I hope I don't have to." "you won't." "fine," I said.

the elevator hit the top floor. she swung out and I watched her movements, shimmering and sliding; shaking and jolting me all through.

"the key says room 41," I said.

"o.k."

"by the way, you ain't interested in mysticism, flying saucers, etheric armies, witches, demons, occult teachings, magic mirrors?"

"iner-ested in WHAT? I don't get it!"

"forget it, baby!"

she moved along in front of me, high heels clicking, her body wobbling all over in the dim hall light. I couldn't wait. we found room 41 and I opened the door, found the light, found 2 glasses, rinsed them, poured the whiskey, handed her a glass. she sat on the couch, her legs crossed high, smiling at me over the drink.

it was going to be all right.

at last.

for a while.